Praise for A J Dalton's w

Fantasy-Faction.com: 'Unique ideas and a story that ~~~~~~~ ~ an unpredictable manner.'

SFX: 'Gives you an interesting setting and a devilishly good villain.'

SciFi Now magazine: 'Engaging, filled with sacrifice, adventure and some very bloody battles!'

Waterstones central buyer: 'The best young British fantasy author on the circuit at the moment.'

Sfbook.com: 'Very, very clever and manages to offer something different over the traditional fantasy fare. Different, fresh and unique.'

FantasyBookReview.co.uk: 'With its rich tapestry of characters and incident there is never a dull moment.'

The Eloquent Page: 'There's interesting world building to discover and a surprising amount of dry humour to enjoy. A great deal of fun and certainly worthy of your time!'

IWillReadBooks.com: 'A. J. Dalton's world building is fresh with new ideas.'

Amazon.co.uk: 'Fast moving and keeps you gripped at all times, while also creating a world with immense depth and complexity. Five stars!'

GoodReads.com: 'A J Dalton, thank you, what I've read will stay with me for a long time.'

The Book of Dragons

Edited by

A J Dalton
Michael Victor Bowman

www.kristell-ink.com

All rights reserved. This book or any portion thereof may not be reproduced or used in any manner whatsoever without the express written permission of the publisher except for the use of brief quotations in a book review.

All characters appearing in this work are fictitious. Any resemblance to real persons, living or dead, is purely coincidental.

The Lecturer and the Dragons of Manchester A J Dalton © 2017
The Non-Dragon A J Dalton © 2017
The Last A J Dalton © 2017
Black and White Michael Victor Bowman © 2017
The Meeting of the Twain Andrew Coulthard © 2017
Dragonfly Andrew Coulthard © 2017
Illumination Joanne Hall © 2017
The Anxiety Dragon Rob Clifford © 2017
Dragon's Bane C.N Lesley © 2017
The Dragon Daughter Isabella Hunter © 2017
Forefront Garry Coulthard © 2017

Paperback ISBN 978-1-911497-31-8
Hardback ISBN 978-1-911497-32-5
EPUB ISBN 978-1-911497-30-1

Cover art by Charlotte Pang
Cover design by Ken Dawson
Typesetting by Zoë Harris

Kristell Ink

An Imprint of Grimbold Books
4 Woodhall Drive
Banbury
Oxon
OX16 9TY
United Kingdom

www.kristell-ink.com

With thanks to Patrick Rothfuss,
who's brought some poetry into the world of fantasy.

Contents

The Lecturer and the Dragons of Manchester

A J Dalton

HE SAW DRAGONS EVERYWHERE, AND THAT WAS WHY they'd put him in a secure unit. They told him there was no such thing as dragons. But he'd seen unprovoked attacks on the street, violence break out in an apparently quiet bar, rage overtake people on crowded pavements, and supposed peace-keepers use shocking degrees of force. In such moments, the beasts revealed themselves. They could be glimpsed louring from beneath ridged brows, snarling in the corner of your eye and leering between your rapid and confused blinks. You had to be quick, mind, and know what to look for. But once you knew about them, it was somehow harder for them to convince you that you'd imagined what you'd seen, that you'd been mistaken, or that it had all been some trick of the light. Once you knew about them and properly believed in them, it seemed they had less power over you, less ability to blind you to them and less general *impossibility*. What really worried him, though, was whether they suspected he saw them. And if they began to suspect, what might they then do to him?

*

HE WONDERED JUST how secure the secure unit was. Could it keep him safe from them or did it keep him trapped so that they could dispose of him at their leisure? Hopefully they were in no hurry – the world thought him mad, after all. And the attractive Dr Andres was working hard to persuade him he was delusional. Maybe he should play along.

*

HE HADN'T ALWAYS been able to see the dragons, of course. He'd been a regular lecturer on sci-fi, fantasy and horror at Manchester Metropolitan University. He'd lectured about the myths, history, beliefs and philosophies informing modern literature and cultural identity, and then led the students in writing workshops. And they'd paid him for it too . . . not much, of course, but enough to get by. Then, towards the end of one lecture, the student Zoe had asked a question.

'Why are there so many dragons in fantasy?'

'Oh, I know this one,' he'd smiled. 'The dragon was a horned beast synonymous with the devil. The dragon sleeps on a bed of gold, which is Mammon. The dragon breathes fire, the flames of hell. The dragon has a forked tongue, speaking lies. Think of the myth of St George and the Dragon – the Christian saint vanquishing the monstrous and venal creature of the pre-Christian era, the corrupt nature of pagan worship. There's probably some memory of dinosaurs wrapped up in the dragon too, just as Christians back in the day truly believed the devil walked the earth.'

Zoe had tilted her head. 'So there might actually have been dragons?'

'Of a sort. Our fascination with them today is that cultural memory and belief in their once having been real.'

Enough of the students attending the lecture had nodded for him to be satisfied that his answer was sufficient – that, or they were eager to end the Q&A in order to get to lunch or the bar. Yet Zoe had sought him out after the lecture as well.

'So we still think they are real?'

'Sorry? Dragons, you mean? In a way. That's why people read fantasy and take it seriously. They're looking for descriptions and clues to confirm what they already suspect.'

'Clues to finding or seeing dragons,' she'd murmured, eyes fixed on his, unblinking.

'Seeing, Zoe? What do you mean?'

'It's not easy,' she'd asserted. 'They're good at disguising themselves. Like demons and the devil. Like you said in the lecture. And in your books. I've read *Necromancer's Gambit*, you know.'

'Er . . . my books are just fantasy, Zoe.'

'You said we have a cultural memory and belief in their being real. You said that's why people take fantasy seriously. They're looking for answers and clues. You said people believed the devil walked the earth.'

The hairs had risen on the back of his neck. 'Zoe, I know I said all that,' he replied carefully, 'but I was talking conceptually . . . almost metaphorically. I'm not saying that there are actually . . . that there are actually . . .' For some reason, he'd become too unnerved to finish, as if they might be overheard.

She'd shaken her head. 'I know what you meant.' A bright smile and a turn of the heel: 'See you in the workshop later.'

*

HE'D BEEN UNABLE to shake off the conversation. Was the poor girl ill? It would be a shame, because he'd always liked her. And it would mean he'd seriously misjudged her. How many more might he have misjudged? If he couldn't tell who was well and who was ill, then how did he know he was well himself? How could he know the real from the delusional?

Stop it!

*

KNOWLEDGE CHANGES HOW you see the world. It even changes *what* you see. If you don't know how something amazing works, you think it magical, wondrous or slightly scary. When you know the secret, it's just a mundane and disappointing trick. What you thought was impossible becomes real, and what you thought was real becomes a meaningless charade. It's all about your knowledge and perception. If you *know* there are no dragons or demons, then you do not truly perceive them for what they are. But when someone describes some new understanding to you, your knowledge of it means you start seeing it. Don't believe me – it might be safer that way. Some knowledge is just too dangerous. I understand now why the Bible bangs on about knowledge being the forbidden fruit.

*

WALKING DOWN OXFORD Street that evening, he wasn't really paying attention. He was vaguely aware of the lean and stubbled man stepping out of the dark alley, but didn't really see him. He smelt the stale and sour sweat upon him, and he didn't really take it in. He felt the man's trembling anticipation, but was somehow numb to it. He sensed the danger, but he carried on towards him as if in a fugue, as if mesmerised or bespelled.

There were umpteen stories and articles about muggings in broad daylight, let alone in the evening. He knew what could happen, but didn't believe it would. Yet now it seemed to be happening. To him. It hardly made sense.

He experienced confusion and then a curious detachment when he saw the knife taken out of the hoodie's pocket. He tilted his head – like Zoe had earlier that day – wondering how the man could have such fanglike teeth and shining eyes. The nearby streetlamp flickered and blinked, exaggerating then speeding up movement, creating an otherworldly second image or phantom afterimage.

'What do you want?' he mumbled distractedly.

'Money.'

'You want money?'

'Always.'

'I've got nothing. You're welcome to that.'

The man's crazed eyes and knife came close. 'You ssscared, laughing boy?'

He didn't really feel anything. 'Should I be?'

Fire lanced across his cheek. He'd been cut. He suddenly came back to himself and cried for help.

The man spat in his face. 'That's for being a twat. I'll be seeing you again. Make sure you've got money next time or I'll slice your gizzard open.'

Blood and spittle dripped onto his shirt. He looked down at the spreading scarlet. It was his own blood. *You're in shock.* Just as well, or he'd be vomiting and collapsing to the ground. He'd be gibbering at people, telling them about the monster. *Get a grip.*

But he *knew* now. And he saw the world differently. There were dragons or demons all around, looking to prey on the ignorant, unwary and weak. He had to be more careful. At least he could now see them and would be able to keep a watch.

*

'So, Adam, why did you attack the policeman?' Dr Andres asked him in the sort of special voice she clearly used for patients.

He watched her warily. There was nothing unusual – nothing reptilian – about her gaze. There was no hint of any scaling about her skin. Maybe she was better at maintaining her disguise than some of the others. 'I was trying to get away.'

'According to this, you thumbed him in the eye, nearly blinding him permanently. That seems like more than trying to get away, doesn't it, Adam?'

'I . . . I had just been mugged. I reported it. The officer was sent to interview me, but . . .'

'But?'

She seemed genuinely curious. 'But he didn't believe what I told him . . .'

'I understand,' she nodded. 'Do you want to tell me what you told him, Adam?'

He chewed on his lip. 'You'll think I'm crazy.'

'Adam, if you're aware it might sound crazy, then you still understand the difference between the normal and the abnormal. If you can still differentiate, then I would say you are *not* crazy. Clearly something unusual happened to you. Whatever you tell me, I'll take it seriously, because you're a highly educated individual with no history of mental disorder.'

She sounded reasonable. What if she was one of them? He decided that things couldn't get much worse than his current situation anyway. 'I was attacked by this guy in a hoodie.'

'Okay. Go on.'

'There was something monstrous about him. His teeth were long and pointed, and his eyes weren't . . . weren't human.'

'I see. The policeman didn't believe you, you said. What did he do or say?'

'He grabbed me on the arm, here, and said I had to accompany him. Then I saw . . .'

'Saw what, Adam?'

'In that moment that he grabbed me, just for a split second, his face changed. His forehead became bigger. His eyes looked like a lizard's. His teeth . . . were like the guy's who had attacked me.'

Dr Andres was silent for long moments. She penned a few notes in the book in her lap. She looked back up and gave a weak smile as she said, 'I'm keeping an open mind on all this, as I told you. Have you ever seen other people who seem like . . . er . . . lizards?'

'No, I can't say that I have.'

She held her expression. 'And what association do lizards have for you? Perhaps you saw one when you were young?'

A natural human smile doesn't last more than four seconds. Politicians smile too long – that's why no one trusts them and how you can tell when someone's lying. She doesn't believe me. And now she's going for some bullshit psychoanalytic explanation of childhood trauma. He sighed inwardly. 'Lizards have no particular association for me. Do they for you?'

'This isn't about me, Adam,' was the smooth response.

'I see,' he answered more sharply than he'd intended. *Torn it now.*

Something flashed. Her skin rippled.

He let out an involuntary gasp.

'Adam, I feel you've become defensive. Perhaps you're tired or still a bit overwrought.'

'I-I do have a headache,' he said, keeping his eyes down.

'Let's end it here and talk again tomorrow. Get some rest.'

*

Fortunately, they'd only put him in a 'medium secure' psychiatric unit. Setting off the fire alarm without being seen that night wasn't difficult. After that, it was simply a matter of scaling an eight-foot chain-link fence when the sole duty officer had to re-enter the unit to ensure it was fully cleared. Some of the other detainees whispered good luck to him, and he was away.

He speed-walked out of the industrial wasteland where the unit was located and back into town. He glanced over his shoulder periodically – there didn't seem to be anyone following him. He stopped at an ATM and withdrew fifty quid in cash. Surely the Manchester police weren't sophisticated enough to be tracking him through any sort of real-time red-flag system.

The police couldn't deal with all the homeless on the streets, let alone anything else.

Who knew how organised the dragon-demons were, though? Had they already discovered his escape, circulated his image and set lookouts? Was he becoming too paranoid? He certainly felt close to the edge. Yet he really didn't know what he was up against. Surely not the devil himself? It was better to be safe than sorry. He stepped into a cheap clothing store and bought himself a beanie and an over-large puffer jacket. It would have to do until he got the chance to dye his hair, get coloured contact lenses, or some such.

Feeling more anonymous, he stepped into the city's flow of night-time revellers – hen-nights, girls baring enough flesh to show they weren't 'nesh', guys exposing even more to show just how much they worked out or injected, trans people who disdained the ghetto that was the Gay Village, corporates who'd strayed on their way home, underfed and grinning students, Saudi women herding children and husbands, Pakistanis with stronger Mank or Scouse accents than most, and directionless Chinese. He decided that maybe he stood out more than he'd realised. Maybe they'd all peg him as a drug-dealer or professional beggar, though.

He made it to the Temple Bar – ornate underground toilets from the Victorian era that had been converted into just another drinking-hole – and cautiously descended the steep and greasy steps. He was sure she'd said in one of the workshops that she sometimes barmaided here. He just hoped she was working tonight.

Inside, he approached the bar, where a pretty girl with green hair was serving drinks. He realised she was wearing a wig.

'Z-Zoe?'

The girl was startled. 'Adam! Mr Dalton? Is that you? What are you doing here?'

He leaned forwards. 'I need to talk to you.'

She stepped away, apparently slightly taken aback by his intensity.

'This guy bothering you, Zed?' rumbled a well-built hipster on one of the stools, his nostrils flaring and smoke wreathing from between his teeth.

Where's his cigarette? People aren't allowed to smoke in bars anymore.

'No . . . it's okay. He's one of my tutors from the university.'

One of the hipster's eyebrows arched. 'Really? That writing stuff you do? He don't look like no writer.'

'I'm an international fantasy author,' he informed the hipster blandly, 'but there's no money in it so I have to teach as well.' He turned back to Zoe. 'I have to talk to you.'

'What about?'

'Not here.'

'I'm working,' she told him, eyes flicking towards the hipster. 'I can't just leave.'

He sighed in exasperation. 'It's about what we spoke about before. I've *seen* them.'

She looked alarmed. 'Who?'

'You know who! Come outside.'

And a little frightened now. 'I-I don't know who you mean.'

'You sure he's not harassing you, Zed?' the hipster growled, his face suddenly looking redder under the mood lighting, and smoke billowing all around.

It became hot, an aggressive scent filled the air and he tasted the acid of fear at the back of his throat. 'He's one of them!' With both hands, he pushed the being off the stool, dodged around the bar and pulled Zoe after him. 'Run!'

Zoe yelped but didn't resist. 'You madman! Up the stairs! Come on.'

They thundered up the back stairs of the bar. There was a roar from below, but Zoe was laughing as they came up into the cold air. 'Adam, you must be on something. No one's ever dared do anything like that to Pete. He's over-protective, though. Likes to get too close to all the barmaids if you know what I mean. This way, down here, before the blowhard can get after us. You maniac!'

Then he was laughing with her, giddy with panic, exhilaration and relief. The stress and horror of the last six hours was all released in that one moment. He hiccupped his words: 'I certainly feel like I've been on something. They gave me pills in the secure unit.'

'Secure unit? What are you like? My flat's this way.'

'I mean it. I was mugged. There was an altercation with a police officer. They put me in a place full of crazies. I've just escaped. I've just assaulted some demonic muscle mary in your bar. And now we're on the run together. Ain't it great? You couldn't make this stuff up.'

'You're shitting me!' she screamed joyfully. 'I want some of what you've been having. You been watching A Game of Thrones? I'm on season six already.'

He felt dizzy and light-headed. When had he last eaten? It would have been some lacklustre and damp sandwich from the university canteen. When had that been?

'Thanks,' he said as she held the door open and let him into her place.

It was small and pokey, little more than a bedsit really. She set about hiding dirty plates, removing knickers and socks from the radiator and sweeping Metro newspapers onto the floor so he could sit.

'It's not much, but it's cheap, that window has a view across Manchester and it's a central location.'

'It's your own and you can shut the world out. I feel like a bit of an intruder.'

'Well, you are,' she agreed, handing him a beer from the fridge.

'Sorry about that.' He took a swig. 'Wow, I needed that. Thanks.'

'You're welcome.' She took a sip from her own bottle and flopped down on the sofa next to him. 'So what's been going on?'

He sat forwards. 'I've seen them. The . . . the . . .'

'Dragons?'

'Yes! They look like us mostly, like they're wearing skin. But their disguises slip sometimes. How do you know about them, Zoe? You've seen them too, right?'

She rubbed the back of her neck. 'Maybe. I'm not completely sure. There was this woman at the supermarket who got angry that I reached ahead of her and got the last burgers on the shelf. I swear her tongue forked and bumps like horns appeared on her forehead. It was like she couldn't contain herself. If a store worker hadn't overheard us and told her not to worry because there were more in the back . . . anyway, I blinked and she seemed normal. I'd dropped some E's a few days before, so kinda shrugged it off . . . till you gave that lecture and I was given this. What do you think?'

She'd reached behind her and picked up a leaflet, which she gave to him. He studied it. *For many demons walk amongst us, looking to spread discord and anxiety, looking to create the fear that makes us act recklessly or paralyses so that we are easier prey*, it declared. Below, there were quotes from the Bible, a picture of a knight fighting a dragon, an exhortation to join 'the eternal battle' and an email address. 'What do I think? It's like the junk those religious nuts give out by Sainsbury's next to Oxford Road Station every morning.'

'Ha! Precisely. That's where the guy gave it to me when I was on my way to class one time. After the episode in the supermarket, I stopped to speak to him. He was kind of freaky, with a wild or haunted look in his eyes, you know. Said his name was Simon Hobbs and that there were dragons or demons everywhere working against us, against peace and order. Said he had to let people know and asked me to tell others. I didn't believe him, of course, but thought I could base one of my writing assignments on him, you know. I emailed him once or twice, but he stopped replying and I didn't see him outside Sainsbury's anymore.'

His scalp prickled. 'What do you think happened?'

Zoe reached behind her again, snagged another piece of paper and gave it to him. It was a newspaper cutting. *Canals claim another victim!* declared the headline. *A dog-walker reported seeing what appeared to be a body floating in the Manchester Canal and reported it to police. Several hours later, police pulled the body of Simon Hobbs, 33, from the water. There was no sign of foul play, so police are calling it a tragic accident or possibly suicide. "The sides of the canal are high and vertical, and the water is very cold. Anyone falling in, especially under the influence, can quickly get into trouble," said a spokesperson. The spokesperson refused to comment on speculation concerning The Pusher, the individual whom imaginative locals believe is responsible for the deaths. A total of 87 bodies have been pulled from the canals of Manchester in the last two years.*

'Eighty-seven victims?' he whispered. 'Have there really been so many? They can't *all* have been accidents. Do you think it was the dragons looking to keep this Simon Hobbs quiet about their existence?'

'Him and others. This Pusher has been busy.'

'But eighty-seven. That's almost one a week over the two years.'

'Yup.'

'Why aren't the police doing anything?' He paused before answering his own question. 'Because there are dragons amongst them, that's why. Damn it! We can't let them get away with this.'

'What can we do? We can try getting the word out like Simon, but looked what happened to him.'

'Well, they're already onto me, so I don't think I've got a lot to lose, Zoe. I could try disappearing, but they could be everywhere. No, the only way is if I get word out to enough people to expose these dragons once and for all. They can't kill everyone in Manchester, after all.'

'Are you sure?'

'No.' He shuddered. 'Have you got any more beer?'

'Sure. And you'll have to sleep on the couch, I guess. You can't exactly go home – it won't be safe.'

*

The next morning, nursing a double-strength coffee from Greggs, he read his work computer screen in bleary-eyed dismay. The message and appeal he'd spent all night crafting and getting out on Facebook had received just 26 likes and only been shared twice, once by Zoe. There were comments like 'Great story! You really had me going there. Is this one of the tales for your new book? The Book of Dragons, isn't it?' and 'Why have none of the dragons got wings?' and 'Dragons are cool. Have you seen Eragon?'

'Why won't you go viral, damn you?! How can the fucking Grumpy Cat meme get everywhere, not to mention Kim Kardashian's arse, but not information about dragons being real? It's insane. How can I get them to believe me?'

Surely the lecture would work. The sixty-nine students on the BA in Creative Writing were the sort of arty geeks that were likely to be receptive, weren't they?

As it was, only thirty turned up, which wasn't too bad, given that it was a morning lecture. The dragons couldn't risk killing thirty students from the same course – it would be impossible to pass off as a coincidence.

'One of the biggest challenges to any writer of fantasy literature,' he began, 'is convincing the reader to believe magic might be real. It's no mean feat. Look at George RR Martin. He takes thousands of pages wandering about before he manages to get any sort of magic going, and even then it's all very much in the background. Or look at Joe Abercrombie, the biggest selling British author of adult fantasy, the biggest selling that's still alive anyway. Mr Abercrombie's wizard doesn't use real magic; he just uses science others don't understand. Real magic is very difficult to pin down or create, and just as difficult to describe convincingly. So how's it done?

'Well, the easiest approach is to write second-world fantasy in which magic is a matter of fact. Your main wizard will have a particular way of accessing the power that is magic. So, Bilbo will have a magic ring, Harry Potter has a wand, and so on.

Because the story happens in a second world, like Middle Earth or Hogwarts, a world that is not our own, the reader is happy to *suspend their disbelief*. That's second-world fantasy and the easiest way to do it.

'Far more difficult to write is first-world fantasy, a story told in our real world. It is very difficult to introduce a credible sense of magic into such a world. Usually, the writer has to use some sort of *ambiguity*. So, something magical or supernatural might *appear* to happen, but then a rational or mundane explanation for what happened might be offered. If this device is used three or four times in quick succession then it begins to feel like more than coincidence, it begins to feel more than the mundane, it begins to feel like there's some greater supernatural power or intelligence at work. The rational explanation each time should become more and more stretched as well, so that the rational explanation actually begins to lose credibility. Done well, and with a delicate touch, the reader will be utterly convinced that magic can operate in this world.

'And let's face it, readers of fantasy *want* to believe that magic is real. They're on the author's side, and very much along for the ride. They *want* the magical reveal or climax moment, but they enjoy the anticipation of it just as much. They want you to spend time rooting the story in the real first, because they ultimately want to believe that magic is real.'

He cleared his throat and gathered himself. 'Let me give you an example of magic as real in the first world then. Say, I had seen dragons and wanted to convince a stranger of it. I wouldn't go up to the stranger and simply tell them that I'd seen a dragon and needed their help. The only help they'd get me was some men in white coats. Heh! No, what I'd need to do is first tell them about a normal and ordinary context. I would describe it matter-of-factly, objectively and sensibly. Then I'd mention that something strange happened that I didn't quite understand. I'd ask them if they could help explain it for me. They wouldn't immediately think I was nuts, because I'd already demonstrated how sensible I was. Instead, they'd begin to think something in the environment had affected my perception. They'd make suggestions. As I mention another strange event, one which frustrates their previous suggestion, they become unnerved. Their next suggestion becomes stretched. The hairs on the back of their neck rise as they begin to believe.'

Here it was. 'Let me tell you that story then. Do you remember at the end of the last lecture I was asked why there were so many dragons in fantasy?' Most of the students nodded. 'And that I answered by describing how the dragon represents the real danger that is the devil walking this earth? Well, later on, I was asked by a student from the lecture if people therefore read fantasy for clues to know about and see the dragon, the dragon that they strongly suspected or feared was real because of their cultural memories of dinosaurs, a pagan past or a Christian tradition. I felt awkward because it seemed like I was being asked if dragons were actually real but hidden amongst us, like demons in disguise.

'Then I was walking home that evening and I was mugged by this thin, crazed-looking man with a knife. The light from the lamp-post was flickering, and it was hard to see clearly, but his eyes seemed to glow and, for a fleeting second, his teeth – and, honestly, I don't think I was imagining it – his teeth were fangs!'

There were gasps. They watched him with wide eyes, some had mouths hanging open and others looked frightened. They'd stopped taking notes. They only listened now. They were his, and he told them everything, right up to checking his Facebook that morning and entering this lecture.

*

WITHIN FIFTEEN MINUTES of the lecture finishing and his returning to the staff room, he was summoned to the head of department's office.

'Adam, how are you?'

'Fine, David. Just given a lecture on magic. Went well.'

'Ah, yes. It was that I wanted to talk to you about actually. We had a complaint.'

'Oh really?'

'Yes. It seems you think dragons are real?'

'No, no. I was talking about how to make magic believable for a reader. Sounds like one of the students got the wrong end of the stick, that's all.'

'Hmm. It was a group complaining. They were quite incensed and upset. Adam, you've been taking on a lot of hours recently. I'd like Jane to give the lecture next week and for you to take some time off till the end of term.'

'What? You can't do that!'

'You'll be paid till the end of term of course.'

'It's constructive dismissal. I'll have to talk to the union rep.'

'We're not dismissing you. As I said, we'll pay you till the end of term, when I believe your contract expires.'

'But–'

He stopped. He glared at the Professor, noting the abnormal darkness of his eyes, the mottling of his skin, the exaggerated width of his mouth, the ugly undulation of his tongue and the baring of his teeth. He realised now why he'd instinctively never liked or trusted his boss. The Professor was of course one of *them*. He also realised he'd been a fool not to anticipate there might be some of *them* amongst the students in the lecture.

He schooled his expression and then forced a smile. 'Do you know what, David? I think maybe you're right. Overdoing it. Yes, that'll be it. Thank you for this, truly. It won't go on my record, will it?'

The Professor waved magnanimously. 'Of course not.'

'Excellent.' He slapped the arms of his chair as he got up. 'I'd better go and get some R&R then. Have a good one. Good day!'

'Adam, you'll be talking to someone soon.'

'Of course, of course.'

'I'll send them to see you. Goodbye, Adam.'

*

He was in no doubt they'd be right after him now. He hurried out of the Cornerhouse building and ducked into the crowds of people heading out of their offices for lunch. He chanced a look over his shoulder – sure enough, the thin, crazed-looking man was pushing past people to get to him.

He took a sharp left and ran up the ramp towards Oxford Road Station. A dozen metres further on and he was past Java café and onto the narrow stairs that would lead him back down by another route. He bounded down, went round the Duke of Salisbury pub and emerged onto the main road once more. He went straight to the nearby taxi rank and got into the first cab.

'Hi . . . Ashraf! The northern quarter, please.'

The vehicle pulled away from the kerb and entered the flow of traffic. 'The northern quarter is a big place, mate. You know an address or street?'

'Don't worry. Anywhere.'

'Okay.' Ashraf eyed him in the mirror. 'Busy today?'

'Sort of.'

'Lunchtime traffic.'

'Sure. No rush.'

'Got a meeting with someone?'

'No, no. Off shopping.'

'Anything nice?'

'Underpants, Ashraf. Anything else you'd like to know? The size of underpants, maybe?'

'Sorry, boss. Just making conversation, you know?'

They lapsed into silence, which suited him just fine. After a few minutes, Ashraf put in an ear-piece and began to speak quietly in Urdu, although it might have been Punjabi.

'Stop here. Right here . . . Thanks. Keep the change.'

He got out and waited for the taxi to move away again, but Ashraf sat there having his conversation while watching him. He ground his teeth in irritation and deliberately walked off in the wrong direction, down a side street. He followed it and boxed round to the left, until he was safely heading across town. He took off his puffer jacket and put it in a bin along the way. He concentrated on strolling at a natural pace.

At last he reached his intended destination: Manchester Cathedral. As far as Catholic churches went, it was a surprisingly austere building. There were neo-gothic flourishes, but no hints of gargoyles and not much stained glass. He wondered if he'd made a mistake.

*

HE STEPPED INTO the hush of the holy house and was relieved to see there were candles lit. There was someone home, someone who observed the basics of the faith.

He passed the confessional booth, but it was empty. He went on towards the altar and made a rough sign of the cross, half bending a knee. Looking right, he saw that the door to back-of-house was ajar. He moved closer. 'Hello? Is there anybody there?'

As if by magic, a small man appeared, dressed in black shirt and white collar. The fellow had quick features, pale green eyes and the sort of forbearing smile that said he had been tested in his time. 'Hello, hello! What can I do for you?' was the tolerant enquiry in a gentle Irish lilt.

'Father . . . ?'

'Reverend Michaels. And you are?'

'Adam . . . Adam Dalton. Reverend, I'm not a particularly religious man, but I need your help.'

The Reverend seemed pleased, the lines at the corners of his mouth and eyes deepening in a way that made him appear older and a bit more careworn. 'You are not particularly religious but adjudge me the person best suited to help you? Intriguing. Is it a religious matter or do you simply have no friends or other place to turn?'

He was a bit disconcerted, not sure if the man was joking

with him. 'Er . . . all of those? I'm hoping they can't follow me onto holy land. I'm hoping you can't be one of them for the same reason.'

'I see. Let's sit.' They went to the front pew. 'So, it's sanctuary you want, is it?'

'Maybe. Reverend, do you believe in evil?'

A single blink. 'Evil is real, my son, I am in no doubt. I have seen enough to know it exists in this world. Just as Satan tempted Jesus in the desert, so he tests Mankind.'

'And do . . . do you believe in demons?'

'Of course. The Bible tells us Satan was cast out of heaven with his followers. Are you beset by them, my son?'

'I-I think so. If I wear a crucifix, will that keep them away?'

'Only if you have true faith in the power of God. You said you were not particularly religious.'

'What if I pin pages of scripture to my clothing?'

'The same as with the crucifix.'

He sighed raggedly. He looked around, at a loss. The statue of Mary and the marble knights gave him no answers.

'My son, tell me what troubles you. I will not judge you. I will listen until you are done.'

'I see dragons everywhere, Reverend,' he whispered. It was easier once he'd said it out loud. The story came out of him, faster and faster. A burden lifted and his breathing was better. '. . . until I came to you!'

Frowning, the Reverend nodded, not replying immediately.

'You *do* believe me, don't you? A-are there dragons in the Bible?'

'Dragons in the Bible?' the Reverend murmured. 'Revelations, chapter twenty: "He seized the dragon, that ancient serpent, who is the devil, or Satan, and bound him for a thousand years."'

'You *do* believe me? Reverend?'

'What? Why of course I do, Adam.' The Reverend put out a reassuring hand. 'You were worried you were going crazy?'

His laugh was brittle. 'It's just that my friends on Facebook and the students didn't seem to believe it. That, or they just don't care. How can I make people believe me?'

'You're asking a servant of the Church how to make people believe?' was the wry reply. 'Fewer than a million people a week now attend Church in this country, probably the fewest it's ever been in history. I fear we are losing the battle, although we must not give in to despair. I do not, Adam, have all the answers as to why people have turned away from God. Clearly, the temptations of the devil are great. Yet I can tell you this – Manchester has had a particular problem with demons for centuries.'

'It has? How so?'

'Well, you'll have heard of John Dee, yes? You're a fantasy writer, after all.'

'Er . . . I'm a bit hazy . . .'

'Don't worry. John Dee was a member of Elizabeth I's court. He was officially her spiritual advisor, but many termed him a dark magician. He possessed an obsidian mirror in which the spirits of the dead could be seen. It's still in the British Museum, I think, along with one of his almanacs of spells. Anyway, when he retired from the court, he was made Warden of Christ's College in Manchester. It was a religious college at the time, but is now Chetham's School. It's barely fifty metres from here and you can visit Dee's original rooms. While Warden, Dee continued his work as an astrologer, mathematician and hermetic philosopher. He also continued to pursue magic. He believed he had discovered and deciphered the holy language used by angels, and perhaps God Himself. He attempted to summon an angel, but it is thought he conjured a demon instead. He was soon after accused of facilitating the demonic possession of six children. In the end, locals rose up against him, ousted him from the college, and stole and destroyed his scientific instruments and extensive library of rare books. He ultimately died in poverty and shame, but ever since his time Manchester has been plagued by rumours and reports of demons.'

He released a slow breath. 'Wow. You mentioned demonic

possession. Could that be how demons manage to remain amongst us? Could there just be the six that you mentioned?'

'I don't know exactly. I need more information. Maybe I should go to see this Professor David Edwards myself.'

'Would you be able to perform something like an exorcism? You priests can do that, right?'

The Reverend shifted uncomfortably. 'I've never been involved in such a thing. It's not really my area of expertise. I'll need to consult the bishop. Yes, I'll do that before doing anything else, for this is no trifling matter. We're talking about confronting the ancient enemy himself. There is none so subtle and malign as he.'

He wanted to make a joke, but it caught in his throat. He felt cold. 'I understand. What about me? What should I do? Will you grant me sanctuary?'

'Of course, Adam.'

'The police can't arrest me here?'

The Reverend pulled a face. 'Well, government officials tend to respect the sanctity of the Church. As you said before, demons can't enter this place, but hopefully no one even knows you're here.'

'Is there anything I can do to help?'

'I would counsel patience for now. Rest a while, and recover yourself. Perhaps look up sections of the Bible pertaining to demons and dragons in the Bible? You might consider praying for guidance, or at least engaging in quiet contemplation. I find answers will often come to a person in such moments. Lastly, you should consider using the gifts God gave you, for He will have given you those gifts for a reason.'

'What do you mean?'

'Adam, you are a writer. That is your main skill, is it not? Follow the example of those who came before you, those who led the way against faithlessness and evil. Follow the example of the disciples, the apostles and scripture itself. Write down your story as testament! Imbue your words with truth so that others might be moved and convinced. Inspire their faith. Use all you understand of beauty, virtue and the soul, then show them ugliness, evil and despair. *Make them believe that dragons are real!* Be a latter day prophet. For if it does not go well for you and me, then your words might be all that survive to save others from these dragons.'

'I partly tried that on Facebook, but I know more now. I can make more sense of it.'

'Come with me.'

He followed Reverend Michaels through the door to back-of-house. They entered a small office that contained an old oak desk, a chair and little else. The walls were whitewashed plaster, bare except for a wooden effigy of Christ on the cross. Upon the desk was a leather-bound Bible, a sheaf of unused paper, a set of pens, a wine glass and an open bottle of red wine.

'This is where I write my sermons. You may work here. When you're done, I'll have my secretary, Mrs Downes, type it up. Copies will be made and sent to those within the Church who have a better understanding than I. Help yourself to wine. I'm sure you're in need of a generous glass or two. The Lord knows I am often enough.' The Reverend gave him a kindly smile, kindly in a way that Adam could not remember encountering in many years. 'I'll leave you now. Remember, the Lord is with you and none is more powerful than He.'

Adam sat down and picked up a fountain pen. He couldn't remember the last time he'd written with one. Back at school? He still had the bump on his finger where he used to clutch the pen. The nib hesitated above the page for a second and then began to set down the opening words of his story:

The Lecturer and the Dragons of Manchester

He saw dragons everywhere, and that was why they'd put him in a secure unit. They told him there was no such thing as dragons. But he'd seen unprovoked attacks on the street, violence break out in an apparently quiet bar, rage overtake people on crowded pavements, and supposed peace-keepers use shocking degrees of force. In such moments, the beasts revealed themselves. They could be glimpsed louring from beneath ridged brows, snarling in the corner of your eye and leering between your rapid and confused blinks. You had to be quick, mind, and know what to look for. But once you knew about them, it was somehow harder for them to convince you that you'd imagined what you'd seen, that you'd been mistaken, or that it had all been some trick of the light. Once you knew about them and properly believed in them, it seemed they had less power over you, less ability to blind you to them and less general impossibility.

The Non-Dragon

A J Dalton

'I HAVE COME TO VANQUISH THEE!' BRUITED THE KNIGHT, his horse rearing. The sun shone prettily off the killer's plate armour.

She retreated further into her cave and called out: 'Do you really have to? I'm not that bad once you get to know me, honestly.'

'You are a fearsome dragon and a menace to all.'

'No, no! I'm a giraffe. It's really just a case of mistaken identity. I'm here in the middle of nowhere just minding my own business, not doing anyone any harm.'

'You have been troubling the kingdom's sheep. The King has promised his daughter's hand to the valiant knight who slays you.'

'It wasn't me. I'm a vegetarian. It must have been someone who looks like me. Some of my best friends are sheep.'

'You are a fork-tongued beast!'

'Now you're just being plain rude. If I had a forked tongue, I'd thalk all fhunny like thith, wouldn't thigh?'

'Enough! Leave your bed of stolen gold and face me.'

'Stolen? How dare you. It was already here when I found this place.'

'Very well, then I will come in there and find you, worm.'

Partly from fear, and partly in anger at how unfair it all was, she roared at him, the cave amplifying the sound a thousandfold.

The horse shied and skittered backwards. The knight fought to turn his steed back the right way.

She saw her chance and came barrelling out and past him, before he could get his deadly lance back in place. She took to the skies and was away.

It couldn't carry on like this, she knew. Everywhere she went, no matter how remote, they eventually found her. She had only just managed to survive the last few knights, suffering grievous wounds in the process. She had not dared to face this new one.

There was nowhere left to run. She would have to go confront this King.

Under cover of darkness, she winged down into the royal gardens of the palace and secreted herself amongst a stand of trees, only snapping one or two of them. Sighing, she settled into wait, dozing with her eyes open.

'Hello!' said the young girl the next morning. 'My, but you're pretty. Do you want to play with me? I'm a princess, you know.'

She blinked. 'Um . . . hello. I'm waiting to meet the King. Is he your father?'

'Yes. I could order you to play with me, you know?'

And I could eat you up. Yes, that would put an end to the knights looking to slay me in order to win your hand in marriage. 'Do you really think I'm pretty? No one's ever said that before.'

'Ooo, but you are. Your eyes are brighter than my cat's. And you're covered in rainbows. Have you seen my cat at all?'

'No. Cats tend to avoid me. Most people do.' *Except knights, of course.* 'You couldn't fetch your father for me, could you? Perhaps I can play with you after that.'

The princess nodded excitedly and ran off. *If I'd eaten her, there would have been outrage and every knight in the kingdom would have been sent after me. Besides, there didn't look to be much meat on her. Scrawny things, these princesses.*

The princess was soon leading a fat and kindly-looking man towards her. Was this the King? The man stopped in amazement. 'Go find the Chamberlain, Isabelle, at once! Tell him there's a dragon in the royal gardens. Tell him to call out the guard!'

As she watched the princess run off again, she said, 'I'm *not* a dragon, you know? Can't you just stop sending all these knights to slay me?'

The King gave her a look of practised sympathy. 'I am of course a reasonable man but, the thing is, the kingdom needs a dragon. And you're it.' He lowered his voice. 'Between you and me, it's very useful you getting rid of my more aggressively ambitious knights, as otherwise they'd only start trouble elsewhere and destabilise the kingdom. With you around, we've never known such peace and prosperity.'

'But that's just it. I'm not going to be around much longer if you keep sending these knights.'

The King smiled and nodded. 'And that's the beauty of it. Whoever slays you will become the people's hero and the kingdom will rally around them. The hero will be named my successor, they will take the hand of my daughter and the people will be happy. See? It works out both ways.'

'Not for me, it doesn't. I could have eaten your daughter, you know, and put an end to all this.'

'Don't worry, I have lots of others.'

'Come to that, I could eat you right now.'

'I see your point, but I don't think that will really change anything. The Chamberlain will continue to administrate things just as he always does, and every knight in the realm will be out to hunt you down, not to mention every farmer and peasant. I doubt you'd live more than a week. Eating me would be a very dragon-like thing to do, to be sure, but you say you're not a dragon, isn't that right?'

'Then I shall find another kingdom.' She knew it was an empty threat even as she said it, for pretty much every kingdom was the same. Humankind was everywhere now. There were no remote places left. There were no peaks distant or inhospitable enough. No caves deep or dark enough. No forests impenetrable and haunted enough. And that was why so few of her kind now remained.

The King looked almost hurt by her last statement. 'Come now, there's no need for that. Look, no one really minds if you take a few sheep here and there. Would it help if I sent, say, only one knight a month?'

'What would really help is if you didn't send any at all! Can't you just accept I'm not a dragon?'

The King shrugged sadly. 'My hands are tied on that, I'm afraid. There's not a lot I can do. You can't deny your own nature, not with such scales, wings and size.'

'But I don't *want* to be a dragon!' she cried.

'Each of us has their role to play. Yours is to be a dragon. Mine is to be a King who sends out brave knights.'

'But you can stop being King if you want to.'

'If only that were true. If I abdicated and tried to live a normal life, people would still *know*. As soon as the new monarch did something unpopular, people would nag me to compete for the throne again. Or the new monarch, anticipating such problems, would send knights to slay me first. Even if I were somewhere no one knew me, there would still be people hunting me. Sound familiar? It should. There's just no escaping it, you see.'

The princess, a stooping Chamberlain and a host of nervous-looking guards suddenly appeared and advanced purposefully towards them. With a bellow of frustration, she took to the skies once more.

She flapped on and on, into the night, through rain and storm. She headed north, desperately looking for some sort of wilderness where none would find her for a while.

Exhausted, she finally descended towards a small and deserted-looking farm. The barn was largely intact, so she manoeuvred her way inside and fell into a deep and dreamless slumber.

'Who are you?' a ragged boy asked her the next morning, upon discovering her.

'Oh, just your invisible friend. I am hiding in here because it's out of the way and seems safe.'

The boy gave a serious nod. 'Yes, that's how the raiders missed me. I should like to have an invisible friend, I think. It's lonely now that my family is gone. Would you like something to eat?'

'Do you really have much to spare? You look very thin.'

'Oh, most of the animals were still out in the fields and woodland when the raiders came. There's still quite a few cattle and such about. I just don't seem very hungry these days, you know?'

She grinned at him, trusting that he would not be alarmed by the sight of her teeth. 'Tell you what, if you bring me a sheep, I'll make us dinner. I can even cook it for you. I can breathe fire.'

The boy's eyes went wide. 'Ooo! Can you really? I'd like to see that.'

'Go on, then.'

They spent every day together, the boy and his invisible friend. She told him of far off places, of battles with knights and fights amongst dragons. He would listen all agog and then curl up next to her to sleep at night. On the first few occasions like this, he was restless and fitful, presumably with troubled dreams, but soon he was sleeping better. He began to eat better too, and put on a little weight.

As for her, she had never been happier. She could not remember ever having had a proper friend before, someone who listened so closely and found joy in the stories she told, joy she had not realised was in those stories, and joy that she now shared in and learned to appreciate. As with the boy, her wounds healed and she put on a little weight.

Then the cruel-eyed raiders returned, with wickedly sharp metal and a bloody smell about them. In abject terror, the boy fled to her.

THE BOOK OF DRAGONS

And his invisible friend rose up and killed all those men who would so think to hurt others.

'Thank you,' the trembling boy whispered as he kept warm beside her. 'You're the best invisible friend in the whole world.'

She lowered her head and nuzzled him. 'I am your friend, and perhaps not so invisible. For it would seem, after all, that I am a dragon.'

The Last

A J Dalton

THE STORY OF MY KIND IS NOT A PROUD ONE. NOR IS IT glorious, no matter its battles, kings, sacrifices and damn golden hoards. Indeed, it is so ignoble that I hesitate to tell it and have it recorded. Yet maybe its lessons will do some good and benefit others, even though it is too late for me. Maybe my kind will be reborn in some distant future and something that is put down here can help them to avoid repeating the mistakes that my age made. Maybe not. Maybe we were always doomed. After all, a beast cannot escape or act beyond its own nature, can it? And our eventual demise shows better than anything else that we were nothing but *beasts*, just as the humans always said.

Oh, it would be easy to blame the humans for all that happened, but enough of it was down to our own vanity that blaming the humans would be just one more example – one last ironic example – of that vanity. No, right here in this graveyard, you see what that vanity brings. Look at the bones all around – they are all that remain of those magnificent giants and fabulous fliers that humanity once feared. In the end, they were no more or less than any other creature in this world – mere flesh and blood. They had no special right to survive, no true reason to see themselves as greater than all other species, and no faith, magic or philosophy to allow them to transcend beyond all. Soon, even these bones will disappear to dust and all that will be left of us is these words that you take down for me, scribe.

Words. The scratchings and scrawlings of a scribe. There are things I will forget to recount to you, there are events that I did not witness firsthand and there are reasons of which I will be ignorant. All that is lost. And so much more will be lost in the telling too. What I relate here and now will not even be properly understood by all readers. Those who never encountered my kind will wonder if this description is a mere fantasy or fiction. They will doubt the truth or accuracy of what I tell you. And, with the passing of time, when there are fewer and fewer humans with an actual memory of us, where there are fewer and fewer to testify that we truly existed, then we will be considered a mere folktale, myth or yarn to entertain children. None will *believe* that dragons actually existed. What you write down, scribe, will be considered the whimsy or delusion of your mind. It does not matter what protestation you append, what testimony you give or what declaration you make. None will know these words to be true.

Given that, maybe it is futile for me to narrate all this. Maybe I should eat you up instead, scribe, as one last meal, and then lay my head down to enter the eternal sleep. What say you, scribe? Huh. You are right. You are here to hear my words, not vice versa. Besides, I am glad of your company, I think. It has been a long time since I last spoke with anything more intelligent that the complaining wind and the busy water of the river below. You are the only living thing that has dared venture close to the wreathed peaks of my home, to the remote fastness that will be the final resting place of my kind. Come now, scribe, no need to take on so. I will not eat you. It was just humour. You humans are fond of humour, yes? Ah well.

Stay a while. You will still have all the gold you can carry when we are done. And the book you are now writing might also make you rich and famous? Surely it is a fair reward for your company. After all, no dragon gives away their gold lightly. In fact, they guard it quite jealously. Perhaps that was where it all began. As it begins, so it will end, eh, scribe? It was rumours of gold and treasure that brought you here in the first place, was it not? So you should hear this from me so that you may warn other humans not to go the way of my kind. It is the only way to know peace, I think, and I would know a measure of that peace before I finally rest.

If the mighty Blackhorn, the eldest of the dragons of my time, had not guarded his gold so jealously, then perhaps our demise would never have come to pass. If the celebrated human thief Longfingers had not thought to steal from Blackhorn . . . ahh . . . if.

*

The Rage of Blackhorn

"He was so large that when he spread his dark wings all would think night had suddenly fallen. Thunderstorms would quail before his roar and turn tail. His fire burnt so hot that the ground that he laid waste stayed barren for a hundred years. When he trod the earth, buildings and trees would topple, rivers diverted in their courses and lakes jumped in their beds. To feed sufficiently, he was forced to turn to the sea, until the Bitter Sea was completely devoid of sea-monsters and whales. In desperation, he turned to eating vast tracts of the earth, and its minerals gradually turned his fangs and scales to gems. He ate out a huge cavern for himself beneath the Needle Mountains, discovering gold as he did so. The gold's lustre enchanted his eye and its substance appeased his hunger better than anything else, although his desire for it only grew and went beyond what he could gather. As last he settled down to sleep upon his hoard, to wait until the earth had recovered enough to sustain him properly once more.

Now the Needle Mountains were quiet, the soft-stepping

Longfingers came stealing in to see what the dragon might have left unattended and what chance might offer. He found Blackhorn asleep and could not resist helping himself to more than a little of the dragon's gold. Longfingers did not know that Blackhorn slept with one eye open and was watching him the entire time. As the human crept away, Blackhorn slowly roused from his sleep of many years and trumpeted his rage. They say his cry was heard across the land.

Longfingers fled to the town called Steppeberg and used some of the gold to pay soldiers, knights and other such humans to protect him. They manned their battlements with archers and brandished weapons of the finest steel. They rode out in bright plate mail, pennons fluttering and lances borne skywards. The townsfolk cheered on the proud display, as drums were beaten and war horns were sounded. It would all be for naught.

The vengeful Blackhorn descended upon them with such violence and noise that they must have believed the heavens themselves were falling. The snap of his wings hurled them from the walls and from their mounts. His fiery breath cooked them in their armour. His shoulders and girth brought their presumptuous towers crashing down, and when he landed upon the town's bulwark it buckled beneath his immensity. He devoured stone, animal, wood and human alike, using them as fuel to release a new inferno from his maw.

Scenting the air, Blackhorn moved down through the town, tumbling dwellings and crushing wagons underfoot as he went. He found the town's treasury and smashed it open. He scraped through the debris until he uncovered the gold shining there. He swallowed it down. It might have satisfied him were he not also intent on finding Longfingers. Where was the wretched human?

Scour the kingdom though he did, Blackhorn could not find the man. That should have been an end to it, but the human King Ironshanks was furious by what had been done to Steppeberg. Ironshanks promised the hand of his daughter in marriage to whichever knight could bring him the head of Blackhorn.

Human after human sought out the black dragon's lair – Sir
Ealred with his longbow, Sir Ilfoot with his glittering shield,
Sir Chattin of the silent approach, Sir Effodd with his mazing
run, and many, many more. There were so many that Blackhorn
inevitably received wounds. It is thought that some of those
wounds were delivered by poison blades. Or that some withering
magic was used. You humans are so numerous and multiply
so quickly that perhaps he simply did not have enough time
between encounters to heal properly. In any event, by the time Sir
Perival – dressed in the scales shed by other dragons – ventured
into the Needle Mountains the mighty Blackhorn must already
have been greatly lessened. Perhaps the Great Drake was unable
to defend himself. Perhaps he was already dead. There can be no
other way to explain how Sir Perival came out of those mountains
carrying the head of the most fearsome of my kind, one who
saw the First Days.

What became of the human thief Longfingers? Apparently, the
thief somehow escaped, had songs written about his audacious
courage, and lived out the paltry number of his days enjoying
his ill-gotten wealth."

*

The Rights of Cobaltskin

"FOLLOWING THE DEATH of Blackhorn, my kind decided to
avoid humans as best they could. They took themselves off to
the inhospitable places of the world, to unscaled heights, unfath-
omed depths, sucking marshes and windswept uplands. They fed
meagrely, on fish, birds, crawling and scurrying things, and the
occasional goat or goblin. We became smaller in size, and many
felt that we had lost something, but we survived without conflict
for a good hundred years or more.

During that time, however, just as we diminished so the
humans grew in number. They claimed more and more of the

land for themselves and soon came close to where the dragons had retreated. So it was that Cobaltskin was flying over his hunting grounds one day and spied sheep wandering and grazing below. It had been a long time since he had tasted the meat of a sheep, but remembered it had been sweet and tender, so wasted not a moment streaking down upon them. He would have appeared as lightning, for his scales were so bright he made the sky seem dull. He was so sharp of eye that he could see the sheep move before they had even thought to do so. His bite was so fierce and clean that they would have been dead before they could wonder at seeing lightning on a clear day.

As magnificent a display as it would have been, the old shepherd that then went scampering and hollering down the hill can't have been too impressed. Cobaltskin considered giving chase, but he was now full of sheep and feeling unusually sleepy. Besides, there didn't look to be much meat on that particular human, and then there was the story of Blackhorn. The Great Drake should never have gone after Longfingers in the first place, as he'd only got all the humans worked up.

'They were on my territory!' Cobaltskin called. 'Fair game and mine by rights.'

That should have been an end to it, but it never is with humans. The very next day, a warrior came riding up the hill, in plain sight. He had weapons aplenty, his shoulders and jaw were set firmly and there was a glint of intent in his eye as he scanned the rise and the skies above.

'What do you want here, human?' Cobaltskin asked curiously from where he perched nearby on a low crag.

The warrior jumped and fumbled for his bow. His horse snorted and reared in panic. Arrows fell from the man's quiver and scattered hither and thither upon the ground.

'What are you doing?' Cobaltskin asked mildly.

The warrior's shoulders slumped in defeat. 'I was fumbling for my bow . . . in order to shoot you.'

'Really? A strange idea. An arrow would be unlikely to penetrate my hide.'

'What would you recommend?

'Well, you could try a sword and shield, I suppose, but I'd incinerate you before you even got close. Hmm. You might be better off just leaving me in peace.'

'You ate the shepherd's entire flock. His family would starve were it not for the charity of others. The mayor says we simply can't have it. I've been ordered up here to sort you out.'

'I see. But the shepherd will not actually starve?'

'Well, no.'

'I see. The thing is, I was out hunting yesterday, and this is my home. I don't usually do you humans any harm up here going about my life, now do I?'

'Err . . . I s'pose, if you put it like that.'

There was a moment of silence. Cobaltskin's tongue tasted the air and his nostrils flared as he caught the scent of the man's mount. He hadn't had horse before, but it certainly smelt . . . No, he wouldn't think like that. He didn't want to upset yet another of the humans. Besides, it was speaking again.

'. . . I go and speak to the mayor and explain? The shepherd was trespassing.'

'That's a good word,' Cobaltskin encouraged.

'Yes. Yes!' the warrior smiled. 'It's simply been a misunderstanding. There's no real need for me to . . . well, you know.'

'Precisely.'

'Good. Good! That's settled then. I wish you a good day, dragon, and sorry for bothering you. You have pretty scales, by the way.'

'Why, thank you,' Cobaltskin preened. 'I wish you a good day also, human.'

With that, the warrior set off down the hill a sight faster than he'd come up it. Cobaltskin watched him go, shrugged and wondered what he might like for his next meal (although dragons do not always think about food, scribe, honestly!)

That, of course, should have been an end to it, but the mayor of the humans had other ideas on the matter. The very next day, the mayor and a large group of other humans (many carrying forks, hammers and other tools) came to visit Cobaltskin.

'Dragon, we will give you one sheep a month if you keep the woods and roads hereabouts free of bandits, thieves and cut-throats,' the portly one who had identified himself as mayor declared. 'Beyond that, you will not touch a single sheep or cow.' Someone whispered to him. 'Or chicken. Do you agree?'

'I'd prefer it if you simply left me alone,' Cobaltskin decided.

The mayor tutted and shook his head. 'Come now, dragon, you did eat the shepherd's sheep. We need to come to some sort of *accommodation*, especially if we are to be neighbours. It is important to get on with one another's neighbours, to do each other small services in order to keep the peace. Wouldn't you like for us to get along? Do this thing by way of *reparation* and we will otherwise leave you alone.'

Cobaltskin thought about refusing, but suspected the warrior would return, and that he'd be followed by another, and another, and another. 'Two sheep a month.'

'Done!'

'And what should I do with these bandits, thieves and cut-throats? Eat them?'

There was some consternation at this amongst the humans, and much discussion. Finally, the mayor announced: 'Yes. They would have been executed for their crimes in any event. You'll be saving us a job, and it'll be in the way of extra reward for you. Agreed?'

Cobaltskin pondered for a goodly while. Humans were generally more trustworthy than goblins (they couldn't exactly be *less* after all!), but no dragon had actually ever entered into a bargain with a human. A dragon's word is binding and never to be broken, you see, and dragons can live a very long time. Yet at last Cobaltskin nodded. 'Agreed, human.'

The agreement made, Cobaltskin was left alone as had been

promised. True to his word, the blue dragon cornered and consumed all those in the surrounding wilderness who might molest the merchants travelling to and from the mayor's town, a place called Ambleside. As might be expected, Ambleside began to prosper and profits were put into improving roads and expanding the town. Soon, there was work for all, including all those who might once have been desperate enough to turn to banditry, theft and the cutting of throats. Inevitably, Ambleside grew into a powerful city and the mayor was referred to as a potentate. Naturally, the city required more land to feed its people, until hunters and farmers alike began to occupy territory that Cobaltskin had always considered his hunting ground. And so the time came when Cobaltskin arrived at the place where the two sheep were always tethered for him, only to discover that there were no sheep. Assuming that there had been some mistake, Cobaltskin waited for several days, but still no sheep came.

'Dragon, you need to understand that Ambleside now has many new families and mouths to feed,' the potentate patiently explained. 'We can no longer afford to give away two sheep a month to a creature who doesn't do anything to earn those sheep. We want to see the number of sheep increase, not waste them on making you, well, quite frankly, fat.'

'I keep the woods and roads hereabouts free of bandits, thieves and cut-throats. It is the *accommodation* that we came to,' Cobaltskin rumbled.

'Dragon, you know full well that there haven't been any bandits, thieves or cut-throats in this area in years. Our city guard would easily deal with them if they were ever a problem.'

'It matters not. We have a binding agreement.'

'I'm afraid I cannot permit you to hold us to ransom like this. I have greater concerns that simply will not allow it. Some say that it's because we keep feeding you that you keep coming back to upset the farmers and livestock hereabouts.'

'They have encroached upon my hunting grounds.'

'Dragon, you have used all the woods and roads for miles as

your hunting grounds. They cannot be for your exclusive use. It's just not realistic. Surely you can see that. Our farmers own the land that they work, for possession is nine-tenths of the law.'

'Dragons are not ruled by human law!' Cobaltskin spat. 'You humans will honour our agreement or you will be known as oath-breakers and I will take the sheep as I choose.'

'Dragon, this is foolhardy. Perhaps it would be better if you kept to that distant mountain range. Surely there is enough food for you there.'

'That territory belongs to other dragons, foolish human. *This* is my territory here. You will respect that or you will be failing to get on with your neighbour. Did you not say it was important to get on with one's neighbours? Now bring me the sheep or I will take them from you.'

The potentate tutted and shook his head. 'Such a shame that you cannot be more reasonable, dragon.'

No sheep were brought, and so Cobaltskin ripped them from the farm that most encroached upon his hunting grounds. 'Menace!' shouted the farmer as Cobaltskin winged away. The next month, again there were no sheep, and so Cobaltskin returned to the farm. The farmer loosed an arrow at him, but the dragon's scales shrugged it off. As was his right, Cobaltskin helped himself to two of the farmer's sheep. The month after that, again there were no sheep, and so Cobaltskin returned to the farm.

This time, the city guard were there. They had with them a giant crossbow mounted on wheels, a weapon you humans call a ballista, I think. As Cobaltskin descended to collect the two sheep owed him, the guards fired the weapon. The giant bolt that had been released skewered Cobaltskin's chest, stealing his breath from him so that he was unable to answer with flame. He tumbled out of the air and broke upon the ground that was his by rights but no longer belonged to him.

That was Cobaltskin's end.

Scribe, there is one more thing to tell of that dragon. Cobaltskin was my father."

The Lament of Greenfang

"HER COLOUR WAS more verdant than a meadow in summer and the moss upon the Unreached Mountains. Her eyes were brighter than emeralds. She was greener than nature itself. To look upon her was to be mesmerised, to catch her scent on the wind was to be intoxicated with something primal and glorious, to touch her was to know thirst and hunger, to hear her call was to know the joy, thrill and fear of life. And she would see to it that humans would know fear like never before, for the outrage that they had committed. She would see mountains tumble upon them and her flames engulf a vast pyre of them, till all trace of their ever having existed was removed.

She had not wanted to leave her cave in winter, but hunger had driven her out and she would need her strength in the time ahead. Game had been in woefully short supply, and she'd had to roam far for several days. Upon her return, she'd discovered the theft and her shrieks of anger and distress near shattered the world.

Greenfang flew faster than the wind, trying to turn back time itself. She could not manage it, though she tested her every fibre. She thumped down in the hamlet of Haver's Brook, the human habitation closest to her cave, and proceeded to tear it apart. 'Where is it, miserable humans?' she screamed as she tipped over wagons, spilling their contents, and her lashing tail decimated their sheds and shelters. People fled in all directions, making no sense. Greenfang tried to grab one, to wring answers from it, but it scuttled like a beetle and evaded her. Suddenly she loomed over a human child, which stared up at her in wonder. There was a cry and a human female – presumably the child's mother – put herself between Greenfang and the child.

'Mercy!'

Greenfang displayed her teeth. 'Where is it, human? Which of you came to my cave while I was away hunting? Answer me!'

'Dragon, a troop of royal guard galloped through here but two days ago. Is it them you seek? They will be heading for the capital.'

She was in the air again before the woman had even finished speaking. Royal guards? Well, she would take on their entire kingdom if necessary. Which dragon would not do the same? Which creature would not? Only the humans perhaps, who were appalling in every way.

Greenfang flew hard for a whole day, then into the night. On and on she went, through storm clouds and violent winds. She would not relent. She had to overtake them if she could, before they reached their defensive walls and their army. Things would be more difficult then, although it would not save them.

Yet there was no sign of them, even as she flew through a second day and night, and then a third. At last she reached the sprawling human capital that was called Dur Mannoch, but she was so exhausted she could no longer stay aloft. Barely controlling her descent, she hit the soft bank of a river, rolled and came to a rest. She took several mouthfuls of the nearby water, but otherwise her strength was entirely spent. Greenfang was pulled down into a dark slumber.

When she awoke, she immediately knew there was something wrong. She tried to rise, but found herself constrained by something that bit cruelly into her the more she struggled. Attempting to spread her wings, she found that they pulled on one another – chained together, with attaching loops piercing her leathery membranes. Greenfang craned her neck, but even that was difficult – she wore some sort of collar that was attached to a large spike sunk deep into the ground. She roared her rage, and would have sheeted flames all around had she taken in enough fuel.

'It is no use, dragon,' spoke a voice on the other side of her. She turned to find a whole host of humans there ready and waiting. A white-haired, lavishly-robed man addressed her: 'Your restraints are magical. They turn your own strength against you.'

'Where is it, wretched humans?' she hissed. 'There can be no forgiveness for what you have done.'

'Keep a civil tongue in your head, dragon,' White Hair warned, his voice thrumming with power. 'You are in the presence of His Highness Prince Raylon. Your Highness, it is safe to address the beast.'

'Thank you, wizard,' a pinch-faced youth in unnatural looking colours smiled. 'Dragon, I am anointed by God and rule all the land up to the sea in every direction. I am prepared to tolerate your kind as long as there is a check upon your unruliness. You will swear to serve me or you must be considered a threat to be ended once and for all. How say you?'

'Where is it?' Greenfang railed, testing her ties again.

The dozens of hard-eyed soldiers accompanying the Prince lifted their weapons. The Prince looked to each side of him and then nodded smugly. 'The egg is safe. It will be returned to you once I have your oath. You will be permitted to hatch it in the royal stable that we are having specially constructed. Your oath now, dragon.'

While oath-breakers themselves, the humans had clearly worked out from their dealings with Cobaltskin that a dragon's oath was binding and forever. 'Very well,' Greenfang said carefully. 'Once my egg has been returned, I will serve you, human prince.'

The soldiers visibly relaxed. White Hair raised the spike that tethered Greenfang out of the ground, and she was led inside the city. They led her through the streets, where crowds gathered and cheered. She was taken inside the palace to a large stable.

'Bring me the egg!' she insisted.

The Prince signalled for it to be done and presently two servants arrived bearing the silver-veined boulder. 'Now,' began the haughty ruler, raising a finger to Greenfang. The dragon rattled her chains and rolled her massive bulk over the human wizard standing nearby, smearing him across the cobblestones of the courtyard. The Prince's mouth fell open in surprise. The magic in the chains that bound her failed. The Prince was still wearing the same expression when, with one casual swipe, she broke him against the ground.

Men screamed in horror. Arrows and pila began to pepper her, but she ignored them. She yanked at the chain connecting her wings – it tore through the fragile membranes but at last she was free of it. She grabbed the egg in her talons and leapt skywards.

She was wobbly in the air, but managed to gain some height. Raggedly, she made for the city walls and just about cleared them. A ballista put another sizeable hole through her wing and she cried out in pain, but she was away now, with the egg unharmed!

The journey home was a hard one for her. With her injuries, she'd fly a mile or two and then have to land and go on foot for a while. She was also significantly weakened for not having fed in three days. Yet nothing was going to stop her, and at long last she made it back to her cave.

There, Greenfang settled down with her egg, surviving on some of the rats she'd deliberately allowed to infest the cave some months before – her offspring would also need this ready supply of meat once it was born, and with such vermin around it could learn to hunt within the safe area of its own home. A week later and Greenfang knew only joy, for the egg hatched.

'Your name is Silvereye,' she crooned. 'You are dragonkind and you are loved.'

Mother and child spent weeks together, forming the bond of dragonkind. Eventually Greenfang sighed. 'It is time for you to leave, beloved daughter. An army of humans approaches, and you must get away while you can. Far away.'

'Come with me, mother!' young Silvereye begged, unable to stop her tears.

'I still find flying difficult, young one, and so do you. If we both try to fly, they will catch us both, for these humans are vengeful and determined. I will hold them here a goodly while so that you may escape and thrive. I will hurt a good number of them too.'

'I cannot be without you. Please, mother!'

'Hush, young one. It happens to all of us in the end. You will go as your dam commands it. Always remember that I love you and that I have known the greatest happiness for seeing you come into this world.'

'I hate the humans, mother!'

'Child, promise me that you will not seek to revenge yourself on them. You must get away and hide from the humans instead. Promise me, for I cannot bear to think they might have you after I'm gone. As you love me, so promise me.'

'I promise, mother,' Silvereye said in a small, sad voice.

'Good. Go now, sweetest child. Enjoy the world, grow, find other dragons and know a comfort of spirit. Goodbye.'

That was how Greenfang ended.

Scribe, there is one more thing to tell of her. Greenfang was my mother."

*

The War and Wane of Dragonkind

"How do I know of my parents in such detail? Why, I have their memories, scribe. What one dragon knows and experiences, all dragons know. (I think it is not the same among humans, that humans do not share mind and spirit. It is why dragons are born wise, but humans must learn by their mistakes.) The loss of a parent is all the keener because of it. It is beyond despair – it is desolation and diminishment. All dragonkind suffers for the loss of just one.

And so the crimes committed by humans against Blackhorn, Cobaltskin and Greenfang were crimes committed against all dragonkind. The attempted enslavement and subsequent murder of Greenfang was considered the ultimate offence, and dragonkind decided humankind had to be punished and properly curtailed. Their numbers had to be culled and our rightful territory had to be reclaimed. Humans had to be taught their place once and for all.

We were led by the formidable Redclaw, whom none could match in the air. He scorched the place you called Fairview from the earth, and probably from your history. He allowed no quarter to any of your kind, even when you pleaded for mercy, offered sacrifices and sued for peace. Finally, you brought the Great Sorcerer Siderus from the plains to the north to save you. The conflict was terrible, and many humans died to exhaust the giant red, but ultimately it was done. It is said Siderus cried to see such a great enemy belittled by strangling magicks, and to hear the whimper of his final breath.

Even though so many humans had died, the loss of Redclaw to dragonkind was the greater tragedy. You see, a female dragon will only have offspring once every hundred years or so, and often never lay more than one or two eggs in a lifetime. Given our size, there would not be enough game to sustain us if we bred more than that.

And there was our weakness – that we could never breed in the numbers required to prevail over humankind. Even once we realised our plight, pride would not allow us to give up our war upon you. There was our second weakness, scribe, a weakness that saw us give up our lives even when humans began to cede us new territories and demand that we save ourselves as much as anything else. Still we would not hear of giving up the war, for we had sworn to see all humans displaced, and a dragon's promise is binding and forever as I have already told you. There was our third and *final* weakness, scribe. That was how dragonkind was ended.

Perhaps it was inevitable. We could not escape our own nature in the end. From the moment the human thief Longfingers stole from mighty Blackhorn's cave, my kind was doomed.

I am the last of the dragons. I have only lived so long because of that promise I made to my mother, Greenfang, to hide from humans rather than seek revenge upon them.

My story is now done, scribe, and soon I will rest. The story of my kind will end as I end. Ah, how I yearn to rest, to finish this desolation and diminishment that are beyond despair.

Dry your tears, scribe, for none remain to blame humankind. I speak for my kind now, so hear me when I tell you that we knowingly undid ourselves while humankind was unknowing throughout. Ours was the greater fault and therefore ours was the price to pay. So put your pen and parchment away, for I must rest. Take what gold you wish and leave me here amongst the bones of my ancestors. Fare you well."

Black and White

Michael Victor Bowman

A NAKED MAN WALKS ACROSS THE FROZEN CALDERA OF an Icelandic volcano. His bare feet crunch through the fresh snow covering the frozen, rocky ground, but he does not flinch. His paper white skin is exposed to the subzero caress of the freezing air, but he does not shiver. He walks tall, stepping confidently and with an easy stride, while the bright sun of the far north gleams in the pure white hair that covers his head and nestles at his crotch.

At the lowest point of the caldera a thin plume of smoke curls up out of a fracture in the ground. The smoke is steam and is the only outward sign that this volcano is alive; that a ten-mile deep and two-hundred-mile wide lake of lava pulses and throbs like a beating heart entombed in the earth's cold stone. The naked man walks towards it but, before he reaches the plume, he stops. His hair casts his face in shadow as he tilts his head towards the ground at his feet. Then he stoops and sweeps away the surface layer of rocks and stones to expose a sheet of glassy ice, beneath. For a moment the ice is a mirror, showing him only his own reflection: a pale shadow against the blue sky, beyond. Then a rare wisp of cloud gusts across the sun and, suddenly, the mirror becomes a chasm that knifes down into the black rock. Something moves down there, far down where the warmth of the beating heart can still be felt, something that coils and flows, like black water pouring itself endlessly through ancient and winding passages, carving paths between deep caverns that have never seen the light of day.

The wisp of cloud burns away to nothing and the ice becomes a mirror once more. But the man does not look away. In the shadow of his face, his eyes flash a brilliant blue that makes the cloudless sky behind him seem dull and lifeless by comparison. His invitation is answered by a paired flash of molten red from deep below, and a distant rumbling.

'Have you learned your lesson?' he whispers, and far below the glowing red eyes dim slightly, as if in reply. 'Then you are free,' he says and, balling his fist, he punches the ice at his feet. Shards as tall as he is stab upwards all around him and the caldera resounds with a sound like a thousand tree trunks snapping in half. The naked man withdraws his fist and smiles with pure white, perfect teeth as the ground begins to shake. And in the days that follow, ten million stranded travellers look up into the ash-filled sky from which they have been temporarily exiled, and are reminded that nature, not mankind, rules all.

*

SHE IS LIKE a bird, skimming over the ocean. The wave tops wash over her like the caress of an old lover and she sings with joy. I am free! Her cry is answered. Out of the blackness below she hears the familiar song of old friends.

We hear you. Welcome.

Their greeting swells her heart to bursting and in her excitement she screams skyward, moving faster and faster like a shooting star returning to the heavens. But before she touches the clouds, she pauses and, floating high above the world, turns to survey her home of old.

The endless sheet grey of the northern ocean spreads out in every direction beneath her, its beauty marred only by a distant v-shaped dash of white. It is very small and far away, but so vast is the ocean and so uniform in colour that this one tiny flaw in its magnificent perfection consumes her. She dives towards it, slashing through tattered fragments of cloud as she goes. She rushes past an ancient albatross riding invisible currents of air, but its squawks of outrage are quickly left behind. Now the perfect, slate grey, smooth surface has become a heaving mass of high peaked waves whose rising flanks betray hues of deep green and dirty blue, and streaks of pale white. Plunging through their troughs is a strange looking ship, its rounded metal bow carving a white wound through the living ocean. She has never seen the like of it before. Has she been gone for so long? Where are the bellying sails? Where are the rows of weather-bitten men straining at their oars? This ship's unnaturally bulbous body rises vertically from the ocean like a seamless cliff face; smooth and hard, lacking the texture of the hand-carved wooden vessels she knew. The bow, which should be fine and pointed, is rounded and fat while the stern, which should come together like a tail, is cut off in a hard flat line. The deck is strewn with strange shapes: tall masts festooned with spindly yards that bear no sails, angular things like the crooked fingers of a giant, openings large and small, some closed like trapdoors. All is dominated by a great house that straddles the width of the hull, with a row of windows looking out towards the bow. But most alarming of all is the plume of grey smoke rising from a black tube behind the house. A fire! On a ship at sea! The worst fear of every mariner, and yet the handful of crewmen on deck are walking about with no concern.

Fascinated, fearful, disbelieving, she moves closer, sliding between the rising waves, stalking the strange vessel until she can come up alongside it and take a precarious hold of its sheer metal flanks. She pauses to sing to her friends once more, to tell them of this strange new thing she has discovered. But they answer only with a warning.

Danger! Flee!

She is confused. What thing on earth can possibly threaten

her? She creeps up over the rail that lines the edge of the hull, and on to the deck, where now she can hear voices. She almost recognises them: they speak the language of the Vikings, or something like it. She knew that race and they knew her. But there is something else about this strange vessel. Something that explains the fear in her friends' warning. The smell of blood.

*

KRISTOFFER SLURPS HIS coffee as he stares out through the tall, narrow windows of the wheelhouse. The coffee tastes like blood. The whole boat and everything on it tastes and smells like blood after a catch. It used to make Kristoffer retch when he was a teenage deckhand, but in the years since he has learned to like the smell: to him it's the smell of money. He stares out at the sea. The weather is good, he muses, but the waves are rising. It will make hauling their next catch aboard tricky. He sniffs, rubs his callused hand across the nine days of growth that cover his chin, then flicks on the radio.

'Anders!' he grunts.

'Nothing, yet,' comes back a tired voice. Kristoffer fixes his eyes on the top of the vessel's foremast, which rises vertically out of the bows. On top of the mast, painted yellow in contrast to the mostly white decks, is a giant dustbin big enough for a man to stand up in. Around the top of the bin is a row of window slits. Inside is the silhouette of a man's head and shoulders. As Kristoffer watches, the silhouette raises a pair of binoculars.

'Anything now?' Kristoffer growls.

He is answered by a stream of invective as Anders curses the skipper's impatience. There is a pause. Now the silhouette in the spotting top starts jerking excitedly. 'Plume at red two four zero, distance five hundred yards.'

Kristoffer spits and moves behind the wheel, his hand resting on the throttle.

'Moving port to starboard,' the voice crackles.

Kristoffer spins the wheel a few degrees to the right and pushes the throttle forward. Somewhere deep below his feet he feels the familiar background rumble of the engine grow deeper. 'Leif!' he bellows over his shoulder. From somewhere in the warm yellow glow of the stairwell behind Kristoffer there is the sound of pots and pans clanging. 'Leif, get up for'rard, you fat bastard! You can eat later!'

The vessel begins to roll from side to side as Kristoffer turns her bows across the direction of the waves. Now the ocean no longer cuts itself open on her bows, but slams into her broad, flat flanks. Anything hanging from a hook: the coiled cable of the radio mic, paper charts on clipboards, waterproof jackets; it all swings crazily from side to side. So does Leif as he clambers up the stairs, bouncing off the plywood-panelled walls as the ship rocks back and forth. Grumbling, he grabs a jacket, pulls it on over the top of his big, baggy waterproof trousers and stumbles outside. Kristoffer watches him clamber down to the main deck and make his way towards the bow.

'Distance four hundred yards, still moving port to starboard,' the radio hisses.

Kristoffer turns the wheel another few degrees. He still cannot see the target for himself. The waves breaking over the railings wash the wheelhouse windows with spray, blinding them. The skipper flicks on the wipers. The small cabin is filled with the sound of their busy squeaking as they carve a hemisphere of visibility in the diffuse, wet grey outside.

'Kris!' yells another voice from somewhere down below. 'Stop shaking the damn boat! I'm working with knives down here!'

'Shut your face and get back to work, Erik!' Kristoffer roars. 'Get that carcass packed and iced. We'll be hauling a new catch aboard any minute!'

'Ah . . . !' Erik groans. 'Why can't I have help? I need a deckhand! There's too much work for one man.'

'Cause then we'd have to split the profits five ways, instead of four, you stupid lazy mother!' Kristoffer snarls.

'Distance, three fifty,' Anders reports. Kristoffer slams the throttle all the way forward. The engine screams, its regular thumping becoming a fast, hard thud that vibrates the deck plates under his feet. A white wave breaks over the deck, soaking Leif as he wrestles to pull a tarpaulin off a piece of equipment mounted in front of the foremast. Kristoffer remembers the day before they left Skrova, nearly two weeks ago now. Leif's wife and four year old son, Kam, had come aboard. Kam had pointed to the thing under Leif's hands and burbled 'Teh-weh-kope, Daddy!' thinking it was like the telescope Leif kept at his window, pointing out across the harbour.

As Kristoffer watches, Leif finally pulls the tarpaulin free. He reveals something tube-shaped, mounted on a heavy tripod of steel girders welded to the deck. Leif grabs two long curved handles that protrude from the back of the tube and uses his own body weight to swing it around to point at the distant plume that jets skywards between the oncoming waves.

'Two hundred yards, dead ahead!' Anders calls, but it's irrelevant now because both Kristoffer and Leif can see the target for themselves. The engine thuds, the waves slam against the hull and white spray drenches Leif. The hull rolls over under the ocean's constant bombardment then pitches back upright. It rolls again, until it seems that Anders will either be tossed from his high perch or the mast with Anders on top of it will be dunked into the subzero water that surrounds them; then it rises to meet them and swallow them like a giant mouth.

'One hundred yards . . .'

Kristoffer can hear the anticipation in Anders's voice.

'Seventy . . .'

Leif won't miss, Kristoffer thinks, the corner of his mouth twisting into a smile. The beast is as good as packed and iced already.

'Sixty . . .'

Kristoffer watches Leif's body tense and sway as he balances himself against the movement of the boat to steady his aim.

'Fifty!' Anders yells down the line. Anders knows what it means. He knows what happens when the range reaches fifty. Out on the wave-battered bow Leif pulls the trigger. The bang is muted, like a giant balloon popping over a naked flame. The harpoon flies up and out into the grey murk, the anchor line uncoiling itself into a long, vibrating arc in space as the harpoon drags it skyward.

They wait, while the sea hammers them and the hull bobs like a child's toy. And still they wait.

Kristoffer frowns. 'Anders!' he yells into the mic. 'Did he get it?'

Leif is standing up straight now, one hand shading his eyes against the sea spray as he peers after his harpoon.

'I dunno,' Anders replies. 'I thought he did . . . wait, what's that?'

A big wave breaks across the boat's waist, smothering the wheelhouse windows in churning, white foam. The struggling wipers are overwhelmed and the wheelhouse windows fall dark, blinding the skipper to the outside world.

'What's what?' Kristoffer asks. But Anders isn't talking to his skipper anymore. Instead the radio carries back the look-out's voice as he shouts to the harpoon man below him. 'Leif! For God's sake, get away from it! Run! Oh God. Oh Christ! Oh, Jesus Christ, help me! It's not real. It's not . . .'

The mic goes dead.

'Anders!' Kristoffer shouts. 'Anders! What's happening?' The water is draining now and, as the skipper raises his round, frightened eyes, he sees something. Just for a second. Something blurred and almost washed away in the seawater that is sluicing across the windows. Something utterly impossible, and utterly terrifying. And then it is gone.

Kristoffer drops the mic.

'Kris?' Erik calls from below. 'Kris? What's happening?'

Kristoffer opens his mouth, but he has no words. The foremast is gone. Snapped in half. The shattered, yellow stump sticks up from the empty bows. The harpoon gun is gone, the welded steel ripped from the boat's deck, leaving a nasty, twisted mess of sharp metal. Leif is gone. Anders is gone.

'Christ . . . have mercy,' Kristoffer whispers, his eyes filling with tears.

*

SAFE NOW, SHE sings. She is answered by a chorus of relief, then her friends dive away and she turns her own face back towards the sky. But this time she finds no joy there. She is no longer enthralled by the beauty of the ocean, for it no longer feels like hers. It has been polluted, somehow. Drifting on the cold winds she glides into the soft, silent embrace of a dense cloud, seeking a measure of solace in its still, grey heart. She is troubled, her mind a maelstrom of emotions, and in this state of confusion she is an easy target for the White dragon.

Like a freshly seaborne seal pup that has strayed too far from shore, she realises too late that something is rushing up towards her. First she sees his eyes: twin points of cobalt blue that pierce the gloom. Then the grey cloud below her is ripped apart by the twin hurricanes of air that spill from the tips of his outstretched wings, wings that beat with the sound of thunder, shake the sky itself and send her senses reeling. She feels claws each as long as a grown man's arm closing around her shoulders, and only now does she find the strength and will to react. She screams, and a geyser of volcanic fire splits the sky, but too late. He evades the flame, moving as smoothly and silently as a breath of icy wind. But doing so has forced him to release her and she bares her own claws in a counterattack! She strikes for those bright blue eyes, determined to put them out. She anticipates the feeling of her claws gouging into the bone at the back of his orbits, but instead she finds them locked tightly as he clasps them in his own. Falling through the sky, each with their wings outstretched, they begin to spin.

'Let go!' she roars, eyes flashing red as she sees the deep ocean rushing up towards them. He makes no reply. His cool blue eyes barely flicker. How he enrages her! She screams again, certain of her mark, for he cannot evade while they embrace. But this time he replies in kind and her flames are met by a blizzard of ice. The two opposing elements collide, but even he cannot quench her fire. Instead, a great cloud of steam erupts all about them and they plummet towards the ocean at the tip of a billowing tail a mile long, like the smoking remains of a shooting star.

When they strike the water, so violent is their entrance that a wave rises up and rushes towards the distant Lofoten Islands, where four anxious families stare out across the small harbour at Skrova. They watch as a coast guard cutter sails in response to a distant distress call, silently hoping for the best, but fearing the worst.

*

SHE FLEES FROM him, but he pursues her. She is a sleek, black shark powering towards land, but he is a shimmer of flashing silver fish; the prey in pursuit of the predator. Reaching shore, she tries to hide as a forest of black and green kelp clinging to the rocky Norwegian coastline. But at low tide he is a flock of hungry white gulls that descend to peck and tear at her leaves and bladders. In agony, she howls and becomes a black wolf, speeding inland, passing between the trees like a shadow. He is a white-winged eagle, twisting and turning through the towering tree trunks with single-minded agility. When she feels his talons scrape her back, she howls again and becomes an army of scurrying black ants, smothering the forest floor with tiny, shiny bodies. A heavy white boot comes down in their midst, crushing dozens of her as the figure of a man in a bulky white suit stands between the trees. He is carrying a silver metal canister on his back. The ant horde pauses in momentary confusion before him as he raises a long white tube, spraying what looks like water across them.

But this water is agony. It burns inside her until she can bear it no longer. Wailing like a hell-bound soul, the ants evaporate into a cloud that coalesces into a human form: a female with wild black hair, pale skin and oriental eyes that burn with red rage. Breathing deeply from the chase, she stands before him, unashamedly naked beneath the forest canopy. White, similarly, divests himself of his artifice. Once more the white-skinned man from the caldera, he steps forward, barefoot, into the dappled twilight to join her.

She glares at him, her flesh still quivering from the memory of the pain. 'What was that?' she hisses.

'Dichloro diphenyl trichloro ethane,' he replies, calmly.

'What?'

'They call it DDT.' As he meets her uncomprehending look, he adds, 'You have been gone a long time.'

'And whose fault is that?' she yells, jabbing a finger at him. Her eyes flash red, but the effort seems to drain her and she takes a weary step back, her bare feet scuffing the dense floor of pine needles. 'How long?' she breathes, stooping slightly.

White turns his head a little, as if he can see her more clearly through the corner of his eyes. 'One thousand and ninety years, as men count time.'

She raises her head and stares at him through her mane of black hair, her mouth working silently as she repeats the number. Then her eyes widen. 'Bastard!' she snarls and moves to attack, to transform once more. But he stands firm, ready for her, and she halts herself mid-stride because her outstretched hands, which should have become the claws of a mighty bear, are still those of a slim young oriental woman, naked, dishevelled and visibly shaking with exhaustion. With a defiant snarl, she clenches her fists and lowers them to her sides. 'Why do you pursue me?'

White scoffs loudly, the sound echoing among the trees. 'Do you pretend not to know?' His smile fades and his cool eyes harden. 'You have killed!'

She snorts. 'What of it?'

Now White jabs a finger at her, instead. 'You have disturbed the balance. Again!'

She plants her hands on her hips. 'So, will you imprison me, again?'

'If I must,' he replies, menacingly.

'Hah! You must catch me first!'

White spreads his arms wide, as if to encompass the small clearing in which they stand. 'Have I not, already?'

Her lip curls with resentment. 'Then why am I not already entombed beneath rock and ice?'

White gazes at her from beneath lowered brows, as though studying a newly discovered specimen. 'Because I would know what was in your heart when you killed those men.'

She gives him a suspicious look. 'And if I tell you, will you grant my freedom?'

But his eyes are now hidden in the shadow of his flop of gleaming white hair and she cannot read his thoughts. She can only feel the intensity of his stare, and she knows she will extract no promises from him. She rolls her eyes. 'I killed them to teach them a lesson,' she says.

'The dead can learn nothing,' he observes.

'Did I kill them all? No! I made an example.'

'Why?'

'Because they hunt my friends! They hunt beings that also think and feel, as much as any man!'

'They do not understand that. Not yet.'

'Then we must show them! We must force them to understand. We have the power!'

White shakes his head. 'Mankind hunted the whales in the past, when you were free. You did not object then.'

She waves a hand dismissively. 'They took only one or two a year: the old or the sick. And they hunted in small boats and made the kill with spears that they threw with their hands. It was a fair contest that killed as many men as it did whales. But that . . . that thing,' she spits, and jabs a finger wildly in the direction of the distant ocean. 'It was full of dead bodies. It stank of the blood of a dozen different whales, and they were hunting for yet more!'

'And so you killed them.'

'Yes! I killed them. To protect my friends, and to teach the other men a lesson. One they will not soon forget. You talk often of balance. *That* is the balance they must be taught to respect! To be mindful of all living things but, most of all, to be mindful of their place in the world. And if they forget it, I will be there to remind them!'

'Will you?'

'Yes!' she roars, her voice cracking the air with its power, reminding him as if he could forget that within this diminutive woman's body lurked the immensity of a dragon. But it is a heavy burden to bear: even as the echo of her roar fades, she staggers and sits down hard on the forest floor, gasping. Despite this, she glares at him, daring him to speak, and when he does not, she thumps her chest. 'That is *my* balance,' she growls, raising her clenched fist in defiance of him and his hollow philosophy.

'And now what?' he asks, quietly.

She frowns. 'What do you mean?'

'And now what will you do? Tomorrow you will find more men who are not mindful. Will you kill them too?'

'If I must.'

He shakes his head again. 'It is not our place to intervene.'

'Who says?' she snaps. 'You? Who gave you power over me?' she yells, rising unsteadily to her feet. 'We are the only two of our kind in the world. We are equals! By what right did you imprison me?' But even this effort is too much. Her legs fold beneath her and she collapses in an untidy heap. A single sob shakes her shoulders. 'Why am I am so weak?' she whispers.

White's face grows a little less impassive as he watches her. His brows knit together. 'You have slept a long time. Your strength will return.'

'No . . .' she breathes, shaking her black mane, her fist balling around a handful of pine needles.

'Of course it will.

'But you will imprison me again! I will fade away.'

White moves towards her. 'Of course you won't!'

'I will!' she insists, raising her anguished face, showing him the dirty tears that stream down her fine-boned cheeks. 'I cannot go back to that pit again! I cannot! I will die!' she sobs.

White's mouth falls open in dismay at her words. 'I will not let that happen,' he says, his voice breaking. Then he drops to his knees next to her. 'I am sorry for the hurt I have done you, but I had no choice. You would not accept the balance. Always, you fought me and denied the natural order of things.' He reaches out to touch her hair. She does not flinch away.

'In time, you will see that I am right,' he continues in a soft voice. 'And then you can explore the world anew. The wonders that mankind has wrought in your absence will inspire you,' he says, his voice rising with excitement.

'That's all you care about, isn't it?' she snaps, brushing his hand away. 'Watching them. Always, you are watching them. You have watched them for as long as I can remember, until you even started to look like them,' she says, glancing up and down his body.

'To truly know a thing, we must become it . . .' he begins, faltering.

'But we must not forget ourselves!' she insists. She reaches up and places her hand behind his neck to better look into his face, as if searching for something. He is mute beneath her scrutiny, and for the first time his cool eyes seem uncertain.

'There was a time,' she whispers, her face so close to his now that he can feel her breath, 'a time when I was afraid of losing you to them. So I chose their form, also, and since that day we have spent more time in their bodies than we have in our own. But still,' she says, looking suddenly sad and vulnerable, 'still you were always distant.' She breathes a shuddering sigh. 'Oh! How I envied the menfolk.'

He frowns. 'Why? Why did you envy them?'

She meets his confused gaze. 'Because they were closer to you than I could ever be,' she says. 'Even as a man and a woman, we have never been . . . close,' she whispers. Suddenly, her body is touching his. 'I have missed you,' she whispers, their lips brushing together, and her fingers tightening behind his neck, drawing him over her as she lifts her body to meet his.

'I have missed you too,' he breathes, surrendering.

And realises his mistake too late. Her sudden laughter shakes the trees. The gentle caress behind his neck becomes a death grip at his throat and she lifts his body up, one-handed, with her undiminished strength, the muscles and tendons of her arm standing proud beneath the skin. Choking, he looks down with bulging eyes upon her face to see it partially transformed into the likeness of the dragon. A wide, vulpine smile curves across her jaw, revealing inhumanly long and sharp teeth, while bony ridges sweep back across her cheeks and through her writhing, flowing hair.

'I have missed you too!' she mocks in a demonic voice, then slams him down onto the ground beside her with a force so great that the soft earth is stripped away, falling in tattered clods among the surrounding trees. His body pounds the rock beneath him to rubble, while larger fragments stab skywards like the ice of the caldera, tearing thick tree roots out of the ground like gnashing teeth tearing at sinews. 'How I have missed . . . breaking you!' she cackles, her talon-like hand still clenched around his throat as she straddles his broken body. Blood trickles from his nose and bubbles from his mouth, and a dark pool mingles with the stony earth behind his head.

She bends close, her long tongue flicking out to taste the blood before it soaks away into the ground. 'You have grown weak, like the men whose achievements you revere,' she whispers. 'You think too much with this!' she adds, grabbing his crotch roughly in her other hand. White winces, but even this can add little to the pain he already feels.

'You have lost your way. It is my time, now. They have had

their thousand years while I slumbered and you did nothing. The next thousand shall be mine, and I will teach them all the lessons they should have learned from you!' With these words she pulls him out of the crater his body has made and, holding him at arm's length, spins on her heels and throws him with all her might high into the western sky. As she watches the distant speck fall below the horizon, she transforms fully into her natural shape, and the beat of her wings flattens many trees as she rises and heads east, in search of her first students.

*

BEVERLY MASTERS HAS been walking all night. It is mid-winter in New York city in the year 2012, and it is Beverly's busy time of year. She started in Vinegar Hill, worked her way through Downtown and is now heading home parallel to Eastern Parkway. Her trolley is empty now. The white paper and plastic packages of food have found their way into the grateful hands of many homeless folk. She's only been stopped by the NYPD twice; when her trolley is still full and with all her warm layers bulking her out, she looks a lot like one of the homeless, herself, and there are parts of Brooklyn Heights that don't appreciate *her* kind straying anywhere west of Prospect Park.

But the police are old friends. They call her 'Beverly' and wish her a good night, or sometimes tell her which streets to steer clear of when there have been shootings nearby. The grateful homeless, for their part, murmur 'Thank you' and 'Bless you' through cold-bitten lips as they accept her still-warm packages with shaking hands.

Her trolley's wheels squeak as she pushes it along across the uneven sidewalks. They squeak so loudly that she almost doesn't hear the clatter of glass on concrete as she passes a disused lot. The chain link fence has been pushed down in places, and the space within is filled with refuse from fly-tippers. Beverly knows the homeless have used this place in the past so she pauses to listen and, in the still winter air beneath the stars, feels sure she can hear the sound of laboured breathing. As she looks past the fence, she spies a glass bottle lying near a pile of bin bags and, in the pale moonlight, sees a limp human hand on the ground next to it.

The girl is young, filthy and intoxicated. Judging by the state of her ill-fitting clothes, Beverly suspects that whomever gave her the bottle has also raped her. Beverly pulls the baggy jeans back up from around the girl's knees as best she can, then tries to sit her up. 'Hey, hon,' Beverly coos, stroking the tangled black hair back from the young woman's forehead, revealing the curve of half-closed oriental eyes encrusted with grime and dried tears. 'What's your name, hon?'

The girl's lips work soundlessly. Beverly bends her ear close. 'Say that again, honey?'

'I tried,' she whispers in a cracked voice. 'I tried . . .'

'I know you did, hon. I know,' Beverly soothes. 'Let's get you home and cleaned up, all right?' she says, reaching under the girl's shoulders and bracing herself to lift her. Beverly's fifty-ninth birthday has been and gone, and she has been wondering how much longer she can carry on with her personal mission: her back aches most mornings and her hips are stiffening up. But as she mentally prepares herself for that old familiar bite in her joints, she realises that she is already standing up with the girl in her arms. She seems to weigh nothing! 'When was the last time you ate?' she exclaims in surprise and hurries to place the girl as comfortably as she can in the trolley.

'I tried . . .' the girl murmurs over the squeak of the wheels.

'I know, hon,' Beverly replies.

'He was right . . .'

*

'ANY IDEA WHO she is?' Beverly asks.

Luther just shakes his head. Beverly looks over his shoulder across the common room to where the girl sits, curled up in an old armchair. Her silky black hair is brushed and tied in a long pony tail that reaches to the small of her back, and her clothes are clean and fit better. A steaming mug is cradled in her hands while those beautiful, but fearful, eyes stare at the other residents, the staff, the walls and ceilings, and react now and then with shock every time the TV makes a loud noise.

'Has she said anything at all?' Beverly asks, and Luther just shakes his head again.

'Can't get a thing outta her,' he replies, sighing. 'Toughest cookie I ever tried to crack.'

'She musta gone through hell,' Beverly says.

'Guess so,' Luther agrees. 'But it's strange. Why's she so healthy?'

'How'd you mean?'

'You know how people crumble on the streets. Life's hard out there. Half the residents in here have malnutrition, ulcers, infections, missing teeth . . . but her? She's healthier than I am! And that ain't all,' Luther continues, guiding Beverly away a few steps to be sure the girl can't hear them. 'Ain't no one in here never heard of the internet. Right? I mean, just because you ended up on the streets, that don't mean you were born there. Toby, he used to work in social media marketing,' Luther remarks, pointing to a man sitting hunched over one of the centre's ancient computers. 'But this girl, you show her a computer and she's lost. You can see it in her eyes. Hasn't got a clue what it's for. And that's not all. There's other things. She hissed at my cell phone the other day. Like it was a wild animal!'

'What are you saying?'

'I'm saying it's like this girl's come outta the past, and she don't know what the modern world is. You say you found her in an abandoned lot in Downtown?'

'Yeah, that's right.'

'Well, that's where she ended up, but I don't think she's from around here.'

'What, you think third world?'

'Sure, maybe even North Korea, somewhere like that. They say the North Koreans are living like it was medieval times. Most of 'em don't even have electricity.'

'So she's been smuggled out, then trafficked over to the States?' Beverly mused.

Luther raised an eyebrow and nodded again. 'Could be, Bev. Could be.'

'Luther, can I take her out with me?' Beverly asked. 'I've got the trolley out front. I was going over to Brownsville . . .'

'That sounds fine,' Luther nodded. 'Fact is, Bev, I was hoping you'd ask. There's not much more I can do for her here.'

*

The girl soon becomes as well known to the NYPD as Beverly. Bev's Little Helper, they call her, even though the girl isn't actually helping. For the first few weeks the girl trails along behind Beverly, watching silently with those dark eyes. She seems not to see the homeless people at first, seems not to comprehend what Beverly is doing. The trolley slowly empties, the ragged heaps of humanity mumble 'Bless you' and 'Thank you' and Beverly glances at the girl, but her face remains impassive. Sometimes she just stares at the sky, as though waiting for something.

Now and then Beverly gathers up some painkillers and antiseptic and visits people in real trouble: grinding poverty, with life-threatening illnesses and no money for medical treatment. Afterwards, even this experienced charity worker is often reduced to tears once she is back out on the street. But the girl's face never even flickers, and Beverly begins to wonder if she's dealing with some kind of sociopath.

Then one day Beverly turns around and the girl isn't there. She glances left and right up and down the length of the street, until the screech of brakes and the blare of a car horn draws her attention towards the road where she sees the girl, kneeling beside a dead sea bird. One hand is hovering gingerly over the matted, bloody feathers of the road kill while the angry bumper of a Yellow Cab hovers just beside her head. The driver is shouting abuse. Beverly rushes over as fast as her hips will let her and hustles the girl out of the way. Now, as they stand on the sidewalk, Beverly notices tears in the girl's eyes.

'Never fly again,' she says simply.

'I know, hon,' Beverly says and, on impulse, reaches over and hugs her. To Beverly's surprise, the girl returns the gesture and her tears soak into Beverly's windbreaker as they stand and mourn the dead bird.

Then Beverly has an idea. 'Hey, honey, you know what? I know the perfect place we can go visit. Huh? Let's go see a sight! What d'ya say?'

*

THEY STAND ON the Brooklyn bridge, the wind in their hair, a dense mist shrouding the waters below, while the steady hum of constant traffic buzzes in their ears. Beverly looks across at the girl. She is lifting her face to the wind, her eyes closed, a slight smile curving her lips. She seems relaxed for the first time since Beverly has known her. 'You like it up here, hon?' the older woman asks.

The girl nods without opening her eyes. 'It reminds me of flying,' she says.

Beverly raises an eyebrow. 'You've done that, have you? Been flying?'

She nods again, and Beverly is startled to hear her chuckle, although what she finds funny Beverly can't guess. A cloud of gulls rises from somewhere below them, climbing up through the mist. Beverly guesses that a garbage scow is passing below, unseen. Only its hungry hitchhikers are visible, wheeling and diving and squawking as they jostle for pride of place on the refuse.

'Look, hon!' she says, pointing. 'See? All the birds? Don't they look happy?' she adds, hoping to expunge the memory of their fallen comrade. But as the girl looks down and sees them, her smile fades and her eyes suddenly look so sad that Beverly worries she has miscalculated. 'What's wrong, honey?' Beverly asks. 'Won't you tell me?'

'They remind me of him,' she says in her strange, slightly lilting accent.

'The birds?'

Silence.

'Do you miss him?' Beverly asks, probing.

'No,' the girl replies. 'But he was right.' She sighs, rubbing her face with her hands. 'He was right. The world has changed. I don't understand it anymore. I was away for too long.'

'Where were you?'

The girl looks at Beverly directly for the first time. 'I was in prison,' she says, flatly.

Beverly is unfazed. She has met many ex cons. 'Well, you're free now,' she smiles.

But the girl shakes her head. 'I don't deserve to be,' she replies, then looks back out at the misty river, and the towering buildings that rise on either bank. 'I wanted to tear everything down. To make it the way it was when I was young.'

Beverly frowns. When she was young? She couldn't be more than twenty-five. 'We all feel like that, sometimes.'

'You don't,' the girl says, looking at her again. 'You help people. You try to take the pain away. All I ever did was cause more pain.'

'Is that when it happened?' Beverly asks, still trying to guess what 'it' was.

She nods, then sucks in a deep breath of the cold air and holds it. Beverly can see her eyes welling up with tears, can see the tension across her shoulders. The older woman moves closer and hugs the girl tightly, and feels her slight body jerk with each sob as she lets it all out.

The gulls are circling now, rising on the wind, spiralling up into the clear blue, while the city's glass towers sparkle and its red stone buildings glow with reflected light. It is a warm, pure light that hides the grime that coats their windows, that conceals the venality and cruelty of their inhabitants, and washes away the old blood stains that tarnish the sidewalks at their feet. Beverly marvels at how the world can be both beautiful and horrible at the same time, then turns and looks into the stunning features of the girl beside her, and wonders what crimes her unblemished face conceals.

A shape moves further along the bridge. It catches Beverly's eye and she looks past the girl to see what it is. The shape is human, with a dark hood pulled over its head. It is walking towards the railing. Now it is climbing over it as casually as someone might step over a low garden fence. Now it is lowering itself down the other side until it is standing on the narrow ledge of steel girders, and the pipework of cable conduits, that protrudes below the walkway on either side of the bridge. And only now does it enter Beverly's mind that this person is preparing to jump.

She leaves the girl standing by the railing, rushing towards the hooded figure with a speed she has not known in many years. She reaches the spot just as she sees the figure below her edge further out, its arms holding on to the bridge structure behind it, but gingerly, as if preparing to let go. In perhaps a second, the figure will take one final, fatal step into the infinite. Beverly does not hesitate, does not try to call out, does not try to get help from any passing motorists. She just dives forward, the tubular railing striking her in the gut as she pushes off the walkway and reaches desperately for the hood. She grabs it, and as her fingers close around a handful of cotton, she pulls the hood back to reveal the short, scruffy hair of a teenage boy with acne crawling up the sides of his neck and cheeks. But that is all she can see because he doesn't look around. He is intent on his fate. Yet he knows someone is there; he has felt the tug of her grip, because now instead of simply letting go and stepping forward, he leans his body over the edge, spreads his arms as though they were wings and, placing one foot firmly against the bridge behind him, pushes hard.

Beverly is helpless. Her feet are already off the ground and kicking in the air while she pivots on the railing, its hard surface pushing painfully into her midriff. So, when the boy kicks out, she has no way to resist, and she cannot bring herself to let go. So she pitches forward over the railing and falls with him, head first towards the unseen river.

The girl watches in disbelief. She watches the skinny figure of the boy and the rumpled, baggy figure of her best friend grow smaller and smaller against the silvery grey. She takes a sudden breath, like a diver coming up for air, and in that moment grips the railing herself, vaults over it and pushes off the bridge in a perfect swan dive. She enters the mist a second after Beverly and the boy, and it swallows them all without drama.

The bridge is silent, save for the steady hum of the traffic passing by. No cars stop. No other pedestrians rush to look for them. All this is, perhaps, just as well, for no one would have believed the witnesses anyway, when they spoke of the incredible sight they saw below the Brooklyn bridge. No one would have believed them when they described the huge, black wings that opened beneath the mist and the long, serpentine shape that was borne upon them. No one but wide-eyed children, and hopeless dreamers, would have listened. They would have described how this fantastic creature swept away to the nearby shore where, as the mist briefly parted, they saw it gently lay the bodies of two people on the gravelly sand. And only the hopeless dreamers might have tried to guess why, as the black dragon hovered motionless on impossible wings, it had looked down into the eyes of the woman and shared a long, silent moment before vanishing into the mist.

*

FOUR YEARS LATER, a train rocks sluggishly as it rounds the last bend before pulling into Deansgate station, Manchester, on a mild, sunny day on the cusp of spring. A young woman with cherry blonde hair and thick rimmed spectacles boards the second carriage and sits down in the aisle seat of a table. She does not look at the other travellers who are already there and, obeying the unwritten covenant of public transport, they do not look at her, at least not directly, because beneath the thick rimmed frames and the knitted sweater and the flowery jewellery, she is quite attractive. This does not go unnoticed by the black-haired woman in the black leather jacket in the window seat next to her.

The young woman is still fumbling with her things as the train pulls into Oxford Road. By the time it has left, the passengers seated opposite have been replaced by a pair of old ladies in expensive coats who chat enthusiastically while staring into their smart phones. Meanwhile, the young woman now has a textbook entitled 'Learning the Law: an overview of the English Legal System' on her lap and has opened a silver grey Macbook on the table. There is a document on the screen. The document contains a heading in bold, black letters which reads 'Examples of Bad Character'.

The woman in leather smiles. 'Are you writing about me?' she asks. She meets the young law student's startled glance with her dark, oriental eyes, then nods towards the screen. 'Sorry,' she says. 'I couldn't help but notice the title.'

'Er, that's all right,' the student mutters, blushing and the woman in leather can almost read the girl's thoughts. Who is this stranger? Why is she talking to me? People don't talk on the train! The woman in leather smiles, watching the redness spread across the student's cheeks and down the sides of her neck, disappearing beneath the round collar of her knitted sweater. 'So, what does it mean?' she asks. 'Bad character?'

The student takes a breath and gives her a wary look. 'It means there is evidence of, or a disposition towards, misconduct,' she replies, glancing from the screen to the stranger and back.

'Sounds interesting,' the stranger says softly. 'And what defines misconduct?'

'Doing something reprehensible,' the student explains, not looking around.

The stranger tilts her head as though confused. 'Reprehensible?'

The student briefly clenches her jaw, but she maintains a polite smile because it is difficult for the English to be blunt with strangers, no matter how tiresome or intrusive.

'Reprehensible behaviour,' the student begins, 'includes things like bullying, theft or racism.'

'Ah,' the stranger nods.

'You haven't done anything like that lately, have you?' the student asks, flashing the stranger a defiant look. Perhaps she was hoping to scare her off, this leather-clad, black-haired, oriental woman with the suggestive smile. But the stranger doesn't seem to scare so easily. 'No,' she replies, after pretending to think about it, 'I don't think so. Not lately.' At this, the student nods and turns back to the Macbook, presumably hoping to close the conversation, but the stranger isn't finished yet.

'So, what's the opposite of reprehensible?'

The student sighs and rolls her eyes behind the thick rims. 'Well,' she begins, waving a hand, 'anything that's praiseworthy or for the public good . . .'

'Is that what it says there?' the stranger interrupts, pointing at one of the bullet points on the screen.

'No,' she says hesitantly. 'That just gives some . . . specific examples.'

'Such as?'

There was a pause. 'Oh, it just mentions some specific examples, that's all,' she replies, waving her hand again.

'Like what?' the stranger persists, leaning forward so she can look into the face of the young woman beside her. Behind the stranger, through the window, the bright nascent spring sky is darkening above the closely-packed rooftops of suburban Manchester. It looks like it might rain, even though none has been forecast.

The student returns the stranger's gaze and swallows. She seems nervous, her own eyes darting around for something else to fix on. 'It, er . . .' she hesitates, her eyes sliding back towards the screen. 'It says . . . conduct that should not be regarded as reprehensible includes . . .'

'Includes what?' the stranger whispers, and slowly blinks her deep, exotic eyes.

'Includes . . . consensual sexual activity between adults of the same sex.'

The two old ladies opposite lower their phones and look up with flinty, disapproving eyes, while the student snaps her head around to stare at the stranger as though to say 'Happy now?'

The black-haired woman is unperturbed, and her suggestive smile has become a wide grin. 'What's your name?' she asks.

'Evangeline,' the student replies, her cheeks blushing deeply. 'What's yours?'

The strange woman opens her mouth as if to reply, but in the same instant the train carriage is rocked on its wheels by a blast of wind. The window beside the stranger goes black, hail stones hammer against the glass and there is a loud roaring sound. All up and down the train startled passengers cry out. Some, their attention locked away in their phone screens until that moment, wail in panic, imagining for a moment that the train is crashing, and it almost feels like it, with the wind rattling the thin walls and the hail bouncing off the roof. Passengers who are standing in the aisles suddenly sway as the driver applies the brakes and the motion of the carriage begins to calm. Only one passenger seems unruffled. She sits back in her chair, brushes a strand of black hair from her cheek and rolls her head to face the sudden tempest. In the swirling mass just beyond the glass she catches sight of two bright, gleaming points of blue that seem to be fixed in space just beyond her window. Black smiles and winks, and when the wind howls louder, as though enraged, her own eyes flash red in return.

*

Evangeline walks along the winding path between animal enclosures, her girlfriend beside her, a leather-clad arm wrapped about Evangeline's waist.

'Oh, look! Tigers!' Evangeline says, pointing, and they pivot towards the high fence with the low wooden barrier outside it. But all they can see is a sward of green bordered by shrubbery and a few thin trees.

'I guess they're shy,' the black-haired woman says.

'Like me,' Evangeline says.

'You're not shy, Evie.'

'I am!' Evie insists. 'I liked you the moment I saw you, but I wasn't going to say anything.' She leans into her girlfriend. 'I'm glad *you* did, though.'

But the black-haired woman pushes her away and looks stern. 'Promise me you'll never let a chance like that slip away again,' she says.

Evie frowns. 'Okay,' she says, quietly.

Black nods, then purses her lips. 'I want to tell you something,' she says. 'I haven't told you much about what I do . . . what I've done.'

'Charity work,' Evie says. 'Refugees, the homeless, animal conservation. You've told me.'

'No,' she replies. 'That's not everything. I've only spent the last four years doing charity work. It's taken me all over the world.'

'Sounds interesting.'

'Sounds terrible, you mean! I've seen some horrible things, Evie. Been to some horrible places where people and animals suffer every day. And it feels like there's never an end to it, like you can never do enough . . . but I also feel like my work isn't finished, yet. What I'm saying is . . .'

'What you're saying,' Evie interrupts, 'is that you're going away, and you don't know when you'll be back.'

Black nods, her deep eyes full of sadness.

Evie reaches up and strokes her dark hair. 'But aren't you allowed some time for yourself?'

'No,' Black says firmly. 'Not yet. You see, I went to prison once. I was in prison.' Black looks away into the enclosure. 'Does that shock you?'

Evie smiles. 'No, I guess not. I always knew you were a bad character!'

They laugh, but Black quickly grows serious, again. 'I went to prison for a long time, but I didn't learn anything, and when I came out I committed the very same crime, for the same reasons, and it nearly destroyed me. I guess you'd call it depression, or despair, or mental illness. Either way, I stopped caring for a while, until someone showed me how again. Now . . . I still feel guilty for what I did, but I think what I'm doing now is better than just letting myself get locked up again.'

Evie slides her arms inside Black's jacket and pulls her close. 'I don't know what you did, and it makes me sad to think of you being so miserable, but that's all in the past. It shouldn't have to ruin your future. Don't go,' she says earnestly. 'Stay.'

Black smiles. 'Let's not talk about it anymore.'

'Will you stay?'

Black strokes Evie's cherry blonde hair. 'You know what? I'm hungry.'

Evie sighs, looking away. 'Well, I saw a hot dog stand around here somewhere.'

'Sounds ideal! But, um, I'm dry,' Black says sheepishly, pulling out the lining of her jacket pocket.

Evie rolls her eyes. 'I'll get them.' But she doesn't move yet. She seems reluctant to let go. 'You stay here. See if you can spot a tiger for me,' she says softly.

'I can come, you know,' Black says, but Evie silences her with a touch on her cheek.

'Just be here when I get back,' Evie says through tight lips, then turns and walks briskly away.

Black watches her go, then feels a familiar presence drawing near. 'I knew you were watching me, these past years,' she whispers as she turns and stares into the enclosure. Out of the dense bushes steps an enormous White Tiger. The beast looks back at her with pale blue eyes, then takes another step forward. Its huge paws come to rest at the edge of the deep moat that runs around the inner perimeter of the chain link fence. One claw dips in the water, the ripples spreading out but not quite reaching halfway. The tiger slowly sits down, the black stripes that encompass his body doing nothing to hide him against the background of vibrant green.

'Will you stay?' a voice asks in her head.

She cocks her head, then glances in the direction Evie has gone. 'No,' she says. 'I think I'm supposed to be gone.'

'She is wiser than you,' the voice replies. 'And you are interfering with the balance again.'

Black snorts. 'At least I've found a way to do it without killing anyone this time. Isn't that an improvement?'

'No,' the answer comes back sharply. 'This, perhaps, is even worse.'

Black's brows knit angrily, but she makes no reply and stares down at the wooden barrier between her hands instead. A passing family pauses to look at the tiger. Two young children, their mother, and a teenage boy in a wheelchair. The mother is intrigued. The teenage boy seems to share her fascination: he rolls his eyes towards the enclosure and waves one arm. The wrist is permanently contorted, but it's the best he can do to point. But the two younger siblings are fidgeting. They bounce on their feet and loudly ask for ice cream. They are oblivious to the sublime, yet lethal, creature that sits calmly watching them, just a few metres away, contained by nothing more than a flimsy fence, a few feet of water and a philosophical choice.

'Who is watching whom?' Black murmurs with a wry smile, earning a flick of the tiger's ears in acknowledgement.

The children's pleas grow even louder and more incessant and, with a tired sigh, the mother gives in, turns the chair and guides her family away towards a distant wooden shed decorated to look like a jungle hut. The boy's eyes watch the tiger for as long as they can, and the twisted arm stiffens and jerks as though he is trying, so desperately trying, to make his wishes known. But his only view of the world is that which his carers, who are simultaneously his captors, see fit to grant him. Thus, as his chair is pushed away towards the ice cream parlour his fixed gaze sweeps across his surroundings like a searchlight, its beam falling by accident upon this and that, and only rarely on a moment of majesty or inspiration. If it should alight upon a brick wall while his mother's attention is demanded elsewhere, then he must content himself with that. He is condemned to impotence by a single mistake in the transcription of his genetic code. A tiny fragment a few molecules long is out of place. The whole world is his prison cell, and his jailer is barely visible under a microscope.

'You could heal him,' she whispers.

'Yes,' comes the silent reply.

'So why don't you?' she asks.

The tiger turns his blue eyes back towards her. 'What would he learn if I did?'

She stiffens, standing up and gripping the wooden barrier in her white knuckled fists. 'Is that why you allowed *me* to suffer? Is that why you watched and did nothing while I was broken, raped, drugged and trafficked?' she hissed. 'So that I might learn a lesson?'

The tiger does not reply. His eyes drop briefly to the moat, and a fresh hemisphere of ripples spreads slowly across its surface as he minutely flexes a claw. She glares at him, a red flash passing briefly through her eyes. 'I will tell you, old friend, what he would learn. He would learn that there is compassion and mercy in the universe.'

'But is there?'

'In nature, no,' she concedes, 'because it is nature which has trapped him in that chair and broken his mother's heart. But that is why those who can act should act!'

'Is this the lesson you have learned?'

'What else?'

'There is pain the world over. You cannot prevent it all. You cannot heal it all. It is a natural part of life.'

'Then should I do nothing, like you?'

Again, he remains silent.

Black's lip curls, revealing pointed teeth. 'Do something!' she yells. 'For once in your immortal life, just try something new! Help me . . .' she says, pleading with him now. 'Help me to do just one thing. Come with me and save one life. Just one!'

The tiger remains still, save for a fresh hemisphere of ripples spreading out towards her. She looks at them. 'Oh, you and your subtle little lessons,' she sneers. 'You smug, insufferable, immortal bastard. What do you know about life, really? You, who have spent millennia dressing yourself as a man and walking among them, but never living like them! Never experiencing pain or death. Never loving or being loved! Of course, you know about lust . . . we discovered that together, didn't we?' she smirks, and for a moment she sees his perfect blue eyes flicker as though she has struck a nerve. 'But that, as they say these days, is just hormones. You don't know what you're missing and, worst of all, you don't practice what you preach! Or you would have tossed me straight back into that volcano six years ago!'

The tiger lowers his head.

'Help me,' she says again. 'Come with me.' And she reaches out towards the fence with an open hand. 'You tried to teach me a lesson once; are you afraid of what I might have to teach you in return?'

The tiger raises his head and looks at her, and his pale blue eyes burn like the skies above the frozen poles.

*

THE MEDITERRANEAN IN bad weather is as dangerous as any other ocean. But that makes little difference to you when the boat you're on is little better than a flimsy, homebuilt inflatable constructed of leaky rubber tubes. This boat is about fifty feet too long, which means that it flops and bends and twists on the surface of the water like an attenuated piece of seaweed, and is about as seaworthy as a portion of greasy chips wrapped in newspaper. To power this dubious craft through the waves there is one feeble outboard engine manned by a scared, twenty-one-year-old Nigerian in a bulky life jacket. He is the only person on board with a life jacket. He was promised the life jacket by the traffickers on condition that he be responsible for the engine. The other three hundred people are crammed into the floppy boat in front of him. As he watches they rise and fall as each wave passes beneath. Sometimes the bow of the so-called boat is in the trough between the next two waves and he cannot see them. Then, suddenly, they are rising high above him. Then he is high above them, looking down on the swaying, puking, miserable mass of humanity. They have skin and hair of many different colours and come from many different countries, but they all have one thing in common. They are all terrified.

Darya turns her head and looks up at her father, whose unkempt, greying beard makes him seem twenty years older than he really is. He had given his daughter a beautiful Persian name that means 'the sea', never dreaming that one day they would be crossing one. They had fled Syria months earlier after his wife, Darya's mother, had been raped and murdered by ISIS. Her crime? She had been seen, through the window of their war-torn and ruined house, reading a book to Darya. But women were forbidden to read. After the family had buried her, ISIS had come and beaten Darya's father, giving him a permanent limp, blindness in one eye and a scar across his face. The scar was to remind him, they had said, so that every time he looked in the mirror he would remember his lesson. Do not allow your women to read!

After that, Tarek had decided he would not raise his little girl in such a place, that the dangers of the journey were worth the risk. And now, here they were, out of sight of land, packed together like cattle, with a soup of sea water and vomit swilling around their ankles.

Darya tugs on his sleeve and pulls a damp and tattered sheaf of pages out of her coat. It is the book her mother was reading to her. Tarek tries to smile. He understands her silent plea. In every moment of fear since they had left what was left of their home, Darya has asked him to read from that book. That book had been given to her by an aid worker. In between handing out food and water and blankets a slim, dark-haired woman with striking oriental eyes had knelt down to Darya and given her a book of children's stories. Stories about dragons. Tarek had been so grateful: everything they owned, including Darya's books and toys, had burned. Now, after her mother's death, that tattered book meant even more.

Today, the Mediterranean is not the tranquil blue pool that tourists imagine. Today it is grey and angry, with the rising waves obscuring the horizon. Thus, it takes the Nigerian helmsman a while to notice the faint plume of a ship's exhaust dirtying the overcast sky, and then to see the vague shape of a ship's upperworks – the blocky superstructure and multi-coloured cargo of a container ship – slowly rising beneath it as the vessel draws closer.

In a few seconds from now the Nigerian will berate himself for being stupid, for not thinking. But right now, in his sudden excitement at seeing possible rescue, he stands up, leaning on the shoulders and heads of those around him and points, yelling excitedly.

Instantly, he realises this was wrong because the rest of the boat tries to stand up with him. Three hundred or more frightened, desperate people with no knowledge of the sea all try to move to that side of the boat to see the ship that will save them. To be saved by it when it comes. The Nigerian sees too late what is happening.

'No!' he shouts. 'Non!' he calls. 'Hapana!' he yells in Swahili, and then again in every other language he can think of, but it's useless. The flimsy craft is already folding beneath the sudden shift in weight; the rubber tube that forms its bulwark is being forced under the surface and the sea is flooding in. The human cargo screams and tries to clamber back to their original places, but it's too late. The boat begins to slip beneath the waves. It is a strange way to sink: the water gently but rapidly rising up past their knees, their waists and their chests until, at last, they are standing upright on the flimsy deck of the raft as it floats a few feet below the water. Then a wave comes. It breaks over the still protruding bows and smashes down upon their heads. Many are forced under and never come back, while the rest are left desperately splashing in the troughs between waves, treading water with heavy, sodden clothes weighing them down. The air is filled with gasps and cries and pleas for some hidden hand to help them: for God, for anyone. In moments, many of those cries become splutters and gurgles as the strength fades from tired limbs and the heavy bodies begin to sink.

Tarek is a strong swimmer. He treads water in the middle of the floating mass of humanity, clutching his daughter close. But he is struggling. His wounded leg never healed, and his daughter is growing heavy. He panics. He cannot save her! A dark face with black, tightly curled hair appears in front of him. The face is framed by a bright orange life jacket. The Nigerian looks into Tarek's eyes, then starts taking the life jacket off. Together, they manage to fit the oversized vest over Darya's head and tighten the straps. Holding her close, Tarek grabs the Nigerian's hand in his own and clasps it in silent thanks. Now there is nothing left to do but wait. The two men swim beside Darya, treading water, while around them the remaining heads begin to disappear. They listen as the other voices are silenced by the bubbling water that pours down their throats. Those few that remain grow silent, rising and falling on the waves, their expressions grim with the knowledge of certain death, and their reluctant acceptance of it. As a wave carries them upwards, the Nigerian manages to turn and look towards the direction of the container ship. But it is gone. It has sailed by and its busy crew has not seen them. Why would they? They are so small. Just a tiny collection of heads bobbing in the vastness of the ocean. Soon they will all will be gone, as though they had never been there at all.

*

BLACK CIRCLES BENEATH White like an impatient child waiting for an elderly parent to catch up. 'There! I see something,' she cries and darts away. White gazes after her, his blue eyes narrowing, but he will be true to his word. He will follow. This time.

As they touch the water they incarnate as a great, white coastguard cutter with a blue racing stripe angling across its sleek, fast bows. The cutter is crewed by men in smart black uniforms whose shining red eyes are hidden beneath the peaks of their caps. Three bodies drift nearby: two men and a smaller figure in a life jacket. One of the men reaches down and lifts up the little girl, cradling her.

'Hello, Darya,' all of the black-dressed crewmen whisper in a strange chorus.

She murmurs, sleepily.

'It is her fate to die here,' White says.

The red eyes of the crewmen flash in unison. 'We will not abandon her!' the crew snarls.

But White's voice remains infuriatingly calm, the voice of reason and balance. 'What life can she have?' he asks. 'A lost little Muslim girl washed up on the shores of a continent that doesn't want her, that has learned to despise her.'

The crew evaporate into a cloud that coalesces into the figure of a black-haired woman in a leather jacket. Black looks down at Darya's face and strokes her cheek. 'Muslim, Christian . . . what should it matter? Oh, but wait . . .' she says, looking up and addressing the rest of the ship. 'That's your fault, isn't it? Yes,' she adds, nodding, her lip curling with sarcasm. 'I remember when you used to walk among them in your white robes, flashing your white wings and handing down your little pearls of wisdom like they were the word of God.' She frowns, theatrically. 'But wait . . . that's exactly what you said they were, isn't it?'

'I've made my mistakes,' White replies. 'So have you.'

'Have I?' Black wonders. 'As I recall it was you who poisoned their minds against me. You who blamed all their pain on *me*. You who called me devil!'

'There had to be a balance.'

Black's roar silences the sea and she rises into the sky. White follows, dissolving into his natural form, his wing-beats flattening the wild waves into harmless ripples. Sensing him, Black pauses. Hovering above him, she glares down with molten eyes, the child cradled in her enormous claws. 'I know that you have always loved me,' she says. 'But I could never love you.' And then she is gone.

*

AN UNNATURAL RUSH of water propels the bodies of two half-drowned men up the flat beach then, like a black shadow passing across the yellow sand, retreats as quickly as it has come. Tarek coughs and opens encrusted eyes. The young Nigerian is lying next to him. They move slowly, feeling life leak back into numb limbs. Someone is shouting. Tarek raises his head. A man in uniform is standing on the beach defences, calling out to them in Italian. Beside him, holding his hand, is the small figure of a child.

'Darya,' Tarek murmurs, then he begins to laugh. He looks across at the Nigerian and they both begin to laugh, struggling to help each other to their feet as the flashing blue lights of a four-by-four roll down the beach towards them. They exchange a glance. Their troubles are far from over, but they are alive. And where there is life, there is hope.

*

IN A SUBURBAN home a thousand miles away, a busy family gathers around the breakfast table. The hassled father is attempting to orchestrate the feeding of his two young children while the tired mother spoons baby food into the unwilling mouth of her wheel-chair bound son. He is uncooperative this morning. He tries to bat the spoon away with his bent wrist and rolls his eyes towards the toast and jam that the two young ones are eating. But he can't eat that: it would choke him. The mother turns away in frustration, the constant clamour from the two young ones reverberating in her head, and barks harsh words at her husband. Meanwhile, her son's head lolls on his thin neck, turning his face towards the window. Mouth caked in baby food, he begins to verbalise something incoherent. He does this often: no one pays any attention. No one notices when he stops. But he shocks the room into silence when he sits up in his chair, uncoils his stiff arm into his lap and, with his other hand, reaches forward and grabs a piece of toast.

The mother drops her mug of tea. It smashes on the floor. The father swears loudly, and the children look away from their brother and giggle.

The boy's teeth sink into the crunchy bread, the sweet jam dazzles his tongue and, to his parents' astonishment, his epiglottis rises and falls smoothly and easily as he swallows. He does not choke. Mouth caked still in baby food, with the addition now of crumbs and jam, he turns to his speechless mother and says, 'Mum, can we go to the zoo?'

Outside, on the lawn beyond the window, a huge white tiger gets up and walks away into the bushes. His blue eyes flash as a strange new optimism rises within him. Perhaps, he thinks, perhaps it is time to don his white robes and wings once again? Perhaps, he thinks, perhaps he will get it right this time.

The Meeting of the Twain

Andrew Coulthard

WHEN THE CALL TO ACTION CAME, SHUJAA WASN'T ready for it. In fact, he wasn't even listening. He was in one of the newer Nairobi suburbs, slouched in a plastic chair in his father's garden. Together they were watching yet another sunset although, as usual, Shujaa wasn't paying much attention.

Just going through the motions.

"You know, you should really get a grip on your life," the old man muttered.

Shujaa sighed and took another beer from the cooler box at his feet.

"And that's another thing; you do far too much of *that!*" his father said, arching unruly brows and raising his right index finger in admonishment.

Shujaa's shoulders slumped further and his face settled into a scowl.

If you think this is bad . . . you don't know the half of it. "Nobody gets out of this life alive, baba . . ."

"Look, it's science, son. The studies, statistics, they all show . . ."

"Making this choice or that, one might actually make a few years' difference, for some," Shujaa interrupted. "But from what I've seen, on an individual level, health and longevity are at best a bloody lottery." He took a long swig from his beer, finished it and fished up another. "Anyway," he continued, "we all go to hell our own way. That's free will, right?"

His father remained quiet for a few moments, then his eyes blazed bright again in the gathering gloom. "Your brother's been sober for nine months now. I'm glad I could help him, but I won't go through that again, not for him or anyone else, is that clear?!"

Shujaa chuckled. "Let's not kid ourselves, baba. You'd never have done that for me, and I'd never have asked you to, or *let* you for that matter. Not my style, accepting help, and it wouldn't be yours to give me any."

"You were always *stronger*," his father objected.

"Just as well," Shujaa said. "I had to be."

"I expected more of you!"

"Oh sure, and don't I know it."

They fell silent.

Beyond the silhouettes of the city, the horizon was illuminated in patches of hot red melded with amber streaks and glints of gold. Above that, in a band between encroaching night and dying sun, strips of purple and grey cloud twisted and slunk, driven on warm winds too far off to be felt.

Shujaa lost himself in the shifting patterns, actually looking for once, anything rather than returning to the conversation with his father. He recalled being a kid, all the shapes he used to be able to see in clouds. Back then there'd been endless parades: faces, creatures, mountains and valleys; reflections of a child's imagination, he supposed. Now, he saw nothing, perhaps because there was nothing left inside him to see.

As if the sky had overheard his thoughts, however, a recognisable form crystallised out of the changing cloudscape. A lengthy, amorphous stretch of vapour detached itself from the rest. It floated free in a sea of fire, writhing, twisting and elongating before his eyes, becoming serpentine in aspect. What might have been a head took on clearer contours: a narrow snout, a firm brow ridge and the hint of horns gilded in the sun's last rays. Other less well-defined outcrops suggested rippling wings and moving limbs.

Despite himself, he was absorbed . . . entranced. The creature was orange at its heart, its edges white-gold. Then, without warning, the rim of the sun slid from view and the clouds passed from golds to reds and then purple-greys in rapid succession. Night rushed in, chasing the last strip of twilight beyond the edge of the world.

Gone!

He returned to his surroundings to discover his father staring at him intently from the darkness. Shujaa met the old man's gaze for a moment then gave a dismissive wave of his hand and took another beer from the cooler.

*

HE WAS WEDGED into a cleft between two enormous boulders, dark hands gripping moss and rock. He kept very still, muscles aching, especially his back and legs. His left calf twitched painfully, bordering on cramp, but he hardly dared move.

The smell of damp earth and forest filled his nostrils, laced with hints of smoke. Faint wails and cries carried up to him from further down the valley. Then he caught another sound. A hissing which grew steadily stronger and louder, building like a storm wind in the trees. His body shuddered with dread, all petty cramps forgotten. He swallowed repeatedly, mouth dry as old bone. Then a shadow fell across him, turning day to twilight.

Instantly, it was gone again.

He glanced up above the treetops, eyes fixing on a massive form wheeling in the air a few hundred metres ahead, like a Vulcan bomber with flexible wings. Sunlight caught the creature's back and trunk, glittering on mottled black and yellow plates. Its serpent body was held rigid in flight while the wings curled and flexed, steering it through the air like the fins of an enormous fish. The venomous skull, a huge sable and amber arrowhead, turned to face the valley and the creature swooped off downhill in the direction of the town. As it glided low over the treetops a stream of liquid fire jetted out before it, spurting into the trees and setting them ablaze.

Screams and shouting rose in a chorus of despair, growing louder until the roar of the conflagration drowned them out . . .

*

WHEN SHUJAA AWOKE, it was pitch dark. He was sweating, his breathing ragged.

Where was he?

The garden. Baba's garden . . .

He reached instinctively for another beer, fumbling for a few moments until he located the cooler, but it was empty. There was a clicking noise, like small stones moving together followed by a soft scrape; something was there in the darkness.

"Baba, is that you?"

No reply.

He listened. Nothing. Then he caught some little sounds further off – *Might be a small animal . . . or maybe a larger, stealthier one. Shit, has somebody got past the guards?*

He returned to the house and found his father on the sofa in the living room, watching the news with the lights out. Shujaa decided not to call security and, after a quick visit to the kitchen, where he fetched another beer, he slumped into an armchair.

"Anything new happening, baba?"

His father's face was ghostly in the glow of the TV, reflected images dancing on the lenses of his glasses.

"The Prime Minister and her cabinet have been implicated

in another bribery scandal," he said. "And, the government has issued a statement that the continued poor economic performance is due to quantities of unregistered illegal immigrants from Europe . . ."

Shujaa snorted.

"They're urging parliament to pass their bill, you know the one?"

"Registration and identification again?"

"Yes," the older man murmured. "What do they call it again . . . National Residents Registration and Ethnicity Census Bill, or something like that. Poor buggers, have you seen what Europe is like these days?" His father shook his head. "Oh, and the war in the Middle East is intensifying . . ."

Nothing new . . . ever. Shujaa was about to make a wry comment when something moved in the darkness beyond his father. He froze, lips parted, beer can halfway to his mouth.

Should have called security!

His flesh prickled as the dim outline of a woman formed on his retina. She was pale, slim, with shoulder length dark hair and, although her eyes were wells of darkness, he knew they were fixed on him. He glanced at her hands, looking for a weapon, but couldn't see one. She seemed insubstantial, almost ghostly. He blinked, but she was still there. Then he closed his eyes and counted to three. When he opened them, the spectral figure drifted closer to stand behind his father's chair, where the light of the TV brought her into clearer view.

Her expressionless face looked almost East Asian, but her eyes were like nothing he'd ever encountered. They cut through him, leaving him with the sensation he'd been exposed; *naked and defenceless.*

His father turned in his seat. "Oh, hello, Lyn. How are you, my dear?"

The woman released Shujaa and turned to regard his father, her face creasing into a smile. "I'm fine thank you, Baba. I've brought the things you wanted."

"Oh, you are a treasure, but don't go putting them away, I can see to that myself . . ."

"Already done, Baba."

Shujaa's heart was still drumming in his ears. *She's real!* Lyn turned to regard him again, and in the wake of his fright it dawned on him how ridiculous he must look.

"Is this one of your boys, Baba?"

"Oh yes, sorry. This is Shujaa. Son, this is Lyn Yung. Friend of mine from across the town. She often helps me out with shopping and things."

"Hello, Shujaa," Lyn said, her eyes rooting him to the spot.

"Well say something, boy," his father growled. "Honestly, no manners at all, I'm just glad his mother's not here to see it."

*

HE WAS ALONE, in darkness, sweating, heart beating unfeasibly fast, breath coming in short, shallow bursts. Panic, panic, panic . . .

Somewhere out there were the scales . . . The Scales. Tipping back and forth. The knowledge terrified him, made him want to curl up and hide, even though he knew there was no escape. If he could only close his eyes and turn his back to the peril, pray that it would be over quickly. But somehow he had to look.

And then they were there, glinting in the dark. Black iron. A vast, vast, impossibly large assembly. How could he have strayed so close to them without realising?

Events out in the world affected the scales, no question about it. But that was all so far away that even major disturbances hardly set them in motion. Here though . . .

No sudden moves!

He struggled to control his breathing. They seemed still and in balance now, but he knew how easily they could be set off from such close range. They were so sensitive that the slightest eddy in the air would begin them tipping back and forth, gathering momentum as the energy and forces from their motion multiplied exponentially, eventually ripping the fabric of the world apart.

"Ever increasing imbalances, Shujaa . . ." The voice rumbled through the cavernous dark, hinting at a size and power to rival even that of the scales. Shujaa battled to maintain his composure.

Be quiet. Don't you know your voice is enough to set them off?! *he hissed.*

"Am I not right? The imbalances are increasing. Imbalances in what, though?"

Had that been a slight movement? Shujaa was close to panicking and felt he must answer, if only to get the voice to shut up.

"Imbalances, the cause and effect of chaos . . . their motion pervades everything."

"That's right!" the voice boomed, "Everything!"

Oh no. Tiny, slow oscillations had begun and were becoming more pronounced as he watched!

"Swinging cycles, tipping back and forth to ever greater extremes . . ." the voice continued. "In behaviour, in excesses, in approaches and attitudes to the world and ourselves . . .

"In believing and not believing.

"In meaning and meaninglessness.

"In sobriety and intoxication.

"In dynamism and apathy.

"In direction and rudderless indirection."

"Shut up! Shut up! Shut up! Shut up!" Shujaa screamed. "Don't you know what you're doing!"

The scales were gathering force in a dread build-up of energy that would result in the ruin of everything. Before his terrified eyes, something shifted in the murk, a huge form, clad in yellow and black plates.

A long drawn-out shriek drew his attention back to the oscillating pans: the voice of tortured metal! Cracks and lines spread across the iron, and scales of another kind began forming, assuming the same yellow and black hues as the massive lizard in the shadows.

Colossal energies radiated outward, causing his body to shudder and dance as one in the grips of a fit . . .

*

SHUJAA AWOKE TO find his father shaking his arm. "Bloody drunk! Are you staying here tonight?"

He stared bleary-eyed about the living room. Lyn was there, watching him with those uncanny eyes. "Whaa, what? Why?"

"Lyn's heading home. She wanted to know if you wanted a lift?" His father turned away. "Don't waste your time, my dear. Really."

Still more than half asleep, Shujaa forced himself upright, "Yes, wait, thanks. Coming."

*

LYN'S CAR SMELT clean. Like seat shampoo and carpet freshener blended with the scents of one of those wunderbaum things his father used to buy when he was a kid.

"Your father tells me you drink a lot," Lyn said as if it were the most natural conversation topic in the world.

"Do it to relax. Also helps me sleep. Have a lot of trouble sleeping."

"Didn't look like it back at your father's place," she said.

He glanced at her, sure he'd find a smirk on her face, but she was as expressionless as ever.

"Been a lot of ups and downs the past few years," he offered, his words sounding lame even in his own ears.

"Do you dream a lot?" she asked.

"*Dream?* Not really, or not that I remember anyway."

"What were you dreaming when you were in the garden?"

"Were you there?" he said, recalling the sounds he'd heard.

"I came around the back way into the house. Your father gave me a key."

"Right."

"So what were you dreaming?"

"I don't know," he lied. "Lot of weird muddled stuff. You know, the usual."

"You were whimpering. I thought it might have been a nightmare."

"Yeah, might've been, I suppose. Can't remember much."

"I'll tell you what, I've got something that might help you. Let's take a detour, pop by my place before I drop you off."

"What is it?"

"Chinese medicine. Give you very good sleep. Restful. Peaceful."

"Okay," he said, a little unsure. "Why not."

They drove into an area of the town he didn't know well. Large houses and apartment buildings bordered roads lined with SUVs and fancy cars.

"It's just along here," she said turning into another street of residential blocks and expensive autos. "The one at the end there . . ." Keeping one hand on the wheel, she pointed towards a four-storey brick and concrete building. A battered white van was parked directly outside.

"That looks a bit out of place round here," Shujaa murmured.

There was writing on the van's side panels:

D.R. Diamond

Trader in Rare Stones

Lyn braked, a look of alarm on her face. Shujaa stared at her for an instant then returned his gaze to the building. There were figures moving in the glass-fronted entrance hall. Another man was standing on the path, little more than a shadowy outline between patches of streetlight. A second joined him, the glowing orange point of a cigarette flaring against the gloom.

Lyn put the car into reverse, turning to look through the rear window. "Stupid of me . . . *stupid!*"

"What is it? What's happened?" Shujaa asked, his attention still on the murky figures on the path.

"No, I just remembered. I left my keys . . ."

"At my father's?"

"Er, no, earlier, somewhere else. I'd forgotten. I'll have to get them tomorrow."

"But can't somebody let you in?"

"Who?" she snapped.

"I don't know, a neighbour, caretaker, security guard? There were people inside. They'd let you in."

"Not into my apartment they couldn't. It'll be all right, Shujaa. Don't worry. I'll take you home."

The journey across town was made in silence. Lyn pulled up outside the run-down terrace where Shujaa lived and they sat for a few moments. She was staring ahead through the windscreen. Shujaa knew he should say something but wasn't sure what.

"Are you going to be all right?" he ventured.

"Hmm?"

"Without your keys."

"I don't know. Probably . . . yes."

"Okay, then . . ."

Silence resumed. Shujaa waited, making no move to get out of the car.

"Can I stay with you tonight?" she asked.

For some reason, he hadn't expected the question and looked at her without replying. Her eyes changed then, as they had at his father's. He felt the gaze of something alien boring into him, opening him up, like blades, and laying bare his mind and soul.

"I'll sleep on the sofa," he breathed.

Inside he fetched clean sheets, pillows and a duvet and, together, they fixed the bed before making one up for him on the sofa.

"You can sleep in this if you want," he said, throwing her one of his clean t-shirts.

"Thanks."

Shujaa went to the kitchen to get two beers and a glass. On his return he found her sitting in an armchair staring into the middle distance. Her bag was open at her feet, lamplight glinting on something. He didn't react at first until he realised what he'd just seen. Looking again to make certain, he shook his head: there amongst the usual jumble of paraphernalia was a large bunch of keys.

"Why are you really here?" he asked.

She regarded him. Motionless. Face blank. The hairs at the nape of his neck prickled as her eyes began drilling into him again. This time, however, he broke the spell and looked away.

"Somebody was at my home," she said. "A person I didn't want to meet."

"Your ex?" he prompted, still careful not to meet her gaze.

Lyn burst into peals of laughter.

Frowning, he handed her the glass and one of the cans. "I'll take that as a no," he muttered and drained half his beer in a single swig.

"Sorry," she said, composing herself, "but that was unexpected. No, not my ex. This man is something else, a collector you might say." She poured beer into her glass and took a tiny sip.

"Collector?" he repeated, finishing his can and returning to the kitchen for another. "What does he collect?" he called out.

"You shouldn't drink so much of this stuff, Shujaa," she said. "It lowers the quality of your dreams.

"Hah! My dreams eh?" he replied, emerging back into the living room. "What does he collect, Lyn?"

"Stones. Buys, cuts, polishes and then sells them."

"D.R. Diamond?"

She nodded.

"*And?*" he urged.

"He thinks I've got something that ought to be his. Something special he could get a great deal of money for."

"And have you?"

She sighed. "I have a couple of objects that interest him. But they're *mine* and he'll never have them."

"Unless he offers you enough?"

"No," she said flatly. "No amount of money could ever be enough."

"I see. So, is he planning to force you?"

She nodded. "I think so."

"And those other people . . ."

"His employees. He's a desperate man, Shujaa, and one used to getting what he wants. But this obsession is an old one and not at all healthy."

"Obsessions seldom are."

"You're right. Over time they torment those who suffer from them. It has poisoned his mind, made him unbalanced."

*

Unbalanced! The word echoed down dark, winding corridors.

He quivered, head spinning.

Vertigo.

Nausea.

And the overbearing dark – a physical weight.

Iron pans, larger than ships, were swinging and splaying outwards like twin pendulums, their motion growing ever faster. Their momentum sending tremors through the cosmos.

A percussive thrumming began. Then the darkness shifted. Yellow and black plates. Wings. A v-formed skull.

Run!

It's hopeless.

Run!

He tried, but the giddiness was too much and anyway his legs wouldn't obey. Terror. The sound of lizard belly and talons rasping on stone . . .

He fell, hard!

*

"YOU JUST WENT quiet, Shujaa," Lyn said softly. "Your complexion was all shiny, and greyish. Then you collapsed."

Where am I? Home. This is home.

He was lying on his sofa. How had she managed to get him up from the floor?

"You're stronger than you look," he croaked.

"Yes," she agreed. "What happened?"

"It was just like the dreams," he murmured.

"Dreams again? Okay, and?"

"Dragons," he said. "Scales. Terrible *imbalances*." He was shuddering, a castaway on the shores of delirium, waves of anxiety coming at him from within. "It was terrible. Sounds ridiculous, but truly awful."

"You dreamt of dragon's scales?"

He shook his head. "No. That's not it. Get me another beer and I'll explain it to you."

"No more beer!" she said sternly. "Only water or tea."

*

LYN LISTENED AS he recounted the events of his vision and those of the preceding nightmares. When he was finished she regarded him for a long time.

He sipped his tea in silence, enduring the weight of her gaze, battling to keep his anxiety under control. She got up and walked over to her bag. After rummaging around for a moment she returned with a small leather bound box and handed it to him.

"Open it."

His hands were trembling, but he persevered, fumbling with the catch. Inside were two stones the size of mandarins. They were an odd grey-green hue and shiny, their surfaces dotted with nodules and ridged with upraised seams that reminded him of veins.

"This what he's after?"

She nodded. "They're thunder eggs. Ever heard of them?"

He hadn't.

"Like a filled geode that forms in hollow spaces between layers of volcanic ash," she explained.

"I'm no expert," he said, "and they do look pretty weird, but to be honest I wouldn't expect these to be worth a lot of money."

"It's not the outside that interests Mr Diamond. It's what's inside."

"Which is?"

"That's the thing. You never really know until you open them up."

"Ah, that's right. Our Mr Diamond *cuts* and polishes stones, before selling them . . ."

"Yes. These things have centres made of chalcedony, sometimes with deposits of agate, jasper or opal. Quartz and gypsum crystals are common, along with other mineral growths. Put your diamond saw through that and you can uncover some pretty astonishing stone."

"So I suppose these two must be *very* pretty inside, is that it?"

"Maybe, but that's not the half of it. These are special even as thunder eggs go."

"How?"

"Let's just say there's a clue in the name."

There was a heavy knock at the door followed by a muffled growl.

"We know you're in there, Lyn!" The voice sounded British. "The boss wants to talk."

"Shit," she hissed. "Quick, take the eggs out of the box and hold my hand!"

"What for?"

"We're going on a journey."

*

What the . . . ?! Shujaa rolled over on the coarse grass and struggled to his feet. His backside and knees were wet from where they'd made contact with damp earth. Around them, a bare expanse of hillside stretched away on all sides; above an inky sky of cloud, smoke and soot hung so low it threatened to reach down and swallow them.

No flash, no blast of ozone or any weird humming, buzzing or roaring. One moment we're at home, Lyn clasping her hands around mine while I'm holding her egg things, next we're here. Nothing in between.

He should have been angry, confused, hysterical, *something!* But despite the suddenness of the change, he actually wasn't. He knew this place, he'd been here before, and the more the truth sank in, the more he recalled the danger they were in.

Down the valley, dense columns of dark smoke spiralled upward to join the filthy vapour above. At their base lay the smouldering ruins of the town, patches of intense orange betraying the fiercest fires. Other pillars of soot and gas were twisting skywards all across the plain.

"We need to find cover, and fast."

"Okay, where to?" Lyn mumbled.

He pointed and she followed his outstretched arm with her eyes. They were a fair distance from the edge of the trees, too far for his liking. But that was the most logical direction even if it led them closer to the fires.

"Haven't you forgotten something?!" Lyn said, her voice harder and colder.

"Forgotten? You mean like to ask what the hell just happened?"

"These," she snapped, handing him the stones.

"You know, I'd say those were the least of our worries now," he said, indicating the smoke-filled vista with a sweep of his arm.

"Trust me, Shujaa, these stones are at the very heart of our concerns! If we lose them, all will have been for nothing."

He shook his head, but took the thunder eggs from her, stuffing them into his jeans pockets.

"So now we're not *talking* about my dreams," he said as they tramped down the slope towards the woods. "Instead, we're actually *in* them. Surely I must have had other, better ones."

"I'm sure you have."

"Well, couldn't you have chosen one of those?"

Her expression soured. "This was the best I could find."

"And another thing: how do we get back?" he continued. "Or is this like some sort of intense drug trip that'll play itself out in time?"

"Right now, Shujaa, *this* is where we need to be," Lyn told him. "There's work to be done. And as for whether we're dealing with dream or drugs, I suppose you could say *zhui lung*."

"Which is?!"

"Zhui lung means that we're chasing the dragon."

Shujaa shook his head. "Was that meant to be funny?"

They reached the edge of the trees as the light was waning. "There are some big rocks a bit further in," he said, remembering. "Maybe hide there until morning."

Lyn nodded. "Yes, we'll need to get down to the town, or what's left of it. That way he'll be sure to see us."

"And we *want* that?" he asked in alarm.

"Believe it or not, we do."

Stumbling on through the trees, tripping on undergrowth and hidden roots, they eventually arrived at an area of huge, mossy boulders. Shujaa explored the periphery and located a hollow formed by several massive rocks heaped against each other.

"I suppose a fire is out of the question," he asked quietly as Lyn inspected his find.

"Go ahead," she said. "Light one if you can. There are so many out there, one more won't make much difference."

"No?"

"It's in daylight that his eyes will probably pick us out. Although he might detect my scent or the presence of the eggs too."

"But only in daylight?"

"No, that might happen tonight, but a fire won't help or hinder him either way."

Shujaa began searching for dry twigs and branches, but before long night had fallen and he was forced to give up. They sat in the dark, huddled together against chill air and cold stone. Shujaa was shivering. "So what's this about work that's to be done," he said.

"We have to stop him."

He laughed then. "Lyn, just look out there. He's left a whole world in ruins. What can we do against that?"

"We have the eggs."

"Like David and Goliath you mean? Improvise a sling and thwack him between his beady, massive, yellow and black eyes?"

"No," she said, shifting position behind him and pressing closer. Her arms encircled him. The move took him by surprise and he held still and quiet in case she changed her mind. "The eggs are the one thing that can restore balance."

Balance . . . that word and its opposite! His head spun at their mere mention. Somewhere in the bowels of the cosmos a gargantuan metal construction was revolving out of control: *Overwhelming me and everything else . . .*

"How can stones do that?"

"They're dragon eggs, of course," she said as if it was obvious.

"Dragon eggs?"

"We must get them to hatch . . ."

"Do we really need more fire-breathing lizards?"

"These will not be like him, Shujaa," Lyn replied with confidence. "He is a *Western* dragon. Almost certainly of European origin."

"And these?"

"Eastern."

"How does that make a difference?"

"Look at the traditions," she said. "Western dragons are destructive, greedy, twisted, tyrannical, *evil*. They gather, steal and horde the wealth of others; they wield fearsome power and unleash devastating ruin on any who get in their way. They're the embodiment of chaos, born of and giving rise to terrible imbalance in the world."

Whirring forms, shaking the earth at its roots! Shujaa fought to keep from vomiting. Lyn's arms drew more tightly about him and as she held him harder, his symptoms grew less.

"Eastern dragons are *benevolent*," she whispered, her face next to his. It seemed that her words echoed down long dark passages leading into him and beyond into other hidden places.

"No fire?" he murmured.

"Sometimes . . . rarely. They are often wise and bring rains, enablers and fosterers of life."

His head was clearing. "I see. So East is *good* and West is *bad*, yes?"

"No, that's not what I meant . . ."

"I know you're from somewhere east, Lyn, but don't go making me out to be on the wrong side of things. *I'm* Kenyan, remember. *East* African . . . although there aren't many parts of the continent that escaped European influence, so I guess we've all been forged in their dragon fire to some extent . . ."

"Shush. You're delirious," she hissed into his ear, her arms and legs winding about him like the coils of a serpent, restricting, yet comforting. "East and west, good and evil, they're just labels, Shujaa. It is what these symbols represent on a deeper level that counts. We must look beyond outward forms, to discern actions, effects and that which dwells within."

"Maybe that's what D.R. Diamond does to the stones: tries to see what's inside . . ."

"He divides them without ever seeing or appreciating their wholeness."

"Aaahhh, of course. And that kills the embryos?"

Lyn shook her head. "Unfortunately they often survive as tortured, half-creatures that suffer pain and horror all their days. It drives them insane and they become like our Western friend out there."

"So if Diamond gets the stones we'll have two more of those things on our hands?" he breathed.

"Mmm. But if we hatch them whole we will have two benevolent forces to bring rain and restore balance."

Balance . . .

*

Although he'd hardly slept, the next morning, Shujaa was as alert as he'd ever been. He blinked, eyes stinging and watering, the linings of his nostrils prickling as if he'd inhaled a bottle of astringent.

He moved forward again, taking slow, wary steps, every breath scouring his lungs and causing a dry hack, which he struggled to suppress.

Passing from the charcoal pillars of the woods, he emerged into avenues of scorched rubble and cracked stone. A fine, reddish dust covered everything, deadening his footfalls. The air shimmered. Here and there, orange embers flowed from the ashes in winding eddies. Cracked, soot-coated bones lay scattered among the debris, in some places gathered in tangled heaps.

He still couldn't quite grasp what Lyn had told him.

They must be bathed in dragon fire . . .

Oh really? That's it? Easy then . . . He'd been angry. *This is a fool's errand, an impossible mission. Why do you even need me? Why? I could be home, with a fridge full of beer.*

He sighed. And what wouldn't he give for a cold one to quench his thirst right now? But no, he really was required, it seemed. Something about the yellow and black lizard banishing her from this world. *It's only thanks to your dream in combination with the power of the eggs, Shujaa. That's what let me return.* So she had to have him with her to access his dream. Well, perhaps.

A piercing hiss brought him back to the immediate. He stopped. Looking around he caught sight of Lyn a few tens of metres distant. She too, froze. He squinted at her through the haze; she looked worried, and if she was worried . . .

The hissing continued, angry, insistent. It was coming from up ahead beyond a ridge of shattered, ash-choked stone and twisted metal.

He glanced at her and pointed. She nodded, making her way towards him. When she drew level, he leaned close: "Is this it? Is it him?"

She remained expressionless for a moment then slowly shook her head.

"What then?"

Without a word Lyn strode off in the direction of the sound.

He waited a moment before hurrying after her. When they rounded the rubble, it was to find that a large area of ash had been turned to pink-grey mud. Near the centre, a jet of water lanced from the ground, gradually broadening and slowing into a plume as it gained height before falling back to earth in a mist of tiny droplets.

"Water main, probably," Lyn murmured. "Best not go too near. There may be fires below ground. Could be hot . . ."

A stranger's voice interrupted her: "Impressive, wouldn't you say?"

They both started. The voice was high-pitched and reedy, the accent refined. "The destruction, I mean. Rather profound, all in all."

The speaker was standing a few metres away on a pile of blackened brick and concrete. He was tall, his bulky, solid body impressively stout about the middle. His head was crowned in wispy, auburn, shoulder-length hair, the round, pale face framed by mutton chops sideburns. His clothing was, if anything, even more striking: black leather knee boots, antique breeches in garish yellow, a black waistcoat and a black and yellow checked tail coat.

All he needs is a top hat and he'd look like a bizarre incarnation of John Bull! Shujaa thought.

As if reading his mind, the newcomer grinned and began

clambering down from his perch, hopping from one piece of rubble to another like an ungainly bird. Small clouds of ash exploded around his feet as he made the ground.

"I see you have a friend with you, Lyn," he said. "Aren't you going to introduce us?"

"Shujaa," Lyn said, her expression stony, "this is Dawin-Riche Diamond."

"You mean, D.R.?" Shujaa said.

"Yes, indeed! That's me. And who are you?" Diamond asked, a mocking expression on his face.

"I just told you," Lyn growled. "He's Shujaa."

"What's *he* doing in my dream?" Shujaa demanded, utterly confused.

"Well you might ask, young fellow, well you might. Lyn here knows, don't you, eh?"

Lyn was silent for a moment, but then her eyes widened. "Get behind me, Shujaa."

"But . . ."

"Just do it!"

"Haha, the moment of realisation!" the stonecutter exclaimed, clapping his hands with relish. "Now, my dear," he continued, "you have some things I want, and for the *very* last time I'm going to give you a chance to hand them over, without a struggle . . ." The mirth left his face and he pulled himself up to his full height. "I'm waiting."

A tremor passed through the ground, accompanied by a rumble like distant thunder. Lyn glanced back at Shujaa and mouthed the word: *Run!* Shujaa shook his head and made to protest.

"Yes," she whispered, "and remember: place them in dragon fire, the hotter and closer to the source, the better."

Still uncertain, Shujaa began backing away. "Where will I find it?" he mumbled.

"There'll be plenty, right around here very soon," Lyn assured him. Before he could reply, the ground bucked beneath his feet, a ripple passing through the ruins like a wave on the ocean. Shujaa was hurled into the air to float in a haze of ash and debris. He came down, hard, and passed out.

*

IMBALANCE. TOO LATE, too late, too late . . .

The Scales were a pulsating blur in the gloom, the sound of their motion a series of high-speed explosions, merging into one long, drawn-out roar. Shujaa struggled to gain his feet but the ground was shaking so violently he couldn't even make it to his hands and knees. He fumbled for his pockets. The eggs were still there but surely now it was too late? He'd let her down. He hadn't meant to, but he was here again and she was alone facing the stonecutter and, more than that, the fire lizard.

He hopped and bounced across the rock, unable to right himself or halt his motion. Lights were flashing in the dark. At first he wasn't sure if they were real or the by-products of concussion. But they grew in intensity like flashes of yellow-orange lightning, illuminating what appeared to be clouds of billowing smoke and vapour.

Electricity arced and crackled about the fulcrum of The Scales, casting darts of light into the void. Something was out there, a huge form. He knew only too well what. Another, vast cloud of ruddy flame erupted, this time much closer. And then he saw the dragon, its yellow and black plates highlighted in the copper glow.

Yellow and black!

An image of the stonecutter flashed through his mind, a crooked grin on his face, eyes cold as the stones he coveted. The apparition opened its mouth to speak and words echoed inside Shujaa's skull: ". . . the moment of realisation!"

Then he knew.

*

HE CAME TO beneath a covering of dust and cinders. Tremors were still passing through the ground, although nothing compared to those closer to *The Scales*.

He sat up and blinked, eyes smarting. Nearby somebody was choking. He looked around for the source of the sounds. But the air was hazy with ash particles, reducing visibility. A figure rose from the ground and wobbled to its feet not more than five metres away, only to double up, in a fit of coughing.

He raised himself, took up a fist-sized piece of broken masonry and staggered towards the wheezing figure.

"Lyn?"

"Get back," she spluttered. "He's somewhere close . . ."

"Yes, and now I know who . . . *what* he is," Shujaa croaked.

"How very perspicacious of you," came Diamond's voice from up ahead in the haze. Then he appeared, a vague, shadowy form broken up by the mirage effect as he moved towards them. Perhaps it was part of the illusion, but to Shujaa he seemed taller and even bulkier than before.

"Well, you've had your chances; you can't say otherwise," he called, "Now *where* are my rocks?!" With each step, he was growing.

"I've hidden them somewhere you'll never find them," Lyn snarled.

"Really? What a pity," Diamond hissed his voice altering. "Then I'll have to hurt your friend here until you decide to tell me where, won't I?"

He halted then, hints of black and yellow in the grey of his expanding body. He was elongating, limbs stretching, head transforming from its usual waxy ovoid to an increasingly well-defined V.

Shujaa, who had hoped to strike the stonecutter unconscious, dropped the piece of brick he'd been clutching.

"Come on, Lyn!" he yelled, taking hold of her shoulder.

"No. Stay behind me," she said, shaking him off.

"But we have to run!"

"Behind me!"

He tried to grab her arm, but it was already out of his reach as her body also stretched and transformed.

"*Lyn?!*"

"Not Lyn Young," she called in a voice like raging rivers, "I am *Ying Lung! Responsive Dragon of Proper Conduct!*"

Lightning crackled beyond the fog of dust. Staggering back in shock, Shujaa felt large spots of rain splashing on his face. Others struck the rubble around him, hissing where they encountered hotspots.

"Now, stay behind me and remember what you must do!"

All trace of Diamond the man had gone. In his place, a huge yellow and black winged dragon reared on his hind legs. Piercing yellow eyes shone from the arrowhead skull, and sulphurous fumes trailed from the corners of his mouth. He yawned, stretching jaws wide to reveal double-rows of curved fangs. Then he inhaled, sucking air, dust and ash down into his innards.

Lyn too had completely abandoned her human shape and stretched up, a willowy pale dragon with vast wings, a long flickering tail and pearly skin that seemed smooth and scale-less. She turned toward Shujaa, her great head coming down before his own, feathered wings arranging themselves around her like a shield.

Remember what you must do.

A great jet of yellow-white flame engulfed them, spreading in a searing corona about her huddled frame. Shujaa cowered, choking on blistering air heavy with brimstone, yet safe in the shelter of her body.

Remember!

The flames subsided. Small fires crackled and sputtered across the rubble and raindrops hissed against Lyn's smouldering back.

Shujaa was shaking. The torrent of dragon-breath was gone. He'd missed his chance. Would one of the little fires do the job?

Yellow and black bony plates clacked together as their opponent drew himself up to his full height, sucking more air into his lungs. Lyn held her position, remaining his shield. The edges of her wings were cracked and blackened and her eyes were tightly closed in what Shujaa could only assume was an expression of unimaginable pain.

A whooshing blast of white-hot air and gasses struck her back and was parted like a blazing river around a rock. In panic, Shujaa drew out the thunder eggs and cast them into the raging streams of flame on either side of his protector. Almost instantly the stones flared white, crackled with a pattern like scales and shattered. Two tiny dragons unfurled themselves from the coiled, foetal positions they'd held while still within the rock. Then they squirmed across the glowing earth, burrowed down into scorched soil and vanished from sight.

D.R. Diamond, the fire dragon, let out a great roar of fury.

My thanks! Ying Lung straightened herself and spun around, revealing the charred, blistered ruins of her back. Then, wings wide, she hurled herself at her enemy. They collided with a force that split the earth and sky. Lighting flashed, thunder boomed and the deluge was unleashed.

*

SHUJAA WAS DREAMING. He was in a dark place, deep inside the earth. *The Scales* towered over him so close he could reach out and touch them. Now they were still, however, and there was no longer any danger in such proximity. In each huge pan, a tiny baby, pearl-white dragon lay curled up asleep.

Balance.

He woke later in his home stretched out on the sofa. For some reason, he was fully dressed, sweaty and uncomfortable. *Time for a shower.* Rolling onto his side, he winced. There was something round and hard in his pocket. He got up and reached in a hand. *Feels like another one of those egg things*, he thought. But when he pulled the object out he discovered instead that it was a large pearl.

Wisdom embodied.

Later that week he visited his father, taking him some groceries.

"Well, glad to see you sober for a change," the old man said by way of greeting.

Shujaa was putting the shopping away. "Yeah, I've grown tired of beer," he said absently.

"Good. Keep that up. By the way, have you seen Lyn? She hasn't been around since the night she drove you home."

"No, baba, I haven't seen her," Shujaa replied. "I think she had to go away for a while."

Dragonfly

Andrew Coulthard

Zero

THE THIRD TIME CHANA WOKE SHE KNEW THERE WOULD be no getting back to sleep. Struggling upright, she propelled herself with a grunt from the edge of the bed to her feet. Beyond the blindfold of night, she sensed the room swaying as if she were below decks on a stormy sea.

It's just in your head . . . it is your head! She reached out, fingers meeting the cold, immovable weightiness of her grandmother's chiffonier. Something of the old woman's strength remained there. She willed the room to be still and it worked.

Clumsy footsteps took her to the bedroom door and out into the hall. The kitchen awaited. Light on. Kettle switch flipped. She flopped down on the nearest Windsor chair, her breathing shallow, laboured. Her heart was hammering behind her sternum in a rising crescendo of palpitations. Somewhere in the shadows a thought awaited her, an inevitable one that she fought to keep at bay just a little longer. But it wouldn't be denied, and broke through her flimsy defences.

Today you are going back to work.

Lurching forward Chana retched up a mouthful of stomach acid followed by the remains of last night's dinner.

∗

Day dawned slowly, like smudged charcoal. The prison loomed, a glass-sided monolith, impenetrable to the outside world. She stood without moving, telling herself to cross the car park and go inside. She was tiny in its shadow, dwarfed by its towering façade.

Somehow, she made herself walk. But slowly, so slowly, as if the building were surrounded by a zone of resistance and greater density. *The turgid zone.* Thoughts raced, while everything else decelerated. An effect of the medication? She even saw things sometimes. But no. This particular piece of weirdness she'd experienced long before starting on meds.

Then she was at the entrance. Fob against the panel. Code. The steel and glass door swung silently open. She stepped over the threshold. Through a second steel and glass door. It was still dark inside the reception hall. No faces behind the armoured glass booth, no hatred or opprobrium . . . *yet.* Another set of doors. Fob against the panel. Code. Through the glass and steel sluice. Still no lights on. Better that way. Perhaps she wouldn't be seen: staff canteen; changing room; lockers; conference rooms. Other officers were present in this area. Shades in the gloom.

"Morning!"

"How's it going?"

"Not bad. Yourself?"

Some caught sight of her as she glided toward the lockers. A few even squinted at her through the half-light until they realised who she was. She nodded to them, ever hopeful, but they only turned away without word or smile. She really shouldn't, but she still felt the pain, every little omission a deliberate attempt to slight her.

No point in hanging around. Best just pass through access control.

Get to the department staffroom. Grit teeth and get on with getting through the day.

The operator behind the security window nodded to her. Her heart leapt and she smiled while retrieving her glasses, key chain, fob and name badge from the tray. Didn't recognise the operator. Somebody new. That explained it. She passed through the next glass and steel door, collected keys, radio and assault alarm, then took the lift to the department. Two of her colleagues were already in the staffroom seated at the table, drinking coffee. Thomas and Victor. Neither among the worst.

"Good morning."

They continued their conversation without acknowledging her presence. She looked over the duty roster, preparing herself for the people in whose company she would have to spend the next ten hours.

"The medicines need doing. See to it, will you?" Now they were looking at her. Faces cold. Eyes hard.

She wanted to sound defiant, but her reply came out as a hoarse whisper. "I'll need somebody else with me." The two men glowered in silence. "You know I will . . . the rules."

"Just get the medicines sorted out," Thomas told her. "The trainee will be here in a few minutes. We'll send her in to help you when she arrives." They weren't her superiors and had no right to order her around. She could argue, or just ignore them until the intern arrived, but there'd be a price and it wouldn't be worth paying. At least the trainee was nice.

She passed through the heavy steel doors into bleak grey and beige corridors lined with metal cell doors. In the corridor office, she unlocked the secure medicine cabinet and began organizing and labelling individually packaged morning doses with the inmates' cell numbers.

When had it begun? She wasn't entirely sure any more, although she hadn't forgotten who'd started it. How could she? The slightest thought of that little clique of male colleagues was enough to induce a panic attack.

Chana sat down behind the desk, pulse rising. They'd got what they wanted through a combination of good old fashioned chauvinism and a liberal helping of master suppression techniques.

She shivered, nauseous again. Sweat broke out on her top lip and across her brow. *Oh no, please, not here.*

The instigators had long since moved on. Promotion mostly. By the time her current colleagues had joined, however, her status was so securely established that nobody questioned it. Not even her.

She rested her head in her hands and focused on her breathing. You could break the attacks that way stop the hyperventilation, take control. Slower, slower, through the nose. The tip of the nose. Be there. Focus on that place and breathing. *Slowly.*

She'd never completely understood why they'd picked on her, a fact that used to be a source of torment in and of itself. Medication helped. Despite all the counselling and therapy to the contrary, however, she was sure the whole business had to be due to some profound deficiency in her person. What else could it be?

"Aren't you done yet!"

Shock jolted her and for a moment she stared up at Thomas, paralysed. For the briefest moment, there was a look on his face that might have been concern. But it was soon replaced with suspicion. "Where you asleep?" he asked, eyes narrowing.

"No, no. Look, they're here, all except A:4-6. I was just going to get his."

Thomas sighed and stared at her with undisguised scepticism. "The trainee is sick. I'll stand in the corridor while you dish them out," he said. "And hurry. They're waiting to start the morning meeting, and you know how the boss is if we start late."

*

Chana and Thomas made their way into the crowded staffroom as quietly as possible.

Len, the Department Senior Officer, was speaking: "So, that's all the visits. What's next?"

Only one seat left. Thomas's. I'll stand. She kept to the back of the room, trying to avoid doing anything that would draw attention to herself. Didn't help. There were looks, frowns, smirks. Two younger female colleagues exchanged glances. One of them rolled her eyes. She gazed down at her feet. She could take this. They'd be out in the corridors soon. Following routines. Time would pass. She would cope.

Breathe properly. Focus.

Victor was running the meeting, reading from the agenda prepared by the late shift the previous evening. "We have another problem with pests in the building . . ."

"Oh, not bed bugs again?"

"No, thankfully not. Flies. Established themselves in the drains of several cells on floor 5. They're bringing in pest control today or tomorrow. If anybody notices unusual numbers of flies on cell walls, it needs to be reported to Facilities Management."

The question arose unbidden and, before she could stop herself, it passed her lips. "Are we looking for a particular type of fly, or just any sort?" All eyes switched to her. Had she really spoken? Why? What had possessed her? So much malice on those faces.

"Good question," Len said, turning to Victor.

Vindicated.

Strengthened!

Venomous expressions evaporated, all eyes on Victor.

"Drain flies, apparently," Victor said, reading from the agenda.

"Naturally," Len said with a chuckle. "Silly question." There was a ripple of laughter, a few contemptuous glances. Had the DSO's comment been aimed at her? It didn't matter; the effect was the same.

"Right," Len continued. "Time to get to work. Have a good day, everyone."

The meeting broke up and in the bustle of general activity she was rendered blissfully invisible.

*

She got through the morning by doing what had to be done and keeping quiet. No more ill-advised comments. Lunchtime unfolded as usual. She sat down in the staffroom and waited for silence to descend. Her colleagues departed in pairs and threes, their laughter and chat passing out from the room and filling the lift hall.

She wasn't going out. Better to be alone in the quiet.

Her sandwiches tasted of nothing. Maybe that was another effect of the meds. For a while she'd tried to compensate with different condiments, but excesses of chilli and vinegar only gave her an acid stomach. Now she accepted the lack of flavour: just another way she was cut off from the world and herself. She told herself it didn't matter. Elsewhere out there people were starving. She wasn't.

"*Help! Please.*"

Chana's left eye twitched. Four shifts until her first scheduled day off, a single blessed island in an otherwise unremitting schedule. She glanced at the clock. God, it was 12:40pm already. They'd be back soon. Of course, she shouldn't have been left alone. Regulations stated there should always be at least two officers on duty in the department. She wasn't on duty either. According to the roster she was to take lunch between noon and 1pm. But the others didn't care about that. Today, there were no scheduled visits or transports during lunch, so they just did what they wanted.

"*Save me . . .*"

Change jobs, her doctor had suggested. Her counsellor had said the same – find something new. But what? Unemployment was a rising constant these days, and the older you were the harder it was to find new opportunities. Besides, what else could she do? Being a prison officer was a very specific occupation. Much as she'd love to escape, she had a mortgage to pay and couldn't afford a cut in salary.

"*Please!*"

The voice was little more than a tinny, high-pitched squeak. She put her hands to her ears. *It's just in your head, keep it there.* Sometimes she saw things that weren't real: today she was hearing stuff.

"*Don't leave me here!*"

Insistent! Chana glanced around the staffroom, no longer enjoying her solitude. There was a gloominess today that went beyond dingy winter. Perhaps she should've gone out. In fact, she wished she had. She listened, expecting to hear the voice again but her heart was beating so loudly. That's when she noticed her breathing: short, rapid gasps. When had that begun? *Retake control: tip of the nose. Inhale, count, exhale. Slow. Deep. Steady.*

Kicking off her shoes she stretched out on the sofa, heart still clamouring. So tired. She hadn't realised. Had to be the stress of being back combined with a very poor night's sleep. A glance at her watch told her it was 12:49pm. They'd be back in eleven minutes at the latest. If she'd wanted to sleep she should've thought of it earlier. She propped herself up with cushions, but within seconds her head was nodding forward.

Mustn't sleep.

Drifting.

"*Help me. Help!*"

The voice sounded almost like her own when she was at her most pathetic. A piercing whine. Recognition was accompanied by a rush of shame. Snatches of memory surfaced: from school when the other girls rounded on her in the locker room; at home when dad had been drinking. One way or another she'd always been a prisoner, humiliated, held fast without hope or chance of escape, paralysed by her own predicament . . . Yet now she was on her feet. How was that possible? Perhaps it made no difference, she decided. And anyway, this was a dream, wasn't it?

"*Help!*"

Dream or delirium . . . do I have a fever?

"*Please . . .*" A tiny shrill voice, and it wasn't actually coming from her head as she'd thought. She paused in the centre of the room, struggling with dizziness and uncertainty.

"*Please.*"

From over there, on the other side of the room, she realised, staring into the shadowy corner by the toilets. Before she knew it, she was drifting in that direction. Not that she wanted to, she simply couldn't resist.

"*Yes, that's it, come closer.*"

The words were becoming clearer and sharper.

"*Closer, yessss . . .*"

It originated somewhere up in the corner where the lines of the room converged. Then a suspicion arose: was this a trick? Scanning the ceiling tiles, she searched for signs of a mini camera or speaker. Nothing. Next she glanced nervously over her shoulder toward the staffroom door. Were her colleagues about to come crashing in, all mocking laughter and insults, her consternation and humiliation destined for social media?

"*Come closer, please. Save me!*"

Chana looked again: this time there *was* something. She took another step. A cobweb, and in its tattered threads a blurry, shiny, greenish mote. She stood on tiptoes, but she couldn't make it out without her reading glasses. What had she done with them? There on the table. A glance at her watch. 12:56. They'd be back *any* minute. She covered the distance to the table in three strides.

"*Noooo*, don't leave, *please, please!*"

Seconds later she was back, peering into the corner at the object in the web. A fly, no question. Big too. Blow fly? Blue bottle . . . or green? Both?

She craned her neck. The body was a little too large and long to be a fly. It was clad in chitinous panels and segments that had a glossy, metallic sheen, blue-green mostly, in places iridescent. The wings were also larger than she would have expected, yet still the most fly-like feature: transparent, ovoid, veined. *So odd, and . . . beautiful.*

"*Save me, please. I'm hurt. Stuck. I don't want to be devoured.*"

The head was the strangest part. Flat and wedge-formed it would have looked more at home on some sort of miniature viper. The eyes weren't right either: no bulbous compound spheres, just tiny black beads.

"*Please . . .*"

The creature's desperation struck a chord with her . . . then there were voices in the lift hall. Her hand darted forward, encircling and plucking the thing free, ripping it from its bonds.

"*Thank you, thank you . . .*"

*

THE AFTERNOON WAS a drawn out, uneventful torment. One routine after another, each taking longer than the last. The creature was in her pocket, wrapped in a hastily prepared cocoon of kitchen paper. She didn't dare take it out while her colleagues were close, but for once their putdowns and icy ostracism failed to affect her.

On the train home, she risked a peek, uncovering her find with shaking hands. In the anaemic light of the carriage, it looked horrible. Dead. Just a weird, disgusting insect. There'd been no voice since lunchtime and she was beginning to realise she'd probably dreamed their conversation. Chana contemplated dropping the paper and its contents down the side of her seat, but stubborn curiosity stayed her hand.

Once home she took a meal portion from the freezer and placed it in the microwave. Then she unfolded the paper on the counter and examined her find more thoroughly. It only had four legs. *Have they been broken off or is this maybe not a true insect?*

Not an insect. A dragon.

Words in her head. But that hadn't been an external voice, had it? Just thoughts tripping off each other as her mind played tricks, simulating a conversation. And the creature was still dead. Perhaps she could find something about the species on the net. Failing that she'd stick it in a glass jar in the freezer. There was always the option of contacting a specialist.

Half an hour later she was sitting on the sofa with her laptop. Despite an impressive range of bugs, she found nothing that resembled her find. All she'd established for sure was that it wasn't any kind of drain fly. She gave up, tired. Time to catch up on sleep.

Just before retiring she remembered reading something about injured bees – you could sometimes revive them with sugar water. A hasty online check revealed the proportions. She hovered over the kitchen counter. Did she even want to revive the thing? It might have a sting or bite. On the other hand, it was so clearly dead . . . oh why not. She mixed water and sugar in a saucer and gingerly placed the creature beside the pool, its shiny, reptile head on the edge of the liquid. Then she went to bed.

The next morning, she awoke seconds before the alarm sounded. For once she felt rested; how many times had she come to during the night? She couldn't remember waking at all. Dreams? Almost certainly, but she couldn't recall those either.

The only fly in the ointment was her right ear. It was itchy and felt blocked, as if it were full of wax. Sitting up, she placed her little finger into the opening and wiggled it from side to side. A sequence of bubbling, crackling sounds ensued. Next she tried yawning and swallowing in rapid succession, hoping to equalise the pressure, but that didn't help either. She shrugged: it would probably sort itself out during the day. Besides, she felt too good to be coming down with anything.

Up you get!

Wandering into the kitchen she threw the light switch and put on the kettle. There was a saucer on the counter. Without thinking, she picked it up, ready to place it in the dishwasher, then she remembered. The saucer was empty, both her dragon-fly and its sugar solution gone.

She scanned the kitchen walls, cupboard doors and table top. A quick search under the table and chairs revealed nothing. Damn thing could be anywhere. Or could it? The sugar water might have attracted other miniature predators, ones that might make a meal of both her fly and the sweet, sticky fluid.

She shook her head, filled a pan with water for her breakfast egg and began preparing sandwiches. Dead or alive, the fly was gone and it seemed to have taken her melancholy and anxiety with it. Today, even the prospect of work was less daunting.

*

One

AMAZING WHAT A decent night's sleep could do. Chana felt so different, *so* much more awake and aware. With a spring in her step, she sped past the shuffling forms of other early commuters, with their slumped shoulders and drab winter clothing. Today she shone brightly, scattering shadows and chasing the dark from gloomy places both without and within.

On the bus, there was standing room only, as usual. She didn't care. Opposite her another passenger, a young man, was listening to music on his phone.

Look at him, so good-looking. Those eyes, oh and his cheek bones, and that smile . . .

That's when she discovered the whispering in her head.

He'd never so much as look at an ageing, ugly bitch like you. Look at yourself. Sickly pale and your face is baggy and lined. Look at the shadows under your eyes. And have you seen your belly recently? Never mind your backside and thighs . . .

You said you were going to do something about that a year ago. Start training, get things back under control. So very typical of you. Empty promises . . . no discipline, no stamina, no character . . .

At first, she felt her mood plummet. It was true, all of it. She *was* ugly *and* overweight *and* she was weak. For once, however, the storm of negative thoughts failed to overpower her completely. How long had grinding vitriol like this formed the backdrop to her world? She'd scarcely been aware, yet now that she was conscious of it, it felt like she'd been the victim of its malice forever. And there was a weird paradox too: now revealed, the voice held no power at all beyond that which she granted it. It was actually a rather pathetic thing, something she could dispense with easily, just as you might flush muck from a sore.

Your light has just grown brighter.

A new voice. Whose? The new her maybe?

At the station, she made her way to the usual spot on the platform and, humming, began surfing on her phone. The news was typically dull and depressing, but today she wasn't going to let it get to her. She even found herself chuckling at some awful jokes posted on social media. When her train arrived, she practically skipped from the platform into the carriage.

As always there were a couple of colleagues from other departments among the passengers. They never said hello or acknowledged her presence, but maybe that wasn't really personal as she'd so often supposed. Maybe they were immersed in their own pre-work hell just as she often had been, tired, moody and lacking any enthusiasm for the day ahead.

Beyond thick glass panes of the carriage windows, the sky was slowly growing lighter. Everything was going to be all right. She was going to get on with things, get through them. And if she was lonely at work, what did it matter? She should get herself some friends outside the service. Come to think about it she neither liked nor respected her colleagues enough to care about them anyway.

So, sod 'em.

She arrived early. She was meant to be starting at 8:00am but she always liked to be in good time, mostly to avoid criticism from her fellow officers. On entering the building, she ignored reception, didn't bother looking at the people in the canteen and went straight to her locker. Then she passed through access control. She paid no attention to the controller, collected her keys and kit, and went straight up.

Thomas and Victor were there again, and today the trainee was back: what was her name . . . Clarice. People under training always started at 08:00am so the men must be scheduled for today's 07:30am start. She glanced at her watch: 07:36am. They were on duty. Good: she was ready for them.

"See to the medicines, would you, Chana?" Victor said without looking up from the meeting agenda.

"No," Chana replied and flashed a smile at Clarice. Then she busied herself getting a mug from the cupboard and putting on the kettle. When she turned around it was to find both men staring at her. Her breathing quickened and her heart began pounding in her ears. She felt herself flushing and just for a moment she thought her courage was going to fail.

"*What?*" Victor said.

"I said . . . *no*. I'm not on duty until 8:00am. You two are. The medicines are your job today."

Her words were met with stunned silence. The men exchanged glances. "You do know that this job requires flexibility . . . and teamwork," Thomas said.

"Yes, teamwork," Victor repeated.

"And, as colleagues, we have to be able to rely on each other!" Thomas continued.

"Yes, and back each other up," Victor added.

"Sorry, but today the medicines are *your* job," Chana reiterated, folding her arms to hide the fact her hands were shaking.

"Oh boy, you've got a very short future here with that kind of attitude," Victor muttered, shaking his head.

After that they fell quiet. Unsure what to do or say next, Chana returned to spooning instant coffee and sugar into her mug. She felt their eyes on her, however, and caught snatches of whispering. Her hands were still shaking and her breathing remained unnaturally rapid. She didn't think she could turn to face them again. Then she heard the staffroom door open.

"Morning, everyone."

It was Len. *Oh shit. How's this going to go now?*

Her right ear was itching unbearably. She inserted her little finger into the orifice and wagged it rapidly from side to side. There was a series of pops followed by crackling. *Wax. Has to be. I'll pick up something from the chemist's tonight on the way home.*

"Everything under control, here?" Len asked.

"Morning, Len," Victor said. "Yes, Tom and I are, erm, just about to do the medicines."

She heard them getting up.

"Oh right. You know you should really get that done first thing. Morning, Chana, Clarice."

"Yeah, sorry," Tom said as they went out.

Chana heard the door close to and the electronic latch shifting into place, "Morning, Len," she replied.

*

CHANA HAD COMPANY for lunch.

"I was so impressed by the way you handled them this morning," Clarice enthused, eyes shining.

"Really?" Chana said, unwrapping her sandwiches.

"Yes, really. Some of the others told me those two are like unofficial bosses here. That you've really got to watch yourself around them."

"Did the others say that?"

"Yeah. Quite a few of the girls are afraid of them."

"Oh." Chana didn't know how to respond. Thomas and Victor had never been the worst in her opinion, but now she thought about it, maybe that was only compared with the gang who'd started the whole campaign against her. "I suppose you've got to let them know where the line goes," she murmured between mouthfuls.

Is this really me speaking? Her right ear bubbled and popped as she chewed. *The new, stronger, brighter you.*

"Oh, they're beautiful," Clarice exclaimed. "Chana, you're really good."

"Eh?"

"Your drawings . . ."

Have I been . . . ? She had. Unawares, sandwich in her left hand and pen in her right, she'd been doodling on her notepad. Delicately realised flies, butterflies, moths and dragonflies filled the page. Despite realistic detail, each was fantastical in its way. Some had human arms, others reptilian heads or tails. One, a particularly extravagant combination of scaled dragon and butterfly, was emerging from a pupa.

"Where do you get your ideas from?" Clarice continued.

"I really don't know," Chana admitted, shaking her head.

*

THAT EVENING SHE found herself in a meditative frame of mind, scarcely able to believe how she and her life seemed to have changed in the preceding twenty-four hours. She was still smiling to herself when her ear began itching again. Damn. She'd forgotten to go to the chemists. She'd have to do it tomorrow.

A low buzzing accompanied the itching. It was soon followed by a level high-pitched tone and the sort of background roar that usually happened when she yawned. She pushed her little finger into her ear, but the itching was moving away, deeper toward the centre of her head.

I can't reach it.

Patience. It will pass.

Was that me?

No. It was me.

Who?

You helped me.

Who is that?

I'm helping you.

Who are you?

Open your eyes.
They are . . .
Not those eyes: the other ones.
The other ones?
What?
Have I your permission to help?
Okay . . .

The room's normal drabness and grey tones were seared away. In their place was a swirl of pulsing gold.

Where did this come from?
It's always been here. You just haven't been able to see it.
What are you?
Your friend.
But what . . . I mean how *is this possible?*
Let's call it magic.
I don't understand.
I have many names. Some might call me dragon, others fey, others still . . .
Dragons don't exist, except in films.

Chana's body and head were filled with rumbling peals of laughter: *Oh, ye of little faith. Amazing things will happen here soon. You have been favoured.*

*

Two

SHE WOKE FROM a dream of wings. Her excess flesh had melted away, leaving a body that was lean, well-defined, strong and resilient. The lines of her frame were as they had been when she was younger: sleek, smooth, and much more beautiful than she'd ever realised. And then there were the wings that sprouted from darkened nubs on her back: ovate, composed of crystal panels, ribbed with thick, black veins.

Soon she would *fly*.

Her world persisted in shades of gold; light shone from her in needle sharp beams, each piercing the darkness.

Day was dawning.

Outside, the beams were less visible, retreating to a general aura about her glittering, greenish-blue skin.

Inside, something was quickening. Nestled in a chamber between her heart and solar plexus, a swelling form fed from both. *Let unconditional love, confidence, self-esteem and will nourish thee . . .*

Before the changes, she had been invisible to people. Now her new power rendered them blind to her. A necessity.

The building was shadow in an ocean of light. Yet once inside, her aura reasserted itself, making gilded currents of her surroundings. People were darker patches in the weave, some darker than others.

"Ah, Chana, good morning!"

Len. Not so dark a shadow.

"Do you have a minute? We can talk in my office."

What is it, Len?

"Some of your colleagues have reported that you were caught asleep on the job the other day. I'm sorry, but I have to ask if this is true."

Show him what happened. Not just then; show him all of it.

Golden tendrils tipped with gleaming blue-green metallic points snaked toward Len from the centre of her body. She gripped his skull, boring through skin and bone and burrowing into his mind. Then she showed him.

As Len's screams faded away, she released him.

"My lady," he gasped in a hoarse whisper. "I know I have witnessed some of that which you have suffered. I chose then to take the easy road and let it pass. But never did I realise the extent . . . or for how long it has been ongoing. Forgive me . . . forgive us all. From this moment forth I am your creature."

*

THE STAFFROOM WAS full and silent when she emerged with Len at her side. The darkest patches were Thomas and Victor, but even they were nothing in a world of gold. Chana shone.

"Take me first," Clarice begged.

Spikes of radiance burst from her, piercing her colleagues' hearts, dispelling shadow, worming into their brains to form plasticity in her image.

"Now, Len," she buzzed.

"Ma'am?"

"Let's visit the control room, shall we?"

*

Three

ON THE THIRD morning, she woke in the heart of the building: the heavily armoured room from which the Surveillance and Control team remotely operated lifts, electronic gates and doors. She was strapped into a restraining chair, held immobile to counter the shudders wracking her body.

The night staff were in place waiting for the day team to relieve them. None reacted to her presence nor deviated from their duties, unless she willed them to. Len was by her side. Thomas and Victor stood guard by the entrance. The others from her department she had allowed to go home, knowing full well that they would not betray their new regent. Clarice had begged to stay, but Chana had sent them all away.

Amazing things will happen here soon.

Throughout the building, staff went about their business more effectively and efficiently than ever before. Everything was now driven by her light. Personality she subdued in favour of duty and precision. In their cells the inmates dreamed. Behaviour modified and drives muted, they were oblivious to their circumstances, blind to all that she wanted hidden from them, malleable in her hands.

Her shuddering intensified, but she felt no pain. The thing

in her chest was still growing, pressing her outwards until she was no more than a thick rubbery membrane in which the being squirmed and flexed.

Soon!

Chana's silver-blue-green exterior darkened, her panels crisping to the treacle toffee gleam of a cockroach. A new, growing translucency revealed frantic motion within.

The day staff were arriving to relieve their colleagues. Out in the departments, breakfast was being dished out cell by cell to docile inmates. With a sharp crack, a white stress line forked from her throat, down her thorax and across her abdomen. Her carapace split open and her breathing grew laboured, long, slow groans issuing forth with each wheezing exhalation.

The new creature shook itself from the shell of the old. Viper head. Gleaming scales. Wings unfolding, glistening, and drying out in the arid recycled air of the prison. Its tail unfurled and flickered like a snake's.

Len took a step back and bowed at the waist. By the door, Victor and Thomas went down on one knee, heads lowered. From her office, the Duty Commander issued the news by radio: *Our queen has been born, long may she reign!*

The dragon stretched like a cat, then curled up beneath the consoles, where the room was warmest, readying itself for sleep. Len, Victor and Thomas withdrew, their watch at an end, for now.

But what of me?

Chana was blind. She had been diminished to a tiny shrill voice, in a dark, hot, moist place.

Ah my friend, you helped me. And now I am going to set you free, the dragon growled. *Tread carefully and make for the light . . .*

Behind the reptile's right eye, its gleaming ear plates twitched. Something tiny emerged, scarcely bigger than an insect. Its body too long, its legs too few. But the wings that flickered and buzzed on its back were like those of an oversized fly.

*

SHE TRAVELLED THE hollows of the building, passing through conduits and voids filled with peril and the accumulated filth of years. On her way, she narrowly avoided spiders and mice, and fed on the sweet juices of flies and dust mites.

On the third day, she saw the light.

Emerging from one of a cluster of segmented metal vents positioned on the prison roof, Chana clung to her perch with all her strength. The wind was gusting cold, droning as it passed through the angled slats covering the vent. Above her, the skies had broken up like sections of grey ice, white sunlight streaming through the fractures. She waited as her eyes adjusted, holding on.

In a pause between gusts, she launched herself upward, wings buzzing. She swayed, circled and rose, the hulking form of the prison falling away beneath her. Then the wind took her, and she was gone.

Illumination

Joanne Hall

YELLOWED VELLUM, GOLD LEAF.

Gilberd selected the smallest of the brushes and dipped it into the precious pot, holding in his breath until he had applied both leaf and a thin covering of glue to the curlicues around the lettering on the manuscript. Only then, once the pot was set safely aside, did he let out a long sigh. It was flawless. He would never have achieved such satisfaction if he had followed his late father into the wool business. Only in taking holy orders had he found out where his true skills lay, away from the lure of material wealth, towards the purpose the Lord had in mind for him. Only here could he perfect his art in silence, inside the peaceful embrace of stout abbey walls, away from the distractions and temptations of the world.

It had to be perfect. The Earl of Newburgh had commissioned this new Book of Hours to celebrate his daughter's wedding – his coffers were deep and his lands stretched from the coast deep inland to the high moors. The abbey had benefited from his largess many times. As the finest artist in the order, the responsibility for the illumination of the manuscript had fallen to Gilberd. It was an honour, one he took most seriously.

The manuscript was already written; Brother Aled, the abbey's patient and long-suffering scribe, had copied out the prayers and devotions for each day, and now it was up to Gilberd to decorate the lettering that crowned the psalms and the spaces in the margins as he saw fit. Saints and scenes from the life of Christ, hard-working monks tending their vines or bowing their heads in prayer. On some pages he had sneaked the image of their good patron, kneeling at the feet of the Lord or ruling justly over his serfs. In Gilberd's experience, it deepened a man's pockets when he saw himself immortalised in art.

There were hounds and cats – Gilberd was very fond of cats – gargoyles and demons, twisted little faces peeping out from between green leaves. Creatures of the field, and of myth. He drew and painted as the will took him, losing himself in the minutiae of his art, filling page after page until he was squinting in the darkness of the scriptorium, copying the most intricate designs from wax tablets onto the soft and yielding vellum. He missed meals. He missed mass. There was only the work.

Gilberd absently licked the tip of his brush before dipping it in the red lead, letting his hands act of their own accord. He pushed aside the wax tablet. He disliked using it, preferring the feel of the calfskin, the instinct that guided him in his art. Maybe it was the Holy Spirit, flowing through him? That was what the abbot had remarked upon when he viewed the completed pages. Gilberd didn't know. He thought the Holy Spirit would feel different, somehow, and wouldn't leave him with an aching back and squinting eyes. Ten years of this painstaking work had left him with a pain in his head that plagued him at all hours, a hunch to his shoulders and a mottled rash across his tonsure. His nose and throat were as raw as the tips of his fingers when he pressed them to his stinging eyes, just for a moment, before taking up the brush once more.

The whitewashed cell walls seemed to lean in around him. There was a window, high above, but it was a narrow slit, and even craning his aching neck all he could see were grey clouds like smoke piling in on top of each other. Not a day to be outside, and he bent his head once more to the painted page.

A curve of scarlet, just inside the gold. A sinuous shape forming beneath his ink-stained fingers. A poisonous serpent, maybe, come down from the trees of Eden to tempt Eve into original sin. No, not a serpent; this was a legged beast, a wyrm, a wyrm with spread wings and a tongue of flame that flickered out to lick at the gold leaf, to melt it like the fire of a forge. The gold was dripping, running down the page . . .

Gilberd blinked hard. His eyes were streaming, and he saw the droplet fall. He tried to catch it with his roughspun sleeve but was too late. Too late, and the ink was smudged, and the page, the page was ruined. Brother Aled would have to start his scripture all over again, and Gilberd knew he would say nothing in words, but the Welsh monk's sighs of complaint would rattle the feathers of the birds in their trees from here to the walls of York. He felt a deep pang of guilt as he sat back, numbed. He was dazzled by the sudden light that flooded into his eyes as he looked up from the vellum, his hand moving automatically for the blotter, trying to clean up the stain. The script was soiled, unreadable. How could he have let that happen?

Gilberd shook his head to clear his thoughts. A moment of distraction, that was all. He was over-tired again, seeing things that weren't there, and his fatigue made him clumsy. The vellum could be put aside and scraped clean, used for some cheaper work, a palimpsest.

He rejected it, and took up another page. Quotations from the Book of Job, maybe some solace for a wealthy man who had lost two sons, maybe an insurance for the abbey against future financial hardship. The righteous might suffer, but so long as they didn't turn away from the Lord, a man could buy his place in heaven. Gilberd narrowed his lips. He had struggled against the temptations of coin, when he lived in the outside world, and he was sure the Earl of Newburgh could make the effort to do the same.

As was his habit, he scanned the page, seeking inspiration for his illuminations.

"Out of his mouth go burning lamps, and sparks of fire leap out,
Out of his nostrils goeth smoke, as out of a seething pot or cauldron
His breath kindleth coals, and a flame goeth out of his mouth."

The Leviathan. That wondrous beast, the dread wyrm with tongue of flame. Gilberd's own tongue flicked out, licking the tip of his brush and dipping it once more towards his inks.

Indigo, turmeric, vermillion.

Breath of fire, curls of smoke rising from a hell-dark maw. Eyes like charred embers burning from the vellum. Scales of deep crimson, each tiny scale tipped with the faintest trace of gold. Gilberd's brush flew over the pages, dipping and weaving, darting like a serpent's tongue.

The world around him fell away. The drawing, the art of bringing this creature to life, was all-consuming. It had to be the Holy Spirit flowing through him that drove him on. It filled his vision, tiny detail vivid and large. The wyrm seemed to writhe beneath his brush. His fingers, slipping, felt the heated skin of the beast twitch . . .

He pushed his seat away hard, sat back and stared at the vellum. Had he ruined another page with his swift movements? Surely not; the abbot would be angry at the waste. Gilberd didn't often make clumsy mistakes like this.

The page was unblemished. He had not felt the beast move. The strain, the time put in to finish the Book of Hours before the wedding – it was beginning to tell on him. It must be that. He would finish his work, and then he would request light duties for a while. Out in the herb garden, in the sunlight, surrounded by the gentle purple shadows of the high hills that protected the abbey and its grounds. A little light gardening would help clear his vision.

He rubbed his eyes, pinched the bridge of his nose between thumb and forefinger, and looked again.

The wyrm was moving.

It couldn't be. He blinked hard, so hard it took him a long moment to regain his full sight. The dragon-creature rippled down the side of the page, flexing along its muscular length like an eel. Wings no larger than his thumb flapped and rustled, the red maw twisted and put forth smoke, and a tiny jet of bright flame sparked against the vellum only to be immediately extinguished, leaving a dark smudge on the calfskin. Gilberd brushed it with a finger, marvelling at the soot that stained his fingertip. Still warm.

"This cannot be!" He breathed the words, barely on the edge of hearing, not wanting to break the spell with the harshness of his voice. "My Lord, is this a sign?"

He held his shaking hand down flat against the page, willing the creature he had drawn to life to crawl into his palm, that he might lift it to his face and study it more closely. It thrashed about on the page, and he could feel the texture of it, but it was as if a fine sheet of glass pinned his creature down to the vellum, and it moved only in its own plane.

His creature . . . It was not his creature. It was a working of the Lord, a miracle, or a test. A test he would fail if he allowed himself to give in to such delusions of grandeur. Or maybe they *were* just delusions, over-work, the fumes rising from the inks that made his skull throb. He kept a wary eye on the twisting, flaming creature as he licked his brush and dipped it once more towards his inks, the white lead burnishing the snow-cap of a mountain beneath the beast's grasping talons. White the snow, and indigo the deep shadows of the crevasses that laced the mountainside, and black as night the cave where the wyrm dwelled. And there, deep in the heart of it, was that a flash of gold? He felt a sudden desire rise within him, one he thought he had left behind a decade ago.

"My Lord, lead me not into temptation . . . This is but a dream, a vision seen through tired eyes. Give me peace, Lord, to finish the work you set me . . ."

The gold leaf, precious, flaked from the brush as a spasm ran through Gilberd's hand. His fingers were blue, not with ink, but with a deep inner chill, and when he tried to return the brush it was with numbed, fumbling fingers. He pressed his hands into his armpits, trying to clench his jaw to keep his teeth from rattling in his head. Why was he so cold? It was May, soon coming into June, warm despite the gloom of the afternoon and the turbulent sky, but his breath curled like dragon-smoke against his lips, and he squinted into the darkness of the cave. When he looked up, he could see weak sunlight struggling to break through the cloud, shining in faint bands through the cell window. When he looked down, it was into the darkness and chill of the yawning mouth of the cave, with that hint of gold, winking like a burnished eye just beyond his reach.

"Lead me not there, oh Lord . . ."

The walls of his cell were gone. He stood on precarious mountainside, pale snow under his feet, rocks standing proud and ink-black all around him. He tipped his head back to take in the sky, impossibly high, the pale blue of a rich maid's gown, and the beast was there. It circled lazily overhead, the light catching and sparkling off gold-tipped wings. He could see his own work there, in the swirls of scarlet and burnished bronze, in the green of the underside of the wyrm's throat darkening to cobalt blue, in the curving white teeth as it swung its open maw towards him. In the flame boiling at the back of its throat . . .

Gilberd ran. The snow crunched and shifted underfoot, treacherous, slowing him down, but he could see the cave ahead, the one where temptation lay in darkness just beyond his reach.

The wyrm roared, but the sound was far behind him now, fading into insignificance before the prospect of the hoard that lay ahead. He felt the desire well up within him, a hot greed, like a fire in his belly. His vows had taught him to suppress all desire, and that desire was a sin that would only bring suffering, but now, staring at the glint of gold deep in the cave, those same vows were only the sinful jealousy of others. He pitied and despised those who would seek to force such vows upon him. He had to reach it, had to stretch for it even as his breath curled smoky in front of him, and the heat in his torso filled his throat with red-gold flame . . .

White lead, mercury, arsenic.

*

HIS BROTHERS FOUND him face down on his latest manuscript.
As if from on high, he watched them approach. Portly Aled, and
David, who worked in the herb garden. There was barely room
for the two of them in the narrow cell.

Aled laid a hand on Gilberd's neck. He could see his own
body, cold, and stiff, ice-blued fingers curled into claws, digging
deep into the shattered pot of gold leaf. When they turned him
over, taking care not to damage the vellum still further, his lips
were stained. Little dashes of vermilion, of yellow, of white, in
the creases of his mouth, on his tongue, his gums, the tell-tale
marks of the madness that often overcame those who worked in
illumination. He had seen it on others, and now it was his turn
to succumb. His dedication had finally claimed his life, and he
was in the hands of the Lord now. But with his dying hands, he
had immortalised himself as the dragon. Painted himself into the
marginalia of the precious manuscript, a dragon spilling gold from
its outstretched claws, a dragon with the face of a dead man. He
waited there, in the fringes of the pages, for the next reader to see
him take life, take flight, before their eyes. He was eternal now.

The Anxiety Dragon

Rob Clifford

AKING OFF HIS SQUARE, BLACK-RIMMED GLASSES, PASCAL squinted at Bernard, who was sitting nervously opposite him. 'It might help if you could explain when this started.'

Whereas Pascal sat gracefully in the evidently expensive, Scandinavian chair, Bernard edged backwards and forwards: crossing his legs, then deciding that might look feminine and so putting the ankle of one leg on the knee of the other like he'd seen in American films, but then that was uncomfortable so he leaned forward, but was concerned that was too keen . . . and so it went on. Ultimately, he looked skyward, thinking, and then tapping out numbers on the wooden ridges of the chair. It might have looked like he was thinking about how many days, months or years of time had passed, but in reality he was just counting. Bernard counted a lot. 'I couldn't really tell you,' he finally began. 'It's one of those step-by-step things, like backache. It's on and off. There's a time before you had it, and so there must have been a time when it started, but you can't really nail down when.'

Pascal shifted to ease the small of his back, which, despite a special orthopaedic cushion, seemed to have been niggling him of late. He probably couldn't say when it started. He replaced his glasses. 'Well, what's the earliest memory that you do have?'

Bernard exhaled, 'If really pushed . . . the earliest was walking through Whitworth Park and realising that if you're going to carry a dragon in your pocket, boxer shorts are definitely a no-no. That, and you really need heat protection if you're going to avoid a couple of evenings in pyjamas with your bits smothered in cream.' He absent-mindedly scratched himself at this point, then, realising Pascal had spotted the motion, suddenly reddened and put his hands under his legs. 'Course, he wasn't a teenager then, I didn't even know he was called Martin, and like those rescue puppies they use in the RSPCA adverts, I certainly didn't realise how quickly, and how much, dragons grow.'

Pascal nodded, made a few notes with a precisely-sharpened Palomino Blackwing pencil, crossed out a word and then put the pencil down. 'And what does he do?'

'Do?'

'Yes, do?'

'Well, I guess he just hangs out mainly.'

*

BERNARD KICKED OFF his shoes, grabbed the ale that he'd been dreaming about since 9:00am that morning with one hand, and the remote with the other, and then eased back into the spot his backside had been carving out of the sofa for the last five years of living in his 'stop-gap' accommodation. Taking a long drink, he gasped, burped and then nodded to the dragon sitting on the IKEA Furmjsta chair opposite (it had taken a long time to find a chair that worked for a dragon and supported his posture, tail and growing wings adequately, but finally the 'Furmjsta' had proven perfect). Martin looked back at Bernard, copied his actions, and let out a smoking snort that would have set the smoke alarm off had Bernard not disconnected it last month after one too many call outs.

'Why can't you order?' Bernard asked. He could already feel his palms beginning to sweat as he looked at the phone.

'Because I'm a dragon,' Martin replied, flicking Bernard's mobile across.

He stretched for the phone that had fallen between his fingers and under the chair. 'That's your reply to everything that you don't want to do.'

'Well, it's true. My claws don't work on the touch screen anymore; the cat's got more chance of getting it right.' There wasn't much chance of testing this theory as the normally territorial ginger-tom cat had taken to keeping a distance since Martin's presence had increased in the flat. 'I want a spicy hot one with extra chilli and jalapenos.'

'No jalapenos. You destroyed the breakfast bar last time. Nothing hot.' Bernard turned the phone over in his hands, which were beginning to sweat. 'What if I forget something or they ask a question I don't know the answer to?' He was subconsciously starting to count different combinations of lines in the keypad: 5 direct up, 3 across . . .

'I had hiccoughs. It'll be fine. You'll make something up. It'll be practice for your social skills.'

'Fuck off. Will you at least answer the door when they come?'

'I can't, because . . .'

'Because you're a dragon . . . yeah, I get it.' Bernard started to dial. 'Sometimes, I wonder what dragons are actually useful for.'

As they ate the pizzas from an upturned box on the floor, Bernard was aware the flat had seen better days. Dragon teething had been bad enough but, once embers had begun to glow and smoke at the back of Martin's throat, the accidental burning of furniture that occurred was far worse. The wooden table had gone through a phase when it could still be passed off as vintage, but now was evidently just barbecued. What had been a useful breakfast bar, dividing the small kitchen from the lounge, had been significantly shortened by one of Martin's sneezing fits. Looking around at the scorch marks across the walls and carpet, Bernard had reluctantly started to realise it would probably be best not to ask for his deposit back. Still, for now, the Furmjsta was just the right size, Martin seemed to have the thin column of smoke that constantly trailed from his nose reasonably under control, and they had four large pepperoni pizzas to get through. Well, Martin had three and a half, but sharing's a bit different when you're a dragon.

'Have you asked her yet?' Martin flamed the top of his pizza whilst asking the question.

'Asked who?' Bernard avoided looking at him and concentrated on the three slices he'd divided, counting the salami so that each piece had equal amounts.

'You know who,' Martin replied whilst carefully rolling up his entire pizza into a giant burrito.

'She's my boss.' There were four pieces of salami on two of the pizzas and three on the third. A bead of sweat appeared on Bernard's brow. He started to try the maths of halving the salami slices to make them fit.

'Was. She leaves in three days.' The first pizza went down Martin's giant gullet. 'That's all you've got.'

'I know. I'll–'

'Mooning over pictures on Facebook doesn't count.' Martin leant across and grabbed Bernard's phone out of his hand, replacing it with a slice of pizza. 'You'll have to actually speak to her.'

Bernard's calculations had been distracted by Rachel's profile, which was currently showing he'd scrolled down to 2012. He desperately grabbed for the phone, having had previous experience of Martin's claws 'liking' photos.

Keeping Bernard's flailing arms back with a wing, Martin saw the photo and tutted. Whilst Bernard wrestled with the indignity of the fact he had fulfilled the dragon's low expectations of himself, Martin turned his attention back to the giant burrito pizza, swallowed and burped loudly, causing a small flame to shoot out and incinerate the lampshade. 'Sorry, bro.'

*

PASCAL FLICKED A piece of lint from his black polo-neck jumper and smiled. 'I'm glad we've got to this issue, the real problem you're here about. Let's start with the mornings. How is it affecting you before you get to work?'

Bernard nodded. 'Well, bit better and a bit worse.'

*

THE TRUTH WAS that work had felt like a little less of an ordeal with Martin around, but he had also brought new problems. Shower, shave, breakfast, quick quiz on which character from Star Wars you'd be . . . everything was fine. And then, the counting would quietly start at the back of Bernard's mind: the items out of the dishwasher, the number of times he circled each finger as he washed them and so on. Quickly, he'd start to sweat and want the loo again. It'd be time to leave, and he'd be sat on the toilet going nowhere.

Martin looked down at his iPad, rehearsed a sentence with his lips, then looked back up and stared intently at Bernard: 'Everything that happens, happens for a reason.' Bernard stared back, confused. 'Motivation. It's what dragons are good for.'

'You know it doesn't make me feel particularly motivated being stared out with my trousers round my ankles,' Bernard replied, fidgeting with the toilet roll in both hands to try and maintain some coverage.

'But that's exactly your problem, bro! You worry, you over-think, you analyse, you extrapolate.' Bernard was certainly over-thinking right now as he tried to break wind silently. 'You need to relax, to give yourself to the moment: as the air is free to travel, so are your thoughts.' Martin punched the air and raised his eyebrows expectantly. Bernard had been quite surprised to discover that dragons have eyebrows, and these had been a new development on Martin. The momentary trail of thought was too much and he farted. Martin whooped and tried to high-five Bernard. 'There, you've started!'

'What I want is to be able to wipe my backside and get ready for work with some privacy.'

'No, what you want is to be able to leave the house without changing your outfit three times because there's an uneven number of buttons and you're panicking about what people will think . . . particularly her.' Martin showed the iPad, still logged in under Bernard's name. Bernard noticed the dragon had liked all the photos from 2012. He put his head in his hands and groaned, feeling himself turn red as he imagined the notifications popping up on Rachel's screen. Oblivious to Bernard's mortification, Martin continued scrolling forwards, pausing at 2013 to hold up a picture of Bernard's ex-wife and stick his fingers in his throat. Finally, he was satisfied with what he'd found and stopped. 'Freedom is in the choices we do not have.' He looked at Bernard expectantly.

'You can't just read Facebook quotes at me, you know?' Bernard sighed. 'It's just embarrassing crap that makes a fool of anyone who reads it.'

'Says the man who can't get off the loo because he's afraid of speaking to people.' Bernard shifted in his seat, realising that Martin wasn't going anywhere. 'There's Biscuit, Degsy at work, and now her.'

'It's a bit embarrassing being watched . . .'

'Embarrassing, pfft.' A flame suddenly shot out of his nose and the last of the toilet roll was suddenly ashes. Bernard sighed. 'Shit, sorry, I know, I promised, not indoors. Look, I'll get some more when I replace the lampshade.'

'I just want some peace.'

'I'll do you a deal. Let me make your choices, follow my lead and I'll leave you alone in the bog.' Martin paused, waiting for an answer. 'C'mon, it's what you want. Just let me take control. It'll be good for you.'

'You make my choices? At the moment my choices seem to

be whether to waddle to the shower or get shit on my hands!'

'Waddle to the shower! See, it's simple.' Martin smiled proudly.

'Yes, yes, it's perfectly simple.' Bernard stood up and gingerly lifted his legs out of his trousers and into the shower. Bow-legged, naked and having lost all remaining dignity, he turned back to Martin. 'No way!' he shouted before snapping the curtain shut.

It was true that Bernard wanted to avoid the outside in general, even his retired neighbour, Biscuit. Ever since he'd discovered Martin's job, each morning, he had a new 'joke': 'Mind the ice, it's 'elf and safety', 'Watch out for them leaves, it's 'elf and safety', 'Careful with that umbrella, it's 'elf and safety'. He didn't mind the idea of the humour so much as, like Martin's new found fascination with Facebook platitudes, it didn't even mean anything. Bernard realised he could take banter, he just couldn't take crap banter.

When they finally managed to leave the house, Biscuit was there, bringing the bins in. Bernard walked quickly to the battered Volvo estate he'd held onto in order to carry around the dogs that had belonged to both him and his wife but were now restricted to visitation rights. However, he was too slow and Biscuit managed to manoeuvre himself between Brandon and the car door. 'All right, eh, eh.' Each 'eh' was punctuated by a dig in the ribs, making Bernard clench his teeth. 'Don't leave your bin out, eh? 'Elf and safety innit, eh?' Martin just watched disgustedly, although Bernard couldn't be sure if it was at Biscuit or his ineffectual ability to deal with him. Suddenly, he realised Martin was taking a deep breath and the glowing embers in his throat were brightening; following his excited gaze to Biscuit's prize topiary dragon he knew he had to act quickly.

'No!' Bernard shouted.

'No?' Momentarily confused, Biscuit was speechless, not a feeling he was used to. At a loss for what to do, he fell back on what he knew: 'Yes it is. I say, 'elf and safety, call the cops, he's left his bins out. It's political correctness gone mad.' Biscuit wasn't really bothered which nonsense he was lumping together and his slightly less focused jabbering gave Bernard the chance to squeeze around him and get in the car. Martin had used a child seat for a while, but now seemed to prefer travelling on the dog blankets in the back, giving him room to stretch out and the opportunity to abuse the people travelling behind. It was only as they pulled out of the driveway that Biscuit realised he was left talking to himself.

*

BERNARD SAT HUNCHED over in the chair, staring at the floor and shaking his head with embarrassment. 'Why did I ever let him in the house?'

'Is that a rhetorical question, or even a metaphorical one?' Pascal absent-mindedly stroked his moleskin notebook with pleasure at his own question.

'It's a question of how I ended up with burnt furniture and no loo roll.'

'Tell me about work.' Slightly annoyed at the lack of recognition of the quality of his question, Pascal had changed the subject. 'How are things different there?'

*

WITH FOLDERS, BOOKS and papers all around it, Bernard's desk looked cluttered and confused, but it was actually achieving a multiple purpose. Firstly, the papers and blu-tacked Star Wars gonk figures had put paid to the attempt to introduce hot-desking. Secondly, he had moved the desk forward from the wall quite a bit in order to create a space for Martin. Finally, it helped create a barrier between himself and Degsy, the self-titled 'bantmeister' whom he was fortunate to be next to. Some days the only thing that kept him going was being able to retreat into this self-created world.

The only other thing that kept him going was Rachel. Once

he'd finally plucked up courage to add her on Facebook, his wishful thinking had only increased: she liked the same guitar-led singer-songwriter bands as him, the same holidays in ex-communist European cities as him and she must like cats as she went to cat poetry readings in Northern-Quarter vegetarian cafes (although he wasn't entirely sure if the poetry was about cats, to cats, or even, possibly, by cats). But much as it pained him to admit it, Martin was right: she would be leaving in three days, which meant his time to actually move beyond liking Facebook posts from five years ago was rapidly counting down.

'Ey up, Bernie, she's coming.' Degsy pushed his perma-tanned face through a hole in Bernard's wall that he'd created by pushing a book over.

'Don't reply,' came Martin's rasp.

'Who?' he replied, betraying his attempted nonchalance by knocking over a pen holder and then hitting his head on the folders as he bent down to pick up the pens. By the time Rachel reached them, half his desk was on the floor and Degsy had launched into a braying laugh.

'Hi, Rach-el.' Trying to imply a level of informality, Bernard had decided to shorten her name to just, 'Rach', but then realising that she might not appreciate the assumed closeness, added the 'el' after just a little bit too long.

'You all right, Bern-ed,' Degsy shouted, braying again.

'Play it cool, just say hi.' Martin encouraged.

'Do you want a coffee? I was just going to get one.'

'No you weren't, you've just come back with one,' Degsy helpfully noted. In his rush to hide the evidence of his fresh cup of coffee, Bernard knocked the mug onto the fallen folders, causing the contents to spray back up into his face. Stinging from the burning coffee, he swiped with his hands, until he could open his eyes again, and saw Rachel's shocked face and splatters of coffee all over her blouse. The wooden brown owl broach she was wearing had now gained a dark stain on its head and seemed to be glowering at him.

Reaching forward to brush the stain, but then catching himself with his hands out-stretched in front of Rachel's chest, Bernard stuttered, 'I'm sorry, I'm just, I'm . . .' Momentarily lost for words, he felt the coffee start to drip down from his face into his shirt. Recognising the same thing was probably happening to his files right now, he could only wish that he would blur and dissolve in the same way as the writing on the papers, and so he did the next best thing he could think of, and ran.

'Well, that went well.' Martin tried a little chuckle to raise Bernard's spirits, who remained sat on the toilet counting cracks in the dirt-filled tiles.

After a pause, Bernard looked up to stare back at Martin. 'I thought we'd agreed you wouldn't do this.'

'No, I offered a deal and you didn't take it up.' Bernard shook his head sadly. 'After that complete fail, I'm going to offer you one more chance.'

'Why do I always do it?'

'In a parallel universe, our regrets are our successes,' Martin tried. 'Let me help you turn it around.'

'And how will you do that exactly?'

'You're still over-thinking things. That's when you panic and it all goes wrong.' Martin tried to put his arm around Bernard, but as dragon arms are so short, it left them uncomfortably close. This was added to by Martin's tail, which had to wrap around Bernard's legs in order to fit into the cramped cubicle. Bernard coughed and Martin stepped back. 'Let me take away the thinking, the over-thinking, and you can just be yourself.'

'I suppose it can't be any worse.' Bernard sighed.

'Exactly!'

'And you'll give me some peace in the loo?' Bernard asked.

'Of course, whatever you say.' Bernard sighed and started a slow nod of agreement. Before he had a chance to speak, Martin grabbed him even tighter than before. 'You won't regret it. I'll be your wingman, bro.'

'And that. Toilets, and that. Both have to go.' Bernard managed to gasp as the air was squeezed out of his lungs.

'No worries, br . . . Bernard.' Martin stepped back and laughed, snorting so that a puff of smoke came out of his mouth just as the bathroom door opened.

'Jesus Christ, Bernie! What kind of fart is that?' Degsy's voice exclaimed.

*

SUDDENLY LOOKING DISTASTEFULLY at the black coffee he was about to sip, Pascal placed the mug down and picked up his pencil, which he used to punctuate the air along with his keywords as he spoke. 'So, it's about *control* (poke), absolving yourself of your *decisions* (poke) to take away the *anxiety* (poke).'

'Well, it's mainly about not being watched when I'm taking a shit.'

Pascal dropped the pencil into his coffee.

*

WHILST HE WAS looking forward to taking control, Martin was finding it hard to keep his side of the bargain. He had got used to being by Bernard's side pretty much 24/7 but, now he was left to his own devices, he found his thoughts wandering to what exactly he was doing with his life. When Bernard first went into the bathroom, he found himself sat on the breakfast bar stool (minus breakfast bar) examining his tail and realising it was no wonder he'd been so clumsy lately with the way that it had grown. After a couple of sighs, the room was beginning to fill with smoke and so he decided to go back to doing what any dragon having an existential crisis would do: getting himself back on the net and browsing some clickbait. Quickly engaged, he grabbed the iPad and ran to the toilet door, where he shouted through, 'Don't let choices be your cage.'

'That one doesn't even mean anything!' Bernard shouted back.

Martin scrolled again, momentarily hurt. 'Yes it does. There's a picture of a sunset with a cage around it and a bird flying away and everything. Anyway, you need to learn to let go, you know, to let it all hang out.'

'What does that mean?'

'That you're just too uptight.' Bernard was beginning to think this really wasn't the bargain. 'You know how clowns train? They have to find their inner idiot. They think of something totally ridiculous, totally humiliating and then add to it, and add to it, and then do it.'

'Welcome to my life.'

'What I'm saying is you've got to stop being afraid. What's the worst that could happen?' Bernard suddenly opened the door, causing Martin to fall backwards.

'Yesterday. Yesterday is the worst that could happen,' Bernard defiantly stated as he walked out the door.

'Every tomorrow is yesterday reborn,' Martin called after him.

*

BISCUIT WAS WALKING back with his paper when they bundled out of the house. 'You're late,' he announced cheerily. 'That's what you get working for the council: part-time hours!' As he said this, he poked Bernard in the stomach with his newspaper. 'Part-time hours so that nobody is at any risk of over-working themselves!' Bernard tried to just nod and get in the car, but as he opened the door and bent over to get in, Biscuit hit him sharply on the backside with the rolled up newspaper. "Elf and safety, madness, that's what it is.' Bernard's head flew up and hit the roof of the car. Rubbing his bruised scalp, he got in and slammed the door shut.

'Reverse over his hedge thing,' Martin encouraged.

'No!' Bernard was already getting nervous about being watched reversing, without deliberately causing damage. 'Anyway, it's a dragon. I thought you'd like it.'

'It looks like a castrated unicorn, and that's beside the point; we had an agreement.' Bernard had to admit that the idea did appeal to him. He had now completed a three-point turn in the close and was ready to move forwards on his journey, or was positioned perfectly to reverse into the prize topiary if he so chose.

'Come on!' Martin encouraged, the tiny flapping of his wings suggesting his building excitement. Bernard put his foot carefully onto the accelerator, somehow convincing himself he wasn't aware he hadn't changed out of gear, and the car began to move backwards inch by inch. They both watched the mirror intently. Biscuit had originally placed his hands on his hips, pushing his large belly out, but, as the car approached, he was gradually tucking himself inwards, not wanting to believe what might be about to happen. As they hit the curb and rose up, the corner of Bernard's mouth began to curl upwards, a flicker of excitement in his stomach. The bumper was only inches from the topiary when Biscuit broke and rushed around, but before he could reach them, there was an almighty bang. Everyone froze, and then Biscuit started belly-laughing.

'Your driving's worse than your time keeping, mate. You wanna watch that, it's not–'

'Health and safety,' replied Bernard sadly, finishing the sentence for him. 'What the hell was it?' he asked, sticking his head out of the window.

Biscuit pointed at the secateurs sticking up from the lawn and deep into one of the tyres. 'That'll need changing,' he shouted as he went into the house.

Bernard yanked the handbrake up and removed the keys from the ignition. He looked up into the mirror, catching the eye of the quizzical face staring at him from the boot. 'And you can't help because . . .' He said the words aloud as Martin mouthed them at the mirror. 'I'm a dragon.' Martin shrugged as if to say, 'What can you do?' Bernard got out, walked around to the back of the car and opened the boot to get the spare tyre. 'If you were a proper dragon, you'd be able to fly us there.'

'I'm underage and you know it,' came the hurt reply. 'You're meant to be the responsible adult!' Martin turned around so that only his enormous backside was facing Bernard, leaving him undecided which was worse: an over-enthusiastic dragon or a sulking dragon.

When Bernard finally arrived at work, Rachel was waiting for him with a book in her hand. Feeling the panic rise as she moved towards him, Bernard tried to settle at his desk and re-arrange his wall. 'Now's your chance.' Martin nudged Bernard with his tail. 'Take charge, tell her she looks hot.'

'Hi, Bernard,' Rachel started. 'I'm–'

'You look hot.' Rachel's face turned from one of careful concentration about the talk she planned to have to ease Bernard's wounded pride, to one of shock and some horror.

'Come again?' Her usual tone dropped as a little bit of her Geordie-steel crept back in.

'Great start. She's hot and she's going out with you tonight.'

'You look out. You're going hot with me tonight.'

Degsy spluttered on his coffee and Rachel's jaw dropped.

'Wow, one step ahead bro.' Martin wanted to hi-five, but the issue of short arms raised itself again. Rachel continued to stare at Bernard in disbelief.

'You know, I thought you were different,' she stated with disgust. 'I got you this, but clearly you don't need it.' She slammed the book down on his desk before turning and walking away. As she reached the door of the office, she paused, remembering something and turned around. 'And stop stalking me on Facebook!' She turned and left, slamming the door behind her. Bewildered with horror at the situation, Bernard looked around at the faces staring at him. Unable to meet their eyes, he glanced at the cover of the book: there was a picture of a relaxed cat with a speech bubble coming out of its mouth: 'Poetry to Ease the Anxious Mind.'

A clapping sound from Degsy's booth. 'Wow, I'll have some of whatever you're drinking, mate.' His head appeared above the cubicle dividers. 'That was an exceptional fuck up, even for you!' He picked up one of Bernard's Star Wars gonks and, noticing it had a lightsaber, placed it in front of his crotch, swinging it around. 'I'm surprised you didn't ask to put your lightsaber in her.' Martin gagged and snorted. 'Use the force, Bernard!' Degsy continued the motion, now accompanying it with whooshing sounds. He picked up a second character and starting playing out his imagined version of the relationship with high pitched voices and very graphic use of the characters.

Bernard sat down sadly. He decided it wasn't worth pointing out that Degsy had actually picked up a droid and, therefore, the interaction his movements were suggesting were not physically possible. He did this partly because he knew Degsy would not listen but also because, right now, it felt like a pretty accurate symbol of his own chances.

*

PASCAL DISPOSED OF the tissues he'd been cleaning his coffee-soaked pencil with and leant forward, clasping his hands together. 'I'm very interested in this issue of responsibility. You say you gave up your responsibility, your accountability, and the words are not your own, yet the words you spoke are not what you were told to say.'

'Well, it was an accident. It's what I do when I get nervous.'

'In my field, there are no accidents.'

This last statement had Bernard looking suspiciously at Pascal's pencil, which was still damp with coffee. 'All right, I suppose maybe the accident was letting a dragon decide what I was going to say.'

*

EVEN WITH MARTIN back on the Furmjsta, the remnants of a Chinese take-away on the floor and a number of bottles of beer drained, Bernard couldn't quite get into the comfy spot on his sofa and was fidgeting. Every time he got close, the memory of what had happened came back to him and he squirmed again.

'The truth arrow may sting, but afterwards you may heal.' Martin looked up from the iPad.

'I'm going to change the code on that thing,' Bernard sulked, 'and you've got noodles hanging out of your jaw.'

Martin slapped his enormous tongue around his mouth and swallowed the offending food. 'You got close,' Martin stated. 'You've got to admit that.'

'What I've got is a choice between a referral to a counsellor from occupational health or a sexual harassment case. Apparently, my behaviour has been described as 'discordant with enabling a professional culture of mutually independent gender identities.'

'Look, what you've got to—'

'No,' Bernard cut Martin off. 'I'm not a success in a 'parallel universe', or trapped in a 'cage of my choices', or a 'clown' in training, or whatever mixed-up metaphor you want to use. This series of nightmares is actually my life and I don't need your help to make it any worse.'

'But I'm just trying to—'

Bernard snatched the iPad from Martin and locked it. 'Well stop. From now on, I'm going to do the exact opposite of what you tell me to do.'

*

'REVERSE PSYCHOLOGY IS a really interesting idea, you know,' Pascal said whilst turning a miniature phrenology head in his hands.

'No, I wasn't doing reverse psychology. I was just going to stop doing whatever his cocky head came up with. That's the problem with dragons: they're over-confident. He claims it's evolutionary.'

Pascal reached for the moleskin pad and pencil. 'Evolutionary. I see.'

*

MARTIN SAT AS cross-legged as is possible for a dragon outside of the toilet, repeatedly tapping the screen of the iPad. 'What have you done to this?' he shouted through the door. With no response, he started to shout again, but then he heard footsteps hurrying down the stairs. 'Wow, what's the deal with you today?'

'I'm being myself, me . . . I don't need any of this shit.' Bernard jogged up to the door. 'And I changed the code on the iPad.' He grabbed the keys and unlocked the door, but suddenly paused. He held his hand on his stomach for a moment and then threw his bag down.

'What happened?' asked Martin.

'I'm being myself,' Bernard shouted as he shut the toilet door.

As they left, Biscuit opened his front door, evidently waiting and looking a little suspicious after yesterday's events. 'Just go to the car,' Martin advised, forgetting Bernard's promise from last night. 'Ignore him.' Biscuit was already walking round the driveway, garden shears in his hands.

'I don't appreciate being kept up all night by Mariah Carey blasting out.'

'I would have thought that'd be a fantasy of yours.' Biscuit dropped the shears and Martin grimaced at Bernard's response.

'I really don't think you should inflame things,' Martin warned. The word jolted a memory in Bernard's mind and he smiled.

'Perfect,' he replied and nodded towards the topiary. Martin shook his head. 'Do it.'

'Do what?' Biscuit asked confused. Ignoring him, Bernard stared Martin in the eye.

'You owe me.' He then turned determinedly towards the topiary. 'Do it,' Bernard commanded, without turning back. Following his gaze, Biscuit also turned to look at the hedge behind them. At the same time, Martin shrugged, stood up, took a huge intake of breath and then let out a roar of incredible fire and heat. The topiary flashed brilliantly for a moment, then seemed to stand in mid-air, as if it had suddenly been transformed into fragile grey moths, before they all fluttered to the ground. All that remained was a thick odour of salami and garlic that seemed to come from nowhere. Biscuit turned around in a combination of shock and bewilderment, just as Martin collapsed to the ground in a coughing fit.

'You really have to give up smoking,' Bernard said as he unlocked the car.

'But I don't smoke . . .' Biscuit feebly responded as the car reversed, leaving him standing with his shears at his feet, fully speechless for the first time in his life.

A gleeful Degsy made a bee-line for him as Bernard entered the office. But Bernard was distracted by something even bigger. 'What's happened to all my stuff?' His desk battlements had been dismantled: the folders were stored on a new bookcase, the desk had been pushed back and there was a set of filing trays with all his papers in it. As he approached, he found the worst insult: next to the waste bin was a small plastic mesh box; the Star Wars gonks were in there, along with everything else that had made his desk a home.

'They thought you were getting a little bit too 'personal.'' Degsy explained, taking the opportunity to sit on Bernard's desk. 'For a minute there, I thought you had it. You showed a little bit of fire in your belly, but it turns out you were just a bit of a creep.'

'Excuse me.' Bernard was trying to maintain composure but it was a hot day and, as Degsy slid his backside to the right of the desk to allow Bernard to sit down, he noticed the sweat patch the man had left behind. He quickly grabbed a tissue and his emergency antibacterial gel. 'After everything you've been saying, I don't think you can criticise me.'

'The difference is, mate, I don't say it to the boss.' Degsy leant in, giving Bernard a whiff of the egg sandwich he'd had for breakfast. 'Of course I'd like to give her one, but I'm not going to announce it to her face, am I?'

'Give her one?' Bernard had been sitting down, but paused, put his hands on the desk and stood up to face Degsy.

'Bernard!' Seeing where this was going, Martin tried to stop him.

'No, not anymore,' Bernard replied. 'Give her one? Do her? Pork her?'

'Bernard, you need to stop.' Martin grabbed him, but Bernard just threw his arms up in the air. Degsy tried to laugh, but it came out as a nervous gurgle. Bernard had got closer, standing over Degsy and forcing him to lean awkwardly back into the desk. 'What exactly do you mean by 'you'd show her your lightsaber?'' Bernard reached into the discarded collection of gonks and picked up the Darth Vader one that had faced so much abuse the previous day. 'It's about three inches long, is that what you mean?' From behind, one of the secretaries giggled.

Degsy shook his head nervously. Bernard repeated Degsy's thrusting actions with the gonk, 'I want to pork you but my gonk is only three inches.' Whilst Martin swiped for the toy, a horrified Degsy leant back even further into the desk.

'Bernard?' He was about to tell Martin to back off one last time, when Bernard realised the voice was too high pitched and more questioning. 'What are you doing, Bernard?'

He paused, then leant threateningly into Degsy. 'I'll show you what a real man is.' He pulled back, enabling Degsy to find his footing again, and then turned to face Rachel.

'I'm so sorry, Rachel. I'm sorry for yesterday. I'm sorry for this moment. I'm sorry for this excuse of a man that's been saying vile things about you just to wind me up.'

'Hey,' Degsy tried to interrupt, but Martin gave a quick flap of his wings, causing him to lose the footing he thought was secure, so that he fell from the desk.

'Look, I sometimes get nervous. Not 'shy' like people say, 'Oh you're just a bit shy, you need to come out of your shell.' I mean shaky scared, so that I end up spilling coffee all over people. I mean blindsided so that I end up muddling my words. You know what, I'll even go there, I mean shit-scared, quite literally, so scared that if I don't move fast, I'll shit myself. But that's who I am, and I like you and I respect you. Not, as this bozo here put it, because I want to 'pork' you.'

Rachel's put her hands out to indicate he should stop whilst she established if she was being apologised to or sexually harassed. Degsy tried to regain his feet, Martin got ready to flap again, but Bernard shook his head and just pushed Degsy down with his own hand. He turned back to Rachel and continued: 'But because I think you're kind, friendly and funny, and I read the book you gave me and I loved it, and maybe, just maybe, someone who would think of a gift like that would have the patience to put up with a guy like me, and so I'll say it this once and then I'll leave you alone and respect any personal boundaries, even if I have to walk out of this building and get a job in another city, country, or planet, which is quite what I'd like to do right now.'

'Say what to me?'

'Rachel, now that you're leaving and it wouldn't be unprofessional and it wouldn't be weird in work and . . . Rachel, would you even possibly, vaguely consider walking my ex-wife's dogs with me?'

*

MARTIN STOOD IN Bernard's bedroom with his wings completely opened; they seemed to be bigger than they were a few weeks ago, as if he were finally shaking off the last stages of his awkward years. On each wing, Bernard had placed three shirts, and both of them looked at the choices. 'Definitely not the flowers, it's not 2005.' Martin picked the shirt off with his teeth and flung it behind him. Bernard picked up a grey one. 'No, too serious,' and Martin repeated the action. Spotting Bernard had begun to rub his hands nervously as his eyes darted from shirt to shirt, Martin put his teeth into a simple checked shirt. 'This one.'

'But what if . . .' Bernard started but then caught himself. 'It's great.' Martin nodded and went towards the door. 'What are you going to do tonight?'

'I think I might just catch a movie or something,' Martin said.

'You'll be around tomorrow though, won't you?' Bernard clung on to the shirt, mentally starting to count the buttons on each cuff. 'I'll need to go through what I'm going to do next.'

'Maybe I'll give the cat a day indoors,' replied Martin. 'My home is where my heart leads.' Intending to give Bernard a playful flap of his wings, he misjudged their new size and sent the shirts and half of Bernard's bedding across the room. As Bernard collected everything, Martin wandered out to find if the luxury size seats at the cinema would be as accommodating as advertised.

*

'BEFORE I SAY that you are fine to go back to work, this dragon thing: it is just a metaphor, isn't it? You don't actually think you've been seeing a dragon do you?'

'I asked him that once, when he was invading the toilet again one day and I just wanted to get on with my business. I said, 'You are real, aren't you?"

'And what did he say?'

'I'm a dragon. It's like magic, gods, castles in the sky, getting the girl at the end of a story; I'm the world as it ought to be, not the world as it is. I've just shifted your world an inch in that direction.'

'Right, so, do you still see this dragon, this 'Martin'?'

'I haven't seen him in a while. I've cleaned up the flat with Rachel coming round a bit. I thought I'd dealt with everything and then she asked why my boxer shorts have all got little burn marks in.'

'So, would you say the episode is over, and the treatment has been a success?'

'I'd say it's shifted an inch in that direction.'

*

As PASCAL PACKED up his things that night, he gave his pencil a final wipe with a soft tissue and placed the precious notebook inside his leather briefcase. He glanced around the room before turning the light off, checking everything was where it was meant to be: a place for everything and everything in its place. He rehearsed the line in his head, but, somehow, it didn't give him the pleasure it normally did.

He thought of the Marks and Spencer's ready meal for one waiting at home, the chilled bottle of New World wine and the single crystal glass, and he knew that not quite everything was in its place. In fact, something was missing. He sighed, turned out the light and walked over to the door. As he pulled the door to and turned the key, he was suddenly surprised by a sharp and extremely heavy hand landing on his shoulder. Jumping back, he abruptly tasted burnt onions and fried salami in the air.

'All right, bro!' Martin announced.

Dragon's Bane

C.N.Lesley

CONNOR SAT UNCOMFORTABLY ON THE HARD, STONE bench. Bored with drawing symmetrical squiggles on his school slate, he let his mind drift as instructor Kerain droned on about kinship and boundaries. The oldest by a few years of those still confined to the teaching cavern, he wanted to be outside, enjoying the last of the mild weather, not stuck with a bunch of younglings learning their lessons by rote. He'd rather have been helping with the packing, but the adults had driven him off when he'd attempted to offer his assistance. Had his sire and dam still been alive then he would have had backing from them. He desperately missed his family, now long gone in an expedition to find new lands to the north. No one had returned, not Drakkens or even any of the firedrakes who had gone with them. Yes, there was trace of their first camp with a few tents and cooking pots in disorder, with no evidence of bones or marks of scorching, but had any one of them survived they would have returned to the aerie. He had lost hope. He knew the failure of the expedition had led to the choice to move to a different planet, given they had apparently worn out their welcome here with the indigenous people. All knew it was only a matter of time before the tribes rebelled, and he writhed with guilt that it was his parents who had tipped the balance on the choice.

Connor didn't agree with the planned exodus to an unknown world, having heard the arguments his parents had put forth about settling all of them in virgin lands to the north. How did the leaders know the star portal even worked as it had before, centuries back, when all the Drakkens in this clan had flown through to a new home? He would have mounted another, stronger expedition to the northern lands if he had been in charge, and he would have found out the definitive reason why the first group had disappeared. Why move so far just because a few of the indigenous First Born tribes had started asking questions about the Drakkens really being the wyverns, the Drakken alternative form that the tribes revered as gods? It wasn't as if any of them posed a threat for Drakkens, not unless they allied with the Angressi people, who came from elsewhere originally. Given the very differing appearance and character of the First Born tribes and Angressi, that alliance was as likely to happen as rain falling straight up. The worst case would be the tribes ceasing to pay the tithe to his clan for their so-called godhead, but would even that be such a terrible event? Drakkens were quite capable of fending for themselves, as would have happened had they moved north, and Connor didn't suppose the traditional attraction between the First Born girls and the Drakken men would fade anytime soon even if the tribes did cut the aerie off from supplies.

What of the half-breeds? They all had to up sticks and leave their First Born families, for none with Drakken blood must remain, or so the decree from the aerie leaders went. Even the tiny firedrakes found themselves caught up in the orders, whether they wished it or not, but who could tell with them? A fickle and feckless species, they followed the Drakkens for food and shelter they didn't have to find on their own.

The sounds of the youngsters reciting their multiplication tables broke through his thoughts, and he suppressed a groan as he knew these by heart already. Instead, he decided to see how high a stack of rocks he could balance on the broken end of a stalagmite just behind the instructor. It would prove entertaining if nothing else, to see how many he could mind-move before Kerain noticed. Connor had got to the fourth before some of the younglings started giggling and the instructor caught him stacking, mid-rock.

"Go stretch your wings and make yourself useful," Kerain ordered, pointing to the ledge that led to an outside exit point in the aerie.

Connor didn't need to be told twice. He was out of there at a run, launching himself into the crisp mountain air and changing to his other form in free-fall as the wind rushed over and around him. Red mist enveloped him as his flesh and bones dissolved, growing and reforming into what Drakkens called a wyvern for the benefit of the First Born tribes – who worshiped such beasts – but was actually a dragon. Connor didn't know how the original Drakkens had managed to explain away the extra legs. Who cared as long as the tribes paid tithe to the aerie? Wind cupped under the newly formed membranes of his wings, arresting his fall. He flapped for lift, finding a thermal and rising in the warm air to look out over the land.

Thick fingers of everleaf trees crept up the sides of the mountains, but lower down, as the soil level deepened, the dropleaf trees started their incursion. None of them showed more than a hint of yellow in their leaves, with most remaining a rich green. The decreasing day length and the first nip of frost would soon see the vibrant fall colours displayed, and he was going to miss it. He wondered why Kerain hadn't given any lessons concerning the new world. Surely they had known what they were going to encounter before coming here, hadn't they? There had to have been reconnaissance flights and initial sorties, didn't there? Connor wouldn't have had a problem giving his attention to that sort of lesson, for he could see the point in learning of challenges to come.

'Make yourself useful.' Right, he'd get busy with that, he didn't think, not when he was always shooed away from anything important as if there was something being hidden from him.

No, there were other activities he'd enjoy a whole lot more and he was quite certain he wouldn't get the opportunity once they made the move.

If a half-breed girl was willing to flirt with a Drakken, all of them would be far too busy packing the aerie to dally with him at the moment, and he was the youngest of the males too. As for full Drakken girls, no, he had no mind to get embroiled in a formal union, and nothing else would suit unless he wanted his wings ripped off at the shoulders by angry parents. However, there was a certain First Born maiden he had in mind for a tryst. She wasn't a woman of power, so he was safe on that score if he got so lucky. One of the lessons he'd received from Kerain when becoming old enough to mate was a dire warning to stay away from any First Born woman with even a hint of power. Kerain hadn't said precisely why, only that it was very, very bad. The regular girls were safe, though, and he knew how to avoid leaving any small keepsakes that looked like himself. Now, that was another recent stricture decreed the moment the decision to relocate had been settled. No Drakken was to risk impregnating any First Born woman, because no half-breeds must be left behind. Connor thought that reasonable, although harsh on all the existing half-breeds, many of whom visited frequently with their other families. Even the full Drakkens abstained from procreation within their contracted unions, for the younglings still enshelled would not survive the journey, they were informed.

Connor thought about his maiden as he flew. In a pocket of his tunic, now buried within the hide of his other form, were a few coloured crystals the First Born loved to sew onto their clothing. Most of the crystals formed deep within Darkspire Reaches and were the source of the Drakken's power, although not ones this small. The colours he had chosen when he raided were green and white as those were the colours the girl sewed on the garments she made as she sat by the river watching goats belonging to the tribe. Strange to send a woman on such a task as animal husbandry, but then he had noticed the men didn't appear to do much aside from going on the occasional hunting trip. Women did everything else, including setting up and striking a camp when the nomadic tribes moved on. He didn't agree with their way for it was not how Drakkens behaved, letting the woman do all the work for the mostly idle males and yet he kept his thoughts to himself around his little maiden. An aerie rule was not to unsettle the tribes in any way, and this included criticism. Maybe he'd get his first kiss today? That was something to anticipate, for he knew he didn't have time to establish a proper courtship that led to something more intimate. Nor was he sure he wanted more, for then there would be restrictions and demands to be met for the few moments of fun. No, too serious, especially with the aerie almost ready to take wing.

He glanced to the north as he flew, catching sight of the burning ring suspended in the sky. Kerain said it only came once every fourteen years, but Connor didn't recall the thing from its previous visit. As a youngling, he probably hadn't paid any attention, it being of no more interest than a cloud at that time. Perhaps no one had paid it heed, there being no reason to think about how it served as a portal between worlds at that time. In a day or so he'd be flying through the ring of fire to a new home. Resentment set in, for his opinion hadn't been asked even though he was full grown. The only reason he still took lessons was that no one had time – what with the move and all that entailed – to mentor him on any other adult task. A youngling and yet not one. He hoped the elders intended to accept him as an adult once they settled in this new world, wherever that was.

She was there, by the lake with her goats again. Heart soaring, Connor looked for a secluded glade to land, for the aerie restriction on not being seen changing into man-form still bound him. A gap in the canopy caught his eye and he swooped in, low and fast, landing before he realized that trees had been freshly felled in a circle. Curious, he looked around, checking for signs of people, but all seemed quiet as if the cutting had just been abandoned. Satisfied, he let the change happen, wishing it to go faster as his essence condensed into a smaller form. When the ground firmed under his feet, there was the glint of fast moving metal and an arrow suddenly hit him in the shoulder. Pain exploded from within him, but he dared not tend to it now, for where one arrow had come, others would follow. Only wyvern kind had a hide thick enough to withstand attack completely; the Drakken beast form definitely had vulnerable parts. He changed back, safe in the red mist at least. During the process, the arrow fell out, but the damage had been done, and now an evil heat radiated from the wound. Connor sprang for lift even as a volley of arrows struck him.

He flapped hard in the still air, trying to rise out of range. The arrows came thick and fast, most bouncing off harmlessly, and yet there was always a chance one might hit him in the crease of a joint or pierce an eye and then it would be over. Heat already spread through his body, the poison beginning to cloud his mind. He had to find somewhere safe to land before he fell out of the sky. At the same time, they would hunt him down if they had an idea where he landed, so he would have to keep going to the limits of his strength. The arrows tailed off as the distance increased. Yes, they would walk that far to retrieve their shafts and how much further? He kept going, his vision swirling.

Far ahead lay a gorge. Connor had overflown it on the way to meeting the maiden, using it as one of his direction markers. Yes, that would do, for any pursuers would have to climb down the side, cross a white-water river and then scale the other side to get to him. If he could just make it. The stillness of the air wasn't helping. His wounded flight muscles spasmed even as they kept him aloft. In the end, it was too much to move his wings any longer. Connor glided the last bit, crashing to land since he couldn't cup his wings.

*

PAIN AND FEVER took his mind to a strange and cloudless place where tribesmen pierced the confusion of his naked man-flesh wyvern form with their spears. An iridescent ring burned in the sky day and night as he raved at his tormentors, till it faded and winked out of existence. A downpour of rain cooled him and he gained some of the moisture he so desperately needed. With what little strength he had, Connor crawled to a small stream that ran down to the raging river in the bottom of the gorge and, having drunk his fill, he slept.

A light morning dew roused Connor from a fogged dream. He stretched out one stiff wing but winced when he tried to do the same to the other. Flying wasn't going to be an option for a goodly while with his flight muscles damaged. One glance around at the terrain showed him the density of the forest surrounding him on three sides. Getting through that wall of wood meant changing into his man-shape. Something about getting back to the aerie nagged at him, but his energy ran too low to think clearly. Since he could see the peak of his mountain home, it wouldn't take too long to get at least to the foothills, and from there he could access the internal staircase if his wing muscles hadn't healed enough. There was something wrong about the sky around the mountains, though. He'd work it out later, when he got home, although he dreaded the yelling he was sure to earn for being so careless.

The journey tired him more, to the point where he had to rest with his back against a tree trunk. Food would be good, but he had no chance of catching any in his weakened state. Had he anything to make a weapon, even? He searched his pockets and then he came across the pouch containing the gem stones. Not food, but nearly as good as a hearty meal the magic coursed through him as he crushed them against a rock. As his head cleared, Connor began to remember all about the First Born girl, the trap and why he had been flying in the first place. A horrible image of the portal winking out of existence plagued him. No, he hadn't been out of things long enough to be too late. They would have sent out a search party. Surely they would do that, knowing he wouldn't stray far from the aerie. The feeling of dread settled in his gut like a giant rock. Now he could manage a slow running pace, but what he saw when he eventually reached a clearing in the canopy killed all hope. There was Darkspire Reaches, set on the top of the mountain and seemingly deserted. No flying wyverns rode the thermals. Worse, no ring of fire burned in the sky. They had gone, all of them, without him. He'd been left alone, the last Drakken in this miserable place, with no way to reach the others until the ring returned in fourteen long years. Could he survive by himself for so long?

*

NORTH OF DARKSPIRE Reaches a tribeswoman set off on a solitary journey into the forest. She needed to get to a rough shack out of the way of her tribe, for none must see her as she was, not now she had started to show. He had promised to take her when the Drakkens had left this world. He had sworn on his magic that he would care for her and their child, and yet here she was, alone, with a child her people would not accept shortly to be born. Her love had withered to a cold loathing on the morning the ring of fire had faded without him coming for her. She'd go to the place of their trysts and maybe leave his ill-gotten get there once she dropped the brat. Perhaps it would be kinder to crush the child's head? She'd decide after the birth and then she could go back to her people, clear from blame for being with one of the Drakkens. Damn him, why had he abandoned her? Why had he even gone with her in the first place if he knew he couldn't take her when they all left?

As she walked, Running Deer counted out the weeks still to go, aware she needed to catch, smoke and store food for the time she got too heavy. There was a stream near the shack and maybe fish to be caught? She wasn't sure, as he had always brought a feast. By her calculations of her moontimes, she thought the child would come in three months, which meant midwinter. Now, that was an easier solution, for she could abandon the brat in the snow. Resolved, she picked up her pace, walking steadily uphill. Only one thing disturbed her, and that was the shack was a touch too close to the lands of the Angressi people, who hated the First Born tribes. It hadn't mattered while she had her Drakken protector, for no one could harm her then, not with him around. Today the story sung a sad theme of loneliness and desertion.

Half a day of fast walking left her with a stitch in her side as the shack hove into view. She ignored it until the bedding roll was laid out on a pallet of straw and ferns, and then she decided she'd get water to brew an herbal remedy for her pain, something to make her sleep. Yes, that would be nice, especially as she could secure the door from the inside with a stout plank slotted into brackets either side of the frame. Maybe she would put out the fire before she drank her brew, though, in case any Angressi hunters spotted the smoke and came to check it out. She didn't want any of those contemptuous fair folk around what was to be her home for the next few months, for they would be intent on driving her away and claiming it for themselves.

Running Deer settled down with her hot beverage after drenching her fire with half the rest of the water. Hauling it from the stream had made her pain worse, but now she had the brew all would soon be well, for it would give her rest and an ease from the torment. She drifted into sleep, but it was shattered by a rhythmic wave of pain worse than she had felt before in her life. A wetness under her legs on the mattress told her what had happened. The stars be praised she was going to drop the brat early, way too early for a live birth. In a few days, she could go back to her people, and none would be the wiser. She bore the pains, labouring through the night and the following day. They were too savage and too close together to let her move even to light her fire for the brewing of another remedy. Something must be wrong. A half-formed child should have made an appearance before now. Fear gripped her, intensifying the pain.

The moon rose above the sill of a window covered in transparent hide, turning all to a sickly yellow. Past screaming, she moaned, wishing for death to end the pain. But then a change came. The urge to push overwhelmed her. Panting, moaning and clenching her arms around her stomach to force the child out, she strained. Something round slid out between her thighs, something that swiftly ceased to be round when it started to wriggle. This wasn't a dead child. Running Deer looked down to a sight of horror. A small, bloodstained wyvern stared up at her from the birthing mess. Her mind flipped, and she reached out for the nearest weapon – a hatchet – but the creature crawled away as if it knew her intentions and another huge wave of pushing came upon her. Two of them? She'd have them in pieces if it were the last thing she did. The one coming was going to get it first and then she'd deal with the firstborn, busy fanning his wings to dry them.

It didn't work out like that, though. A full-term girl-child followed the monster in a huge surge of pain. Running Deer tried to stay awake, aware there was something she had to do, but exhaustion closed her eyes, sending her into a deep sleep. Her last memory was of the monster locking eyes with the baby girl before he flew up the now cool chimney.

*

ONCE CONNOR HAD staggered to the cavern entrance to the internal passages leading up into the high aerie he could leech energy off the gems in the mountain. Every step brought renewed vigour if not a relief from the pain or the fever caused by whatever poison the archer had used to tip his arrow. Nothing could help the deep heartache that increased with every step nearer his home. He knew it would be empty, for the ring was no longer hanging in the sky. As he'd thought, no one remained when he entered the aerie. The silence was as profound as the aerie had always been full of noise, bustle and life. All around lay discarded or broken goods deemed not worth the taking. They hadn't intended to return so they had left a muddle. Connor just hoped someone had remembered him and thought to leave some food. He checked the pantry area off the great hall where roasts would be turned on a spit, now empty over a dead fire. Half a sack of flour, wriggling with weevils sat, lonely, on a shelf. A small cup of hard and malodorous fat lay on the floor. Nothing else of interest. The cupboard was bare except for a thin layer of dust, which outlined where goods had once stood.

Connor reckoned if he could find a pan to boil the fat then it wouldn't poison him. He could then add it to the flour for biscuits as such, and the weevils would be the added protein. His stomach – empty for so long, because he had been feeding only on the energy of the gems – seemed positively enthusiastic at the prospect and made loud grumbling noises. He formed a flaming fireball in his hand from the gem energy he carried and sent it to nestle in the dead wood and embers of the great hall fireplace. The place began to look more welcoming now, and felt a lot better once the chill had left the air. Fortunately, his people had left all the old and blackened cooking utensils, so he had what he needed to cook up his nasty tasting biscuits. They might have been better with a pinch of salt. Maybe several pinches.

What he needed was meat, fresh, slightly rare meat, running with juices. Connor didn't bother going to the coolest storage cavern to check for carcasses, certain the place would be bare of anything edible. No, he must catch his own and, for that, he needed to fly. Opening his black leather jacket and pulling down his shirt, he reckoned the wound had at least closed. Why the stars did it have to be a flight muscle that had been hit? An arm or a leg would have been preferable to this. Not trusting his luck by going into free-fall from one of the ledges, he trudged up to the aerie entrance that opened up on the plateau. Now he had space not only for a transition, but also to test his wings. Either they would bear him or they would not. If not, he'd only fall a few feet. Walking to the centre of the plateau, Connor willed the change, welcoming the red mist as he dissolved to spread out into a much larger shape. Everything seemed good when the shifting was complete, excepting the dull ache in what had become the flight muscle on his left side. The discomfort increased when he flapped for lift, yet was bearable. He tested it, flapping higher, and then a warm thermal tugged at him. Connor took it as a sign, riding upwards with a gliding motion until near the top, where he broke free to glide down the mountain, his eyes searching for signs of animal movement. He wanted deer since going after domestic livestock wasn't a great idea, given the herder might retaliate, and he'd had enough of arrows. Aside from that, he didn't want to fly far until his wing was a lot more secure.

There, in a grassy clearing, a whole herd of the creatures grazed. The bucks ringed around the outside, while the does and fawns nestled safe in the middle, except they weren't, not from him. He couldn't risk getting impaled on any antlers and nor did he wish to use his flames, killing or injuring far more than he could eat before the meat went bad. A doe or larger fawn it must be, despite the guilty feeling of killing the mother of a family and species. He chose the most ungainly kill he had ever executed or seen anyone else try as he flopped on his victim from the air, crushing the beast as the others scattered. In his beast form, Connor didn't bother to flame his prey. He tore it apart to eat raw, enjoying the warm blood running out of his muzzle. A sense of well-being spread through him, easing his hurts a little and giving him strength for the next kill, for he'd need one to take back to the aerie. He launched, flapping for lift to get high enough to see where the herd had bolted. His next target proved much easier, for one of the fawns had fallen in a ditch, breaking its leg. Putting the creature out of its misery was a mercy, which he gave it with a swift bite to the neck.

After he had dressed and hung the meat in his cool cavern, or what had become 'his', Connor set about trying to put some order into his home. He hoped something could be salvaged out of the trash the others had thrown away, for this was all he had for the moment. Fourteen years of isolation stretched ahead of him. Now he dare not go courting First Born maidens since he'd had a dose of what would happen if he did. However, he did need to re-establish a tithing system with a few loyal tribes farther away from the aerie than the ones who were restive. He needed cloth or cured hides and a small amount of the food they processed, like flour, as he didn't have a clue how to make those items for himself. Engrossed as he was, the calling hit him sideways. Someone Drakken needed help. The caller, weakened beyond speech, could only send a message showing the location. Connor ran to the nearest exit, bringing the change as soon as he was in free-fall. Whoever had summoned help wasn't going to last much longer.

The image faded, but the link with the dying Drakken held, if only tenuously. Connor raced, snapping his wings against the air as he powered in the direction of need. He headed north, near where he had been shot, but that didn't matter anymore. Here was a companion for the lonely years ahead, if only they would stay alive. The clearing below matched the relayed image. He swooped down, worried not to see the body of a Drakken in wyvern form. Surely no one would take a vulnerable man-shape? As far as he could see, there was no prone body of any sort, and yet the yearning plea still whispered of this place in his mind.

The viewpoint was from above and yet strange, as the trees appeared bigger than when he had descended. Why? Was the sender smaller? Connor shut his eyes, allowing his mind to direct his movement towards the sender. A blurry image of himself in his wyvern form entered his thoughts. So he was in sight, was he? He opened his eyes, scanning carefully for where someone might hide. He almost missed the tiny foot sticking out from around a rock. A little drake, and newly hatched by the look of it, but all the firedrakes had left with the aerie. How had this one been overlooked? It hadn't hatched in Darkspire Reaches, or it would be there now, seeming too weak to move. Connor shifted to his man-shape, needing his hands to check the little creature over. The drake was so pale now that it was difficult to judge its original colour. Connor guessed at silver. It was a newly hatched male with not a mark on it. He didn't know what to do for the drake until a faint image of meat came into his mind. It was starving. Connor reverted to a wyvern, carrying his sorry burden in his claws and flying as fast as he could. As it was, he barely arrived in time. Rushing through the aerie on three legs to get to the cool cavern, he simply thrust the baby at a torn section of flesh where the blood still dripped, holding it while the little forked tongue lapped at the blood and then steadying the baby when it would bite at the flesh with its sharp teeth. The drake ate until it had managed to fill itself up to the throat by Connor's estimation. A very tired little huff of smoke and the baby's eyes shut as it keeled over into instant sleep.

Drakes liked the heat, so Connor made up a bed for his new-found charge on a bundle of discarded clothes set in a nice nest shape near the fire. Thinking for a moment, he arranged a bed of sorts for himself in front of the hearth so he would be near the baby in the night. He also cut off a generous helping from the haunch, slicing it finely so the drake wouldn't have to work so hard for his food. One pan he found proved shallow enough to act as a meat dish for the baby. There was nothing else he could do, although something seemed to be wrong with the little one, for it twitched and snarled in its sleep as if threatened.

*

Sunlight glinted off the scales of the golden wyvern as it flew high with something small in its talons. Fury and hatred had told Running Deer what that object might be that was cradled so carefully. She knew her Drakken lover's secret, for she had followed him – Runnel the betrayer – and watched him shift into his wyvern beast form. Was this him leaving again? The colour looked right, although a bit brighter than she recalled. It must be, and he'd taken the monster she'd first birthed. Her heart dropped. He hadn't gone with the rest, and he hadn't come for her either, only for the product of their union. Would he know of the second birth? Would he smell the babe on the scales of the beast? He might for she knew Runnel had an acute sense of smell.

A thin wail sounded behind her in the shack. The child needed feeding, and Running Deer hadn't bothered, thinking to kill the child. Her thinking had changed once she'd caught sight of the wyvern. Now she dared not, for what if he found out? She'd no mind to be flamed to a crisp by his beast form. No, since he was still here, then she would take the child to the stone of gifting, where all half-breed children were left for their fathers to collect. She'd have to feed it first, or it would die before she reached the place and then he might think she had neglected the babe on purpose. Would he be waiting there at the usual place for the transfer of half breeds to the Drakkens? She hoped he wasn't, as she wanted the babe twinned with a monster to die, and if it did, from exposure, then it would be his fault, not hers. Yes, that would work, especially now the sky clouded over with the threat of a storm.

Soon she had the sleeping infant bundled up in a shawl strapped to her back as she walked. The stone of gifting was not near, but not too far that she couldn't get there before moonrise, although the moon might not show through the black clouds rumbling overhead and spitting jagged fire. Great drops of rain started, hissing as they fell through foliage.

*

THE LITTLE DRAKE cried on waking, a pitiful little chirrup stirring Connor instantly. The youngling found his food, attacking it ravenously and then cried again. Pictures of a woman lying on a piece of sacking and a newborn human babe between her legs. This wasn't the drake being birthed, for the child was female, and the view was from quite high above, perhaps rafters? Connor had never heard of a twin birthing, or that a First Born woman would produce a drake instead of a child, but then he hadn't taken a great deal of notice of such things, their being women's issues. Now he worried, for the little drake thought his sister was in danger, and the youngling was probably right. A First Born woman, ignorant of how Drakkens were birthed, could go mad from shock on birthing an offspring that was a flying lizard. He should get the human baby, but then what? Perhaps another woman could be bribed to rear the little girl? A baby would not live if he brought it to Darkspire Reaches, unlike the little drake, whom he could care for easily, and had named Kryling. The drake wanted to come with him and in truth, Connor needed the little creature to locate the baby, for one looked much the same as another to him from the few he had seen.

He still had the bag with the coloured crystals so coveted by the tribes, which would do nicely for a bribe. The woman who took the baby would have more when Connor visited to check on progress, as sometime he'd need to take the girl. One thing was sure and that was he couldn't let her come to maturity in a First Born camp, for as a half-breed she'd have the ability to shift form. Another thought worried him even more. What if the mother was one of those First Born women with power, the ones the Drakken males must avoid? Which one of the Drakken males had been too lusty or too stupid to obey the one restriction they all had when trysting with the tribeswomen? Was a double birthing what happened, or was there something more? Would the girl-child have the magic of a Samara Maiden, revered as a woman of power by the tribes? If she did, along with Drakken power, then she'd become very dangerous to any who crossed her without the proper instruction. Even more reason to get her away before she matured. Connor set off into a thundering night storm with the drake held in his talons, where there would be some protection from the elements.

The shack door swung in the wind to show an empty room. No trace of the woman or her child remained beyond a few bloodstains on what passed for a bed. Connor supposed the child now dead, but thoughts from the little drake disagreed. Kryling felt the presence of his sister among the living. She moved to the south and the west, which meant the woman still had her. He sprang into the sky, flapping for lift in the fierce wind and rain. A woman on foot couldn't travel far, so he flew and then circled when Kryling sent more feelings about the location. A high moorland, almost bereft of trees figured in the little one's thoughts, something he could only have seen through the eyes of another. Images from the baby girl were vague and unfocused. The child cried from the cold and because she had been abandoned on something hard.

Connor circled again, trying to spot the tiny child from above with Kryling telling him when he got nearer. The drake became frantic, trying to push his way out from Connor's talons. Someone had taken the girl, and now he couldn't sense her. Firmly trapping his little drake, Connor circled lower, sending out his magic in waves to see where it bounced back. There, in the north quadrant of the moor, near a flat rock bare of vegetation, something hid. He concentrated, pushing harder against a different sort of magic. This wasn't a child, it was a grown woman, and not a First Born but an Angressi. He could tell by the flavour of her magic and what little trickled through from her thoughts. The woman thought him a threat to the baby and was protecting her. He relayed that to Kryling, who calmed a little.

The woman intended the child no harm. In fact, she intended to keep the baby, although he didn't get the reasons, other than the woman thought they were important, so she'd make a good temporary guardian. He flapped for lift, rising through the storm clouds, out of sight, but not out of range for tracking. Kryling had the ability to track his little sister, but Connor would follow the trail of magic oozing from the woman. He'd let her keep the baby for now, while keeping an eye on the little girl from a distance. Someday, before the ring of fire returned in the sky, he'd take back the girl, for she belonged with him. While he waited, he was going to search the northern lands, mapping them out and looking for any signs of the missing party that included his parents. Something kept them away if they still lived, and if they didn't then he'd find their bones and maybe whatever killed them.

The Dragon Daughter

Isabella Hunter

HOORI WATCHED THE LEAD SHIP CREST A LARGE WAVE and become air born. They still hadn't sighted Ryujin, but with the sea this tumultuous he had to be close. Dark clouds reduced how far they could see across the ocean's surface, and when he looked out he could only count ten ships even though there were over twenty in the fleet. The ship rocked violently as a wave crashed into its side, spraying sea water into his face. The air was thick with the smells of the ocean.

His boat was occupied by other sailors, some he knew and some who had travelled from far off cities to help take down the dragon. There were also soldiers on the ship, but they were staying below deck for now. They didn't know how to sail, so it was Hoori's job along with the other sailors to get them to their quarry.

For a second he thought he saw the long serpentine body of Ryujin between the waves but as quickly as it had appeared it disappeared under the surface. A long bellow rang out across the sea, breaking through the shouts of sailors and the roaring wind. It was here. The lead ship had located him.

There was a lull as everyone stopped, realising what this meant. Then they set to work. Hoori's ship was the closest to the lead, and another ship had changed course, heading towards them. The men worked the ropes and sails, picking up the wind to get into position.

Under the water's surface he saw it. The sea was an inky black but Ryujin was a brilliant blue, the colour of the sea on a peaceful day. He was not peaceful though. Ruler of the tide, he caused storms and would attack any boat that he didn't like the look of.

Now they were his target. The dragon broke the surface between Hoori's boat and the other fleet ship. His fins flared and a loud roar echoed across the water. Hoori could see the treasure of the sea on Ryujin's forehead like a third eye. "Quickly, he's here! Get the harpoons!" Hoori shouted across the din.

Hoori moved over to the mounted harpoon launchers and aimed. He pulled the trigger and a spear flew through the air, lodging in the dragon's body. Ryujin let out a howl and turned towards the other fleet ship that was still moving into range.

The boat listed as the dragon swam away from them. The harpoons were designed for taking down whales, not something as powerful as this. Hoori slipped down the deck as the boat was pulled towards the sea. The other sailors were also struggling, holding onto the launchers or ropes.

They just needed to hold on a little longer. His fingers burnt as he held on to the rope of the harpoon that was still embedded in the dragon. Once the other ship landed a harpoon the dragon would recoil again. He looked over towards the other boat and saw them firing towards Ryujin. Yet every spear fell harmlessly into the water. Hoori could see the fear as the men frantically reeled the harpoons back in.

Before they could reload, the dragon reared up and began to wrap itself around the other boat. "We need to cut the rope or he'll take us down with them!" Hoori shouted. "Knife! Get me a knife!"

One man who was gripping the mast unhooked his sheathed

dagger and slid it down the ship. Hoori reached for it but the dagger slipped between his fingers. Just before it fell into the water he managed to grab the ties of the sheath. He yanked the blade out and cut through the rope. The ship suddenly righted itself, sloshing water onto the deck and throwing Hoori onto his back.

Leaping up, Hoori worked the ropes of the sails and turned them so the ship moved towards Ryujin. The dragon's long body was coiled around the other boat and slowly tightening. With one last rotation, Ryujin crushed the deck of the boat. Many sailors had already jumped ship, but the rolling waves weren't any safer.

The other boats had caught up and made a semicircle around the sea dragon. Each one began to fire, and harpoons rained down on Ryujin. "We have to load new harpoons!" Hoori called to the other sailors. A young lad opened a chest and pulled out a long spear, lofting it to Hoori.

He loaded it into the launcher and fired it at Ryujin. Two more harpoons flew towards the dragon from the boat. Only one landed in his scales, but all the boats had managed to tether him now. This time when he tried to pull away, the boats stayed still except for the rocking of the ocean.

A second horn bellowed across the sea, signalling them to return to port. Hoori and the men got to work turning the ship and sailing home with their mark. It was slow work against the wind and waves. Ryujin had risen up out of the water, pulling against the harpoons.

The boats continued to pull at the dragon's body, drawing it through the sea. It unhinged its mouth and water began to swirl in front of its gaping jaw, creating an ever growing orb.

"Get down!" Hoori cried, hitting the deck. With a deafening cry it unleashed a torrent of water that obliterated the ships closest to itself. Splinters of wood rained down into the ocean and he could hear the screams of sailors and samurai caught by the blast.

Ryujin had destroyed three boats, but still didn't have sufficient strength to pull against the boats. The dragon collapsed back into the sea, causing a wave to rock the boat violently. The wind changed and the dragon could no longer resist. Its energy had been spent and the ships towed it all the way into the harbour.

Large metal walls separated the city from the tempestuous ocean. Each wave spun a turbine that powered the capitol. Here the sound of the waves was drowned out by the grinding of gears, and the smell of the ocean gave way to that of smoke and iron. They moved into the confines of the port, and soon after Ryujin had passed the gate there was the metallic clang of it trapping them inside.

Footsteps came from below deck and the samurai appeared, holding rifles. Two carried up a large cannon and started locking it into place. One of the men shoved Hoori back. "You've done your job," he said. "Now let us finish it."

Hoori nodded and moved out of the way. The men were heavily armoured, and rattled as they got into position. An older man raised his hand and then lowered it swiftly. "Fire!" he bellowed at the top of his lungs.

The air filled with sharp and sudden retort of gunfire. The smoke and gunpowder nearly choked Hoori. He found himself sweating despite the coolness of the temperature.

Ryujin thrashed in the water as bullets struck his body from every side. There was the boom of cannons and the large metal balls smashed into the dragon. A final one all but removed Ryujin's jaw, and he fell into the water, no longer moving. Blood slowly spread from the dragon's body, turning the water black.

There was silence now. No one moved or spoke. Everyone waited to see if Ryujin was finally dead. Then the general on Hoori's ship raised his hand. "Ryujin, Ruler of the Sea, has been slain. Collect the treasure of the ocean," he ordered.

*

OTOHIME GAZED INTO her mirror, searching across the seas for her father. The ocean had calmed over the past day and her father hadn't returned yet. The water in the dragon palace was warm and moved gently through her fins.

Someone knocked softly on the door to her dowsing room. "Come in," she called. The door creaked open and a young maid entered, her eyes lowered. She didn't have hair like a human. Instead the girl had long diaphanous fins that flowed from her head and down her back. Her whole body was scaled and she had two small horns on her head. Using her long tail the maid swam towards Otohime's scrying board.

"We have had reports come in from the scouts that your father was captured by the humans," she said.

"How was he captured? A group of humans could never manage that," Otohime hissed.

The girl shrank away from her, saying, "A large fleet harpooned him and dragged him inside the walls. We don't know what happened after that."

Otohime dragged her nails across the lacquered table, small bits of wood chipping under her claws. "Has no one been able to get inside the walls to find him?"

"No, my lady. Attempts have been made, but all in vain."

She pushed herself up. Otohime was much taller than the other girl. The anger built up and she could feel her fins spreading out like a lion fish. "So you're telling me you've all failed."

"I'm sorry. We are trying everything we can."

"I will go retrieve him myself, if everyone else is incapable. We can afford to lose neither my father nor the treasure of the ocean."

*

THE DRAGON PALACE was on the seabed far offshore from the city wall. Otohime had packed a satchel of essentials, including a dagger and some fish, before setting off. She had already lost so much time before she'd received news of her father.

As she travelled, the water became darker, filled with dirt that had been disturbed by trawling fishing nets. She saw one pass by her, with thousands of squirming and desperate fish already caught in it. She dodged out the way before her tail could get trapped.

Surveying the metal walls, Otohime couldn't see a way to pass them. There were large spinning turbines under the water which would mangle her body or trap her fins. She surfaced and saw that the wall carried on up way above the sea level. They were completely smooth. She had no chance of climbing them either.

She dived below the water again. There had to be a way for her to enter the city safely. Another ship passed her by, churning more sand up in its wake. They must need a lot of food for the people to have so many fishing boats. Otohime swam back towards the net, then into its mouth, letting herself fall onto the other fish.

Otohime smiled to herself. She would just walk in like any other human. More fish filled the net, and as the water grew darker the net was eventually pulled up onto the deck. Still covered by the fish she transformed into her human form. Her horns shrank back into her head and the scales peeled off her body. She was left naked except for her long black hair.

The net was emptied out onto the deck. She slid out on top of the fish, feeling them slap and flip against her. She lay still. The air was cold and she heard someone walk over to the catch. "Hoori, get over here!" they shouted. "There's a woman in the net!"

Another set of footsteps approached. The two men pushed the fish out of the way until they could both kneel next to her. She felt warm fingers softly touch her neck. "She's cold, but I can feel a faint pulse," the new man said. "Go fetch some blankets from below deck."

The other sailor scurried off. Otohime opened her eyes slowly, making sure to hit him with her most vulnerable and beseeching look. "Where am I?" she asked, pursing her lips slightly.

"You're on my fishing boat," he said. "You came up in the net." The other man came rushing back and offered a blanket, which Hoori wrapped around Otohime. "Can you check the catch today, then take us back into the harbour?" he asked the young sailor.

"No problem, Captain. Leave it to me."

Hoori lifted her up off the deck and carried her into the cabin. He lay her down on one of the small beds. "Why were you in the ocean? You're not a mermaid, are you?"

Otohime knew of these women. Ama, they were called. They were divers who collected shellfish off the seabed. With her naked body, she did look the part. "Yes, I am," she said. "I think my cord got cut and I got washed into your net."

"You're lucky we caught you. You could have died if you'd stayed in the ocean much longer."

The other sailor came into the room holding her satchel. "I found this in with the fish. Is it yours, miss?" he asked.

"Ah! Thank you. Yes, that is mine. I'm glad I didn't lose it." He brought it over and placed it on the small bedside table. He smiled shyly before running back up the stairs.

Otohime pulled the blanket around her tighter. "When I was pulled away by the tide I was sure I would be killed by the dragon," she said with a shiver.

Hoori smiled at her. "You don't need to worry about that any more. Ryujin has been killed," he said triumphantly.

She had suspected as much. She feigned joyous surprise and asked, "But how?"

"A fleet of ships harpooned it and brought it inside the walls to finish it off. The sea will be a much safer place from now on."

"And what of the treasure of the ocean? Did Ryujin have that as well?"

"I think it is being held in the city at the moment. Apparently there is a princess due to succeed Ryujin."

"Is she a dragon as well?"

"Some say she is. Others say–"

The younger sailor's voice called down the stairs: "Just coming to the gate now, Captain. I'll need your help anchoring her."

Hoori nodded and got up. "Will you be okay down here?"

"I think I can walk. If it's okay, I'd like to see the city as we sail in."

He thought about it for a second, before extending his hand to help her up. They walked above deck and he directed her to a small bench. Hoori set to work with the other man, manoeuvring the boat. The gate blocked all sight of the city from the outside, stretching between two great cliffs, all protecting the bay within. On the deck she could hear the whirring of the turbines, but it was drowned out by a loud groaning as the gates opened outwards to receive them.

The first thing she saw was the great hall upon the highest rise of the city. That was where the President lived, and most likely where the treasure was being kept. The rest of the city seemed to climb up the cliffs. It was all made of either stone or metal, in various shades of grey and orange. Smoke dirtied the air and under it she could smell decay.

"I will take you to my house and we can get you some clothes, okay? Then we can look at trying to get you home again," he called back to her.

She nodded and watched as he secured the boat to one of the bollards. He placed the gangway down and beckoned for her to cross first. The ship rocked gently and it made the wooden plank move up and down. She went forwards and shakily walked down onto the dock.

Hoori and the other sailor followed after her, not batting an eyelid at the unstable walkway. They embraced each other and agreed when they would meet the next day.

A drizzle started to patter down onto the cobbled streets as they made their way up the alleys. It wasn't long before they were being pelted with rain and the roads had small streams of dirty water washing down towards the bay. The small blanket was soaked through and clung unpleasantly to Otohime's skin.

The streets darkened and lamps began to flicker to life, except with no flames. "What are they?" Otohime asked.

"They're just street lamps," he said. "We power them with electricity generated from the sea."

She stared into the flat light, waiting for it to flicker like a normal flame would, but it stayed steady. "You can create light with this electricity, but can it do anything else?" she asked.

They turned again and Hoori opened the door of a small house. "It's been used to speed up our manufacturing process," he said. "Soon this city will be the largest exporter of metal in the entire country."

Otohime walked into the dwelling. It was made of metal, but on the inside it had light wood panelling and a coral coloured futon in the centre of the room. He had art hung on the walls depicting forests and mountains of brilliant greens and blues.

Hoori struck a match and lit an incense stick, letting the trails of smoke rise to the ceiling. Otohime took a deep breath and let the strong smell of chrysanthemums fill her lungs. The smog of the city hadn't entirely managed to permeate Hoori's house.

She took a seat on the soft futon while Hoori rummaged through the wardrobe. He pulled out a komon with a thin obi and handed it to her. "This was my mother's," he said softly. "I didn't want to get rid of it. But I thought you could wear it to cover yourself."

She nodded and Hoori walked out the door. Otohime unwrapped the blanket and placed it on the wooden floor, before putting the komon over her shoulders. The obi was basic but it worked well enough to close the komon. It felt good to be out of the wet fabric and in fresh clothing. "I'm dressed now," she called. "You can come back in."

Hoori opened the door again and started brewing tea. He placed the kettle on a small apparatus that began to glow. The water quickly boiled, he poured it into the tea pot and he set out two cups on the table.

"What is that thing?" Otohime asked.

"It's an electric teppan," he said. "I can use it to cook or just heat up water." He flicked the lever and the small griddle started to cool.

Otohime poured a cup of tea for herself and took a sip. "My father is quite an important man in my village," she told Hoori.

"If you could get me into the presidential district I should be able to find someone who will take me home."

Hoori cradled his cup in his hands. "I'll see what I can do. We will set off after we finish our tea."

*

THEY HAD WALKED through the spiralling streets up towards the presidential district. Night had fallen, but she couldn't see a single star in the sky. Instead, florescent lights shone down garishly on the wet floor and the metallic buildings.

Up here the buildings were polished like the steel of a blade. The air smelt fresher, but when she looked down towards the harbour Otohime could see the smog swirling through the streets. They came to a set of stairs that marked the border between the labourers and the rulers.

Two guards dressed in the traditional dou stood at the gate. They had their naginata crossed over each other. As Hoori and Otohime approached, the samurai glared down at them. "What do you want?" the shorter one demanded.

"My guest here has a friend she must meet in this district," Hoori told him.

The taller one gave a short laugh. "And does she have a pass?" he asked.

Otohime saw Hoori's jaw tighten and his lips thin. He pulled a small wooden token from inside his clothes and held it at their eye level. "I have a pass. I earned this during the battle against Ryujin. Do not give her any more trouble."

The guards scowled and murmured to each other. Reluctantly they pulled back their naginata. As soon as Hoori and Otohime were past, there was the scrape of the two blades crossing again behind them.

The walls of the buildings were all painted in rich colours. It was a rainbow up here compared to the lower levels. The smell of cooked meat hung in the air as dinner was being prepared in the nearby houses. There was a warmth here, away from the bay, from the fire pits that marked each street corner.

"Where would we find your friend?" Hoori asked.

"I won't need you from now on," Otohime said. "I can find him on my own. Please, head back to your home."

The man lingered behind her. "Be careful," he said. "It is still a dangerous city." He turned and left her alone in the street.

The President's court shone like a beacon above the other buildings. She could feel the pull of the ocean, but it was leading her towards the main complex. That was where the treasure must be. It was close.

Another set of stone stairs lead up to polished red walls. Two guards stood watch with rifles resting against their shoulders. They eyed her suspiciously as she loitered under a glowing street light. One of them shifted his gun slightly, placing a finger upon the trigger.

It took less than a heartbeat for her body to change. From her head, two horns sprouted, and scales suddenly covered her skin. The kimono was shredded as she grew in size and her tail lashed free.

The two guards raised their guns to fire. She was already moving, with jaws wide. In one swift movement, she had them. Metal screeched, bones crunched and the men cried out. The copper of blood filled her mouth, they struggled briefly and then she let their limp bodies drop.

Otohime roared defiantly as she made her way into the complex. An alarm began to clang from a tower on the far side, where another guard was beating a gong. Gun shots echoed in the courtyard and a volley of fire ripped into her side. She hissed, flinching in pain. She slithered through a set of double doors that led into the main household, knocking more guards aside as her tail swung out.

She wound her way down the corridor to the left and bashed through a paper partition wall. It led into a large audience room which looked out onto an ornamental garden. She crashed over a koi pond as footsteps clattered on the wooden floor behind her.

Otohime could feel it pulling her forwards. She took hold of the roof tiles and pulled herself up. From here she could see the entire complex – straight ahead was a large temple. She scrambled onto the slates and towards the shrine.

An altar stood in the centre of the temple. Her father's body was laid around it, and upon the stone top sat the sparkling gem. The treasure of the sea. She moved down at once to Ryujin and touched her nose to his. She expected his breath to brush her face, but it didn't come.

She raised her head and looked into the precious stone as it swirled an entire ocean inside it. Otohime reached out with her claws and closed them around the orb. She felt its power ripple through her.

"So this is the dragon's daughter? I must say I am disappointed." A young man had walked out into the courtyard. He was wearing full formal attire, including a dark haori depicting a raging ocean. Two men stood to either side of him, with large shoulder-mounted cannons loaded with ballista.

"I'm not here to impress you, murderer," she hissed. "I am here to take back what is rightfully mine."

"The power to control the ocean cannot be only for wild beasts to possess," he sneered. "You dragons already have water magic. You have no real need of this bauble."

"The sea belongs to the dragons," she roared. "It belongs to me!" She reared up with the gem and began to summon a blast of water.

The President raised his hand. "Your time is over, snake. Humans rule the world now." He clicked his fingers.

Bullets hit her, piercing deeply. Hot blood trickled down her scales as her bellow of pain echoed over the city. A group of samurai rushed towards her with naginata raised. They drove them at her underbelly. Some skittered off but a few found ways between her scales.

The two guards of the President lit their cannons and the ballista were launched at her. One flew over her head. The other landed in her shoulder. She dropped the orb to the ground and it rolled and bounced down the shrine's stairs. She tried to reach after it, but recoiled as a second barrage of shots peppered her body.

Otohime writhed, knocking guards away with her fore-limbs. Bolts plunged deep into her sides. She reared up and began to draw a water pulse. Droplets formed in the air and flowed towards her, creating a ball of swirling liquid. Warriors ran for cover.

She let the pressure build until it almost overpowered her. Then she released it, to hurl men against the walls. As some of the guards struggled back up, she hauled her protesting body back onto the roof. She had precious little strength left with which to fight them. And there was still the gate blocking her path back to her sea palace. She had to find a way out before they could finish her.

The guards' cries fell away behind her, but occasionally she heard the scream or whimper of city folk that saw her. She still had naginata stuck under her scales, and each movement drove them deeper into her flesh. She got to the dark murky water and stopped to pull them out. As she removed them, blood ran down her stomach, staining her pearly scales. Otohime slid into the water and dove deep under its surface, where she wouldn't be visible. She moved close to the gate but saw there was no way to squeeze through the turbines spinning with the tidal pull.

Breaking the water's surface, she looked up the wall. It was massive, far higher than her body was long. She wouldn't be able to get over it easily, especially in her injured condition. The glow of lights also suggested that guards were stationed on the top. The second she started climbing, they would hear her and begin shooting.

She had to find another way out of the harbour. All around her were bobbing, anchored boats. Her eyes settled on Hoori's ship. She began to swim towards it, but saw men on the pier, shining lights down at the water.

"She's a dragon!" the President shouted. "How could you lose her? Keep searching until you find her!"

She ducked down and swam below the surface towards Hoori's boat. She stayed out of sight while they searched the vessels. Only the larger ones that she could fit into while as a dragon were searched. Once they were satisfied she wasn't on the land they began to send a few men out on small ships to search the deeper water.

The men worked long into the night, but they slowed down as the hours crept by. The lights from the boats became less frequent, and the men on land stopped searching. She broke the surface again and saw the slumped, sleeping heads of the guards rising and falling in time with the tide.

Otohime shifted back into her human form and swam over to a rope hanging from Hoori's boat. It was coarse and burned against her hands as she pulled herself up the side of the ship. She tried to be quiet, but her wounds stung from the salty water and each pull made more blood run down her naked body.

She hit the deck with a wet slap and left a red stain on the wood when she rose to her knees. Her body was starting to go numb, and her movements were slow and heavy, like she was wading through muck. She dragged herself into the bedroom and up onto the bed as the darkness encroached on her vision.

*

VOICES BROKE THROUGH the fog of sleep and Otohime heard footsteps on the deck. She pulled herself off the bed and saw the blood that had seeped into the quilt. She flipped the covers over but it had soaked through to the other side.

The voices grew louder. The other sailor from the day before said, "It looks like the fish made a real mess on the deck."

Otohime looked around the room for somewhere to hide. The room was sparsely furnished, with just the bed and a desk. She lay flat on the wooden boards and slid under the bed. She disturbed dust as she wriggled further in. Each breath tickled her nose.

"It does seem like that," Hoori said. He had walked all the

way up to the door to the room and stopped. "How about you head home for today while I get this cleaned up?"

"It won't take long if we both—"

"It's fine. I would rather not waste your time. If I get it done early I will come get you, okay?"

"All right then. I'll see you later, okay?" the younger sailor said before walking off the deck.

Hoori must have waited to watch him leave, because he didn't move for a long time. Then the door handle turned quietly and he crept into the room. "Who's in here?" he called out to the dark room.

He walked in slowly and a light cast shadows across the room. Otohime could see his shoes as he came towards the bed. He shifted the quilt above her and moved away from the bed.

Otohime came silently out from under the bed. He had walked over to the desk, where her satchel still lay with her knife in it. As he went to place the lantern down on the desk, she reached past him and snatched the knife from the bag.

His eyes widened as she pressed the blade up to his throat. "Take me to the ocean," she growled.

"You're his daughter," he said. "You're the one they are looking for."

"They're looking for a dragon, not me. Now get this boat moving so they open up the gates and I can get home."

Hoori reached up and grabbed her arm, pushing the blade away. "And what will you do then?" he asked. "You didn't get what you came for."

Otohime tried to push back against him, but she was too weak and wounded. "I'll bring an army and tear the walls down and take my father's body and the treasure back."

His grip tightened until the knife dropped from her hand. "Then they will assemble a fleet to hunt you down, as they did your father."

The ship began to rock violently, pushed by waves. "I wouldn't let them!" she screamed. "I control the sea. I will take everything from them, and batter all those who dare venture upon the water." The ship felt like it was moments from capsizing.

"Then take everything. Starve them until they realise they need you, but starting a war that will see countless numbers die on both sides cannot be the answer." He let go of her hand and took a step back. "Now, what are you going to do?"

She turned away from him and picked up the knife again. She ran her finger over the edge slowly. "All right. There is wisdom in what you say. Take me to the ocean and I will show them who the true ruler of the sea is."

Hoori smiled at her. He ran up onto the deck to prepare them for cast off.

*

HOORI HAD TOLD her to stay below deck until he signalled for her to come up. The sea was calm like just before a storm rolls in. Otohime tried to gather her thoughts. The ship's progress slowed.

The door opened and Hoori beckoned her up. "Are you ready?" he asked as she ascended the stairs towards him. The ship had stopped just outside the gates, stopping them from closing again. From here Otohime could see a number of soldiers were still searching along the docks and on the moored boats.

An alarm sounded above them and two men indicated that they needed to move the boat out of the way so that the gates could be resealed.

"I am as ready as I will ever be." She took a deep breath and let her body shift. She coiled herself around Hoori, as there wasn't enough room on the deck for her. Her tail fell into the sea and she held onto the mast with her claws.

The alarm changed, proclaiming the threat to the city. Otohime roared and sent waves crashing into the dock. Every person in the harbour turned in her direction. Many backed towards the safety of the city. Some lifted their guns and started firing, but their bullets fell short.

With them all watching, she began to pull the water away from the city. It came slowly at first, but then in a faster and faster rush. The boats dropped down until they sat on wet sand. She kept pulling it back, raising Hoori's boat on the giant swell.

Now empty, the turbines slowly ground to a stop with a long groan. The electrical buzz of the generators died away. The sea below her was ready to burst, to wash the whole city away, but she held it back.

"Return my father and the ocean's treasure to me and I will do you no harm," she said to the city. "However, if it is not returned to the sea I will take away the very foundation of your homes." She found the cringing President and locked gazes with him. Bracing herself, she carefully let the water return. It rushed into the harbour and splashed up the wall of the pier, spraying sea foam over the city.

The boats were rocked so much they nearly swamped, but the waves gradually reduced in size. She let herself change back into the form of a woman, and was left kneeling on the wet, slippery deck. Hoori lifted her to her feet, "You did it!"

"I showed them my power," she said. "And no one had to die this time. Will you bring my father and the treasure to me?"

"Of course, but where will I find you?"

"At the dragon palace," she replied. She dove off the ship's edge and disappeared under the water's surface.

Forefront

Garry Coulthard

One

RAFE JACKSON STUDIED THE WOMAN OPPOSITE HIM closely. Even handcuffed and wearing police issue paper clothing, she was attractive enough. Blonde hair, blue eyes, petite, mid-twenties: the type he would have gone for in the past, but she gave out an aura of trouble. If there was one thing Rafe knew when it came to a woman . . . it was that if she looked like trouble, or was in trouble, then she was way more trouble than she was worth. Considering the beating she had just administered, she was remarkably unblemished; experience had taught him you don't inflict that much damage on someone without getting caught with a few shots yourself. But even her knuckles were pristine. If he had seen her without knowing why she had been arrested, he'd have honestly said a paper bag would have won in a tussle between the two.

Shuffling in his chair, half bored and half guilty that he'd retreated into his own thoughts, he wondered why he always caught the loonies when it was his turn to act as duty solicitor. She hadn't uttered a single word to him or the police since she had been arrested. He felt he had to try one more time.

'There's much more to this than you are saying, isn't there? Was he your boyfriend, ex-boyfriend, dealer?'

He knew the deal with these scenarios. They eventually came around to drugs, one way or the other. He remembered Paul Allsop, another delightful client of his who had also kept his own counsel. High as a kite on the newest magic powder, he had refused to say a word and just sat there with a beatific grin on his face. That was until the guard had come in to let him out of the interview room and he had showered the guard, and by default Rafe, with a vulgar raspberry of the contents of his mouth, which was blood and the small pieces of his tongue he had been quietly gnawing away on. Although he didn't think that was this woman's style, one could never be too sure. Maybe she was an innocent victim or maybe the man had assaulted her and had just happened to have the misfortune to try beating up on a kick boxing assassin, one with looks to kill and the moves to back it up. The truth was stranger than any fiction, a saying that had often been bandied about by his law professors; Rafe had never really believed it until he had started practising and found it proven right time and again.

'Miss Nobody, I want to help you, but I can't if you don't give me anything to work with. Give me something.'

The woman raised her gaze from the floor, looked at him and then looked away.

'They'll find out who you are eventually, you know. They've already taken blood and DNA. You'll be in the system somewhere.'

Silence regained the room. He decided he was just about done here. With a client with nothing to say, there was nothing to be done. At least he'd get his payment for attending from the CPS. He put his papers back into his briefcase, clicked it shut and stood, putting the chair under the table.

'I'll see you in court in the morning, then, Miss Nobody.' With that he turned on his heel and took the two steps towards the door, raising his hand to knock on the reinforced square of glass in the door.

'Don't knock,' came the voice from behind him. It was a surprise, much deeper and raw sounding than he'd expected. 'I have a question.'

Rafe stood perfectly still, took an extra second, and then turned to face his client. 'What question?'

The prisoner gently kicked back out the vacant chair and gestured for Rafe to sit. He took a step forward towards the table and stood his ground. It was important he kept control of the situation.

'What question?'

'Are you sure you won't sit?'

'Perfectly sure, thank you. I'll answer your questions and then maybe you could answer a few of mine so we can be ready for court in the morning?'

'Sure, why not? Firstly, the man I attacked. Do you know where he is?'

It wasn't the question Rafe had been expecting. Usually people asked 'What's the prognosis? Am I going down? How much is this going to cost me?' or in cases of domestic abuse, and then only sometimes, they asked how the abused was. Not where they were.

'He's stable in hospital. What's your name?

'You called me . . . Miss Nobody? I quite like that. Which hospital?'

'Well, Miss Nobody, I'm Rafe Jackson. I'll be providing your legal representation, unless you have your own solicitor?' She shook her head. 'Since you beat your boyfriend up pretty good, I'm not at liberty to disclose which hospital he's been taken to.'

'But you do know though?'

'Yes, I do. You know, looking at you, I wouldn't have thought you had it in you quite frankly. That said, I think that's something we can use in court. Maybe you were under extreme duress?'

She looked at him and for the first time her face seemed animated. Finally, he thought, progress.

'So, Mr Jackson, or do you prefer Rafe? My other question for you is whether you have ever seen a girl smile like this before?'

Rafe looked on, confused as much by the question as he was by the fact her handcuffs, freed from her wrists somehow, had just clinked down on the table. Miss Nobody's mouth smiled, becoming much larger than a normal mouth. And the teeth, oh God, the teeth! Horrified, he felt the urine trickle down his leg. Paralysed, he watched as the woman who looked like she didn't have an ounce of badness in her melted into a living nightmare and advanced on him. He couldn't move or scream as Miss Nobody smashed her petite fist into the side of his head with the force of a jackhammer. His final thought was the answer to the question.

No, nobody should ever see a girl smile like that.

*

Two

St Paul's Hospital
THE BEEPING OF the monitoring station woke Lucas Gabe. For the sweetest of moments, he lay there, blissful in his ignorance, and then the pain crashed in. Every part of him hurt. He tried to assess what had happened to him and where he was. He tried to open his eyes, but only one would open. Brilliant white stung his retina. He closed his eye and opened it again, this time more slowly. The darkness gave way to light and then the white resolved itself into blurred objects. He realised it was a hospital room, and that was enough. He closed his eye and tried not to panic. Images flashed behind his eyes. At work collecting pizza. In his car driving. Stopping at a house. Getting out to deliver. A woman. Teeth and, as the punches crashed him to the edge of consciousness, a name. Asmodeus.

He passed out.

*

WHEN HE WOKE up again, it was dark. He didn't know how long had passed, but he felt better than he had before. Less hurty anyway. He shuffled in his bed and tried to sit. The plume of pain that erupted from his side made him change his mind. Maybe not that much better after all.

A nurse looked in on him and asked if he was okay, to which he nodded and gave his best, 'No, I'm not, but you don't want to hear it' grin. She offered to make him a hot drink, which he declined, and then informed him a consultant would be in to see him shortly and asked if he could manage anything to eat. The idea of food struck him as both repulsive and essential. He said he thought maybe he'd like something later and that he'd like to try and sleep for a bit longer. Before she left, he asked her what had happened to him, to which she replied she wasn't sure, just that he had been in a fight with a woman and she had come out on top. She told him the police would like to speak to him shortly, probably after the consultant said it was okay for them to do so. The nurse closed his door and left him to rest.

Beaten up by a woman? Lucas didn't quite know how to take that fact. The woman who had developed the horrific mouth of teeth was a regular customer of his who tipped generously. Tuesday night special: ham and pineapple 12-inch with wedges and a bottle of Coke. He'd been to her house many times and never had she been anything but really nice to him. Until last night. Had it been last night? How long had he been in and out of consciousness for? He considered ringing for the nurse, but decided against it, noticing the TV remote on the pull-across table. He pulled the table over and turned on the news. The clock on BBC News told him it was 22:45, just over 24 hours since he had been brought in.

'Survived, then, I see. Disappointing.'

Lucas looked around. The voice seemed to have come from behind him, which was impossible, because there were only pillows, the bed frame and then the wall.

'Stop looking. I'm in your head, idiot.'

Great, Lucas thought. I've gone mad. He flipped the channel on the TV. BBC2 was showing a re-run of The Fugitive with Harrison Ford. He'd seen it before, but it was easy viewing.

'Are you going to say hello, or just carry on pretending I'm not here?'

Scanning the room, Lucas looked for somewhere someone could be hidden and talking to him. There was nowhere obvious. He didn't know whether to be pleased or worried that he was in a private room. Usually people were just stuck on same-sex wards with old men who belched, farted and snored in their sleep, and told you how soon they were going to die. Those in private rooms were either a) rich or b) very poorly indeed or c) lucky. Lucas hoped it was the latter. Unless he was in a private room because they thought he was mad and he had told them he was hearing voices in a period of semi-consciousness.

'Are you real?' he asked just loudly enough to be heard over The Fugitive.

'Are you?'

Not exactly sure on how to answer that question Lucas turned his attention back to the film. Tommy Lee Jones had Harrison Ford trapped in the drainage outlet of a dam.

'He jumps. I've seen this before. I watched it with another host. It's Nichols who's the bad guy.'

Lucas ignored the voice. It wasn't real and would go eventually. He didn't fancy admitting to anyone that he was hearing a voice in his head, unless he had already done so, in which case he'd just put it down to the drugs they'd given him. He put BBC News back on: Fiona Bruce was just handing over to the regional desk. He watched as the presenter delivered segments on the rising cost of HS2 and how a mosque had been defiled with a bacon sandwich. The next story was about how a man had been attacked whilst delivering food last night and police were appealing for witnesses. Lucas realised they were talking about him. He watched mesmerised as they flashed his photo on the screen and said he had been beaten severely and was in hospital in intensive care and the woman who had beaten him was in police custody. The presenter then moved on to a story about a cat that barked.

'It would have been better if you'd died, you know.'

The statement left Lucas reeling. Did he really think that little of himself? Perhaps it was time for him to ring the bell and speak to the nurse, to see about getting something to knock him out. Hopefully, when he woke up his head would have reset itself to his usually much sunnier disposition.

'I mean, she or another will come and finish the job. It's just a shame you have to go through the experience twice.'

Lucas picked up the hospital remote and pressed the emergency button.

'Good idea. Get some pills to help you sleep. You probably won't have to wake up again that way.'

He pressed the button again. The nurse from earlier burst in. 'Are you okay?'

Lucas took a second to answer, weighing up the pros and cons before he waved the remote gingerly. 'God, really sorry, wrong button. Is there any chance of that hot drink?'

The nurse sighed loudly, and went on to admonish him for using the emergency button instead of the assistance button, making him feel like he was back at school and being told how to use a compass for the first time. Once she had finished reprimanding him she said she'd bring him a cup of tea shortly and left.

'Coward.'

'Piss off!' Lucas snapped at himself and pulled his pillow around his head. 'You're not real.'

'I am real, you soft-brained shit, very real. And you should be honoured to have me with you. If you'd scratched that mental itch you've been feeling for weeks instead of watching movies and delivering pizza you'd have found me.'

'I'm not pretending a voice in my head is real because it says so.'

'Fine. Soon you'll be dead. But, as you have a few minutes, why not let me in and I'll show you what you could have been part of?'

Lucas laid back on the bed and closed his eyes. He wasn't sure of the merits of letting the voice in his head tell him a story, or if it was even a good idea.

'You are feeling sleepy, sleeeepy.'

'Seriously?'

He heard a gentle chortle in the back of his mind.

'Just relax and let me in.'

As he allowed the voice in his head to enter his consciousness he started remembering something he had never seen.

*

Three

He was standing alone on the summit of a table top mountain. Beside him was an ornate plinth made of what looked like gold and sitting on it was a great white jewel. The floor was covered in scorch marks, some still smouldering. He walked to the closest edge, and looked down. At the foot of the mountain a circle of luminosity surrounded the foot of the mountain as far as he could see. Inside the light he could just about make out shapes, but what they were, he had no idea.

A low-pitched thrum brought him back to the jewel, which was now illuminated. It glowed brighter and brighter, the light becoming harder and harder to look at, and just as Lucas felt he had to cover his eyes it then purged itself of its brilliance, leaving a pool of light on the rocky ground. He watched as the pool shimmered and started to grow, sliding across the scorched ground. From within the pool a huge ethereal talon reached through the surface, then a scaly head pushed out of the pool, followed by another foot. The feet cut into the earth and the beast dragged the rest of itself through the shimmering portal. Lucas watched in awe as it shook itself, not unlike a dog, and then he gasped as the beast unfurled wings from its back and started to gently beat them, like it was testing itself or warming up. The wings, while not unbecoming, seemed too small to be able support the weight of the beast. No, it wasn't just a beast anymore. He knew what it was.

A dragon.

As if cued to the revelation, the dragon opened its maw and exhaled a brilliant white fire, incinerating the portal from which it had come, leaving a fresh scorch in the earth. Turning its not inconsiderable form, it gave what Lucas interpreted as a bow to the stone, before hurling itself off from the edge of the mountain to join with the luminescence below.

As he watched the dragon fly down the mountain and join with what he assumed were other dragons, he saw a black shape moving at speed towards the glowing base of the mountain. As the shape came closer he saw that behind it many more dark shapes were in pursuit, so many that they looked like a plague of dark locusts enveloping the land. The shape crashed into the dragon shield surrounding the mountain at full speed and bounced backwards with great force. It rose again to its feet and tried again, only to be repelled by the luminous defenders. Behind the shape the darkness was closing rapidly: in a matter of seconds whatever was fleeing from it would be absorbed by it. The stone behind Lucas hummed gently and below a path opened in the circle of dragons, allowing the shape to pass through the glowing perimeter, closing behind it as it passed through. The dark horde arrived at the base of the mountain but, unlike the lone shape, stood off. It seemed to him that they were unsure of what to do now the chase was over.

Lucas stepped away from the edge, backing up as he saw the shape make its way up the mountain, towards the stone and him. He looked about for something to try and defend himself with: there was nothing. Then it was there in front of him, heading for the jewel. It was huge, a far larger beast than the dragon the jewel had summoned, vaguely humanoid, a monstrous living silhouette.

It stood in front of the plinth, removed the jewel and held it aloft it its claw, roaring to the heavens. The noise rattled Lucas's skull. It was like being inside a jet engine plummeting towards the earth but never hitting the ground. Lucas pressed his hands to his ears to try and lessen the sound but then it stopped. The silhouette placed the jewel back on the plinth and knelt before it. When nothing happened, the silhouette crashed its claws against the floor, and then threw itself down in abject supplication to the jewel. And just lay there.

Lucas noted the complete lack of sound. Everywhere and everything was still. He turned and looked back over the mountain's edge. The light had stopped swirling and the dark horde was still, the atmosphere pregnant with expectation. Suddenly the jewel burst into life, thrumming at a rate much greater than when it had summoned the dragon forth. As it vibrated, it glowed and the silhouette before it silently squirmed in what looked like pain. The silence was broken as the creature howled and the jewel once again dispensed its light, this time on the form prone before it. The creature writhed and, as the light continued to spew upon it, the howl turned to a cry, the cry to a whimper. Below him he could hear the rage of the darkness; whatever was happening here was not going down well with the other dark creatures below.

Lucas watched transfixed. The light burned, becoming ever brighter until there was only its brilliance. His eyes burned as he watched, but he couldn't turn away, and couldn't see what was happening before him. Then there was an almighty sound and the light slowed. As the jewel dulled, Lucas saw a huge crack had appeared within it. He then looked where the silhouette had been. Instead there was another dragon, much bigger than the previous one and much more corporeal, with green and black hide, and red flashes on its wings already unfurled and majestic. It bowed, low and humble, to the stone. As Lucas watched on, puddles of water appeared on the floor. It was crying.

*

Four

LUCAS OPENED HIS eyes and sat up. They still hurt from the brilliance of the jewel's light.

'Holy shit. What the hell did I just see?'

'The eternal battle.'

'You were the dark form, the monster?'

'Demon, actually, one of the Demon Kings. What you saw was my repentance. I turned my back on the Dark One and begged the World Stone for forgiveness. It responded by sending me to fight the battle on this world, a battle which I've been fighting for hundreds of years. I have inhabited the forms of some of the greatest warriors who ever lived, yet now I've ended up with you. Something must have gone wrong. The sooner you die, the sooner I can take a more fitting form to take the fight back to them.'

Lucas processed what the voice had shown and told him. It was all too crazy, and he'd have liked to put it down to the strong painkillers he'd been given but he knew it wasn't the medication. So, either he'd had a complete psychic break from reality or he really did have a dragon living in his head.

'I'm not best keen on dying you know.'

'No one is, but you've no choice in the matter. Even if you were worthy of me, and you're not, there wouldn't be sufficient time for us to join together. It's a process that takes time and a certain amount of willingness to accept the realities of what us joining together entails. You don't have the time and I don't have the inclination to do any of that with you before you meet your maker.'

The door opened and the nurse came in with a cup of tea. Behind her were two men. They quickly introduced themselves as Detectives Drummond and Harris from Bathsford CID and asked if Lucas would be okay to answer some questions. The nurse put his cup of tea down and left the room. The policemen walked over to his bed and stood uncomfortably close, leaning over him to ask questions about the night of the attack and what may have caused it. He answered as honestly as he could but he didn't have real answers for them. All the time the voice in the back of his head was calling the policemen names and telling them to let the boy die in peace, which didn't help Lucas's thought process at all. The officers were convinced he was lying and that he had invented his amnesia as a way of not implicating himself in what had really happened. All Lucas could do was protest his innocence, which didn't seem to be going down too well.

There was a knock at the door and Rafe Jackson entered. He quickly announced himself to the two policemen as Lucas's legal representative and said that they should leave and that any future appointments with his client should be made through his office. With that he ushered them both out of the room, closed the door behind them and turned to Lucas and gave a theatrical bow. 'How was that for a performance?'

'*You're out of time, kid. Better make your peace with whatever deity you worship.*'

Lucas sat bolt upright in his bed.

Rafe stood at the door, blocking his exit. 'Nowhere to go. Let's just give the nice policemen time to get far enough away before we get down to it, eh?'

His options limited, Lucas decided the only thing he could do was to try and attract the policemen back to the room. The Rafe-demon saw Lucas take a deep breath and moved with astonishing speed to Lucas's bedside, grabbed him firmly by the jaw, reached inside his mouth and took a firm hold of his tongue.

'Any more ideas like that and I'll rip it out, okay?'

Lucas carefully nodded his understanding and Rafe let go of his tongue.

'Do you think it's been long enough? I do.'

Rafe punched Lucas squarely in the face, the blow laying him back down again and causing his nose to erupt with blood. The Rafe-demon laughed. 'I want to speak to the traitor.'

He punched Lucas again, this time in the midriff, causing him to double up in the bed. Rafe reached over and flipped him out of the bed onto the floor and gave him a kick in the face for good measure.

'Talk to me, Asmodeus. Show yourself!'

Lucas dragged himself onto all fours, coughed, spat blood and collapsed onto his elbows.

'What's an Asmodeus? I don't know what it is,' he wheezed.

'Not a what. A who. Me.'

The Rafe-demon kicked Lucas hard in the ribs, flipping him over onto his back. The demon leapt on him, straddling him.

'Traitor, you're running out of bodies.'

For the first time since he'd heard the voice in his head, he felt what the being connected to the voice was feeling. Uncertainty. Fear. Lucas felt himself sympathising with those feelings.

'In fact, you can tell him he's out of bodies, because yours is about to die.'

With that, the demon opened its mouth impossibly wide, then the top of its head flipped back like a Pez dispenser and the rest of the Rafe skin-suit sloughed away, pooling at the creature's hips. Lucas watched helplessly as the grotesque de-gloving took place. The creature before him looked like it had climbed through a maze of razor wire face first. He couldn't tell which parts were meant to be mouths and which were just gaping wounds. Then the real mouth opened and Lucas knew exactly which part was for biting. Lucas flailed with his fists at the demon. Every time he made contact it sounded like he was hitting a side of meat. He squirmed beneath it, trying to free himself from its weight, but it remained steady. Lucas stopped hitting and squirming – he was exhausted. He closed his eyes. He knew it was over and, just as the voice in his head had promised, he was about to die.

'Asmodeus the Coward. Asmodeus the Traitor. Killed by a lesser. Show your true form and I'll take it easy on the human.' The demon took hold of Lucas's throat and started to squeeze.

'Do something!' Lucas wheezed.

'Lucas, I can't. If he kills me when I'm exposed, I'm dead and they win. I'm sorry.'

The beast squeezed harder.

'Goo umpfing.'

He felt the sadness of Asmodeus in his mind. This being, this passenger he had acquired somewhere along the way, who had the personality of an internet troll, was feeling genuine sadness at what was happening. Lucas's eyes bulged as the demon tightened its grip around his neck.

'I can't.'

As darkness drew about him Lucas uttered one last scream for help, not through his mouth, but through his mind.

'DO SOMETHING!'

Asmodeus not only heard Lucas, but he also felt him, felt the fire of desperation within the young man reach up and engulf his presence. It was fierce and jolting. They shared minds. There had never been a connection so strong in all Asmodeus's time of taking hosts. He had sorely misjudged him.

'All right, don't just lie there! Fuck this guy up already.'

Lucas felt an instant change in himself. It was if someone had plugged him in and ramped the voltage up. They had melded, two separate individuals now operating as one. His hands were no longer just his hands – they were green and black three-clawed talons. He rammed his right claw into the demon's face, extending the front two talons straight through the demon's eyes, pushing it back off him. He withdrew the talons from the eye sockets and delivered two heavy punches to the side of the demon's head, knocking it flat on the floor.

Lucas pulled himself to his feet and delivered a swift kick to the head, snapping it back violently. He felt stronger than he'd ever thought possible, quicker and more agile too. He looked down and was amazed as his enemy rose to its feet again. Lucas threw himself upon it once more. His onslaught was too much for the demon and it collapsed to its knees. Looking blindly up at Lucas with its oozing sockets, it sneered, 'You can't kill us all, boy.'

He felt Asmodeus's will pushing him on urgently. He raised a talon to deliver the final blow. But hesitated. Despite the urgings of Asmodeus, he was still in control of his body. He lowered his hand and stepped back.

'*You need to kill it now. Quickly!*'

When he had been fighting for his life Lucas would have had no hesitation in doing whatever was necessary to save himself, but with a beaten and maimed monster in front of him, the killing urge just wasn't in him. The demon slowly came to its feet.

'Your vessel is weak, Asmodeus. You won't last long with this one. Oh, and here's my new ride.'

The handle to Lucas's room wobbled and the door opened. The nurse entered the room and froze. The demon wasted no time leaping upon the woman, taking her to the floor and forcing its limbs down her throat. Within seconds it was gone, as if she had consumed it. Lucas was unable to comprehend fully what had just happened in front of his very eyes. He heard Asmodeus roaring in his head but couldn't understand what was being said to him. The nurse stood and adjusted her clothes, pulling them about her form.

'Does my ass look big in this body?'

The demon laughed at its own joke and then stopped and started towards him.

'Now, where were we?'

Asmodeus came to the forefront, pushing Lucas's will aside. Hands as talons once more, he stepped to meet the demon's attack. He avoided a swinging punch and raked talons across her ribs. The demon did not slow, spinning to deliver a savage blow to Lucas's face. Asmodeus kicked the demon hard to the middle, pushing it back and putting distance between them. The possessed nurse regained her balance and launched herself through the air. Asmodeus side-stepped and, as the demon went past, pounced onto its back, delivering a one-two-three to the spinal cord.

'*You need to do this!*'

Lucas was back in full control of himself now. He took hold

of the nurse-demon's hair, pulling its head backwards to expose its neck. 'See you soon, traitor!' it uttered, before Lucas tore out its throat with a talon.

As he let the body drop to the floor, Asmodeus quickly warned, *'You might want to step . . .'*

The demon exploded, covering every surface of the room in gore, Lucas included.

'Back.'

'A bit more notice next time? Also, claws?'

'Pretty cool, eh?'

Lucas thought it was. He looked down at his hands. They were his again. No wicked talons extending through them. Just bloody hands. He tried to wipe them on his gown. As the adrenaline left his system, his injuries and the huge effort he had put into staying alive caught up with him. He doubled up and vomited.

'Unpleasant.'

Lucas perched on the edge of the bed and dug around, trying to find an area of the bedsheets that wasn't covered in gore to wipe his mouth.

'We joined. I thought you said it was impossible.'

'Yeah, well it seems we did it.'

'So what now? We hunt monsters and have adventures?'

'Demons. We kill demons and next time you don't be so lame about killing the damn thing when you can. Now get your shit together. We need to go. There will be more coming.'

'What about this mess? How can anyone possibly explain this?'

'You'll see.'

As Asmodeus spoke, the blood in the room started to fade out of existence. The pile of skin the demon had sloughed onto the floor, the skin that had once belonged to Rafe Jackson, turned to ash. The parts of the nurse-demon liquefied and then evaporated, leaving nothing but a dirty watermark on the floor. He watched as an eyeball seemed to stare through him before winking out of existence.

'Best thing about killing demons – they clean up after themselves. Come on, boy, get dressed. We've got shit to do.'

About the Authors

A J Dalton

A J Dalton (the 'A' is for Adam) has been an English language teacher as far afield as Egypt, the Czech Republic, Thailand, Slovakia, Poland and Manchester University. He has lived in Manchester since 2003, but has a conspicuous Cockney accent, as he was born in Croydon on a dark night, when strange stars were seen in the sky.

He is the best-selling fantasy author of *The Sub-genres of British Fantasy Literature* (2017*), I Am a Small God* (2016), *The Book of Angels* (2016), *The Book of Orm* (2015), *Empire of the Saviours* (2012), *Gateway of the Saviours* (2013), *Tithe of the Saviours* (2014), *Necromancer's Gambit* (2008), *Necromancer's Betrayal* (2009) and *Necromancer's Fall* (2010). He maintains the Metaphysical Fantasy website (www.ajdalton.eu), where there is plenty for fantasy fans and aspiring authors.

Michael Victor Bowman

Michael Victor Bowman is interested in everything, and the stress of keeping up with it all has left him slightly disturbed.

Not much is known about his background except that he was a toilet salesman, that he is a biology graduate and that he spent some time being chased by angry hippos in Tanzania. When not running for his life he hammers away at his ratty old keyboard and brews the strong tea that fuels his website, Life Described (www.lifedescribed.com), where he shares his views on everything from natural history to space travel. So if you liked his story 'Black and White', please stop by his website to leave a comment because, as Charles Buxton said, silence is the severest criticism.

Andrew Coulthard

Andrew Coulthard first saw the light of day on the wind-lashed eastern coast of Northumbria. He then spent most of his childhood and youth in the western shadow of the highland boundary fault. Since 1990 he has dwelt north of the land of the Geats – where these days, it seldom gets very cold.

Andrew's short fiction has appeared in anthologies published by Eibonvale, The Alchemy Press, MorbidbookS, Oneiros Books and Omnium Gatherum. He has also featured in Trevor Denyer's Hellfire Crossroads and The Ironic Fantastic. His Swedish work is published by Affront Förlag.

Joanne Hall

Joanne Hall is the same age as Star Wars, which explains a lot . . . She lives in Bristol, England, with her partner. She enjoys reading, writing, listening to music, playing console games, watching movies, eating chocolate and playing with the world's laziest dog.

A full-time author since 2003, Joanne's short stories have appeared in many publications, both print and online, including Afterburn SF, Quantum Muse, and The Harrow.

She has had short stories published in several anthologies, including "Pirates of the Cumberland Basin" in *Future Bristol*, and "Corpse Flight" in *Dark Spires*, and four novels published by Kristell Ink. Her books have been long listed for both the Gemmell and the Tiptree awards.

With Roz Clarke, she has edited and contributed to *Colinthology*, *Airship Shape and Bristol Fashion* and *Fight Like A Girl*.

Jo says she is always happy to hear from readers (https://hierath. wordpress.com/), especially the ones that send her cake in the post . . .

Rob Clifford

Rob Clifford's writing experience ranges from winning a bottle of champagne at Manchester's Frog and Bucket for a poem about trying to pull in Asda, to short-listing in the BBC FutureTalent competition with a feature length script set in an asylum-seeker detention centre. He has also short-listed in a CBBC script competition and had a short drama performed at the Media City 'Turn Up The Talent' showcase. Although originally from the south, after attending a number of Manchester Universities, he has settled in Stockport with his housemate, indifferent cat and collection of gins.

C.N. Lesley

C.N. Lesley used to run a local news publication as the reporting editor before becoming a full-time writer. She lives in Central Alberta near the Rocky Mountains with most of her family. One daughter and family live over on the British Colombia side of sparkling Vancouver Island, which makes for a great vacation visit.

Her books range from paranormal fantasy though to science fantasy and are *Darkspire Reaches* (2013), *Serpent of the Shangrove* (2016), *Shadow Over Avalon* (2013), *Sword of Shadows* (2014) and *The Chalice of Shadows* (2016).

Her website is cnlesley.com/

Isabella Hunter

Isabella Hunter is a recent graduate of English and Creative Writing from Manchester Metropolitan University. She's been writing stories from the moment her parents told her that dragons don't actually exist. Since then she has been bringing fantasy to life through her stories, and is now taking her first steps into the publishing industry. Her writing is heavily inspired by myths and legends from across the globe, but she has come to call Manchester her home. She runs a writing website (https://isabellahunter.blog) which is still in its early days but will host a wide variety of information on writing and other subjects.

Garry Coulthard

Garry Coulthard is a Creative Writing graduate from Bolton University who spends more time writing about unpleasant things than a well-adjusted person should. He once spent a day wearing odd shoes and didn't notice until teatime (true story). He has published poetry in The Bolton Review and a selection of his sort stories can be found on www.kerning.co. Should you feel the need to admonish him or tell him a good joke, you can often find him on Twitter @Grimgarry. Alternatively, you might check out his website, www.garrycoulthard.com.

Acknowledgements

A whole slew of people have helped put together the *The Book of Dragons*. I'd like to thank . . .

Joanne Hall and Sammy HK Smith of Kristell Ink, whose tolerance and good faith are equally rare amongst publishers.

Charlotte Pang, who produced the fabulous book cover.

Michael Victor Bowman, Andrew Coulthard, Joanne Hall (again), Rob Clifford, C.N. Lesley, Isabella Hunter and Garry Coulthard, my inspiring co-authors, who have contributed their work, hearts and minds in return for a small pile of groats.

Mum and Dad, who continue to support the literary ambitions of their son against all good reason and common sense.

Nadine West, my beautiful wife, whose only flaw is that she writes better than me.

And all those fantasy fans who keep insisting it's all worth it!

I humbly salute you all!

– Adam Dalton

A Selection of Other Titles from Kristell Ink

The Book of Orm by A J Dalton

This exciting new collection brings together the writing talents of international fantasy author A J Dalton, Nadine West (Bridport Anthology) and Matt White (prize-winning scriptwriter). Magic, myth and heroic mayhem combine in a world that is eerily familiar yet beautifully liberating.

Fear the Reaper by Tom Lloyd

All Shell has ever wanted was a home, a place to belong. But now an angel of the God has tracked her down, intent on using her to hunt the demon that once saved her. The journey will take her into the dead place beyond the borders of the world, there to face her past and witness the coming of a new age. A stand-alone novella from the author of The Twilight Reign series and Moon's Artifice.

Children of the Shaman by Jessica Rydill

When their aunt is taken ill, thirteen-year old Annat and her brother are sent from their small coastal town to live with their unknown father. Like Annat, Yuda is a Shaman; a Wanderer with magical powers, able to enter other worlds. As Annat learns more about her powers, the children join their father on a remarkable train journey to the frozen north and find a land of mystery and intrigue, threatened by dark forces and beset by senseless murders that have halted construction of a new tunnel. But Annat's doll, her only remembrance of her dead mother, may hold a dark secret - and when her brother Malchik is kidnapped, Annat and her father must travel onwards to find him before it is too late. Between uncertain allies, shadowed enemies and hostile surroundings, it is only in the magical kingdom of La Souterraine that they can find answers – and it may be that only a Shaman can save the family and the Goddess.

www.kristell-ink.com

Also from A J Dalton

I am a Small God

Exclusive Sampler

I

HATE ME IF you want. Love me if you prefer, but hatred is just fine. At least that way you know I exist, or you believe in me. And in large part it's actually my haters who keep me alive. Without them I would be… well, nothing. Literally nothing.

Believe me. Believe *in* me. Please, because I can make it well worth your while. Trust me. I can give you most anything. A woman of great desire? She can be yours. A man? A child, anything. Just name it. Name it.

Naming is important. Perhaps you've heard me. I pray you have. I'm not going to tell you my name straight out. Instead, I'm going to Ecrelis. Sorry? Ecrelis. What was that? Oh, you mean Ecrelis? You said it in your head, didn't you? Yes, Ecrelis. There, you did it again, only a little louder this time. You just shouted it in your mind. Like a prayer, *precisely* like a prayer in fact. ECRELIS. Alright, alright. I'm not deaf, you know. I'm right here next to you. Well, behind you and off up to the right. In your blind spot, over your shoulder where all gods reside. But enough of them. Ecrelis.

You can stop reading now if you like. Seriously. This tome has already done its job. Go ahead, put the book down so someone else can find it and can read this page. Or *give* the book to someone even. Tell them it's awful, that it's soooo awful that they will look at the first page to see just how awful it is. Many awful books succeed like that. Trust me. I know.

You may as well. Why? Because the alternative is you trying not to pass on the book, perhaps burning it even. (They tried that in Constantinople and it didn't work.) Ecrelis. My name is in your head, you see. It is in your mind and memory now, and always will be. No matter how deeply you try to bury it, it is still buried in there. You can't get it out. You are a walking, living, breathing prayer to me. Sorry.

It's tough, I know, but there's nothing you can do about it. Now, if you accept it rather than resist it, then I will reward you. Truly. Trust me. Have faith. Accepting it is your display of faith and all but the reward in itself. For in believing in me, you will be safe in the knowledge that I am there for you. You will *know* that I am watching over you, that your god is real and attentive. Your faith will sustain you and you will not have fear, because I will be walking at your side, or in that blind spot anyway. We will sustain each other, then, you and I.

Accept me and all will be well. Share my name with others. Ecrelis. Repeat it out loud and you will be first among my flock. You will lead others. As leader, great benefits will come to you, all as I promised you. You will be idolised, but only if you continue to share my name over your own. Deny me, and you will have nothing. You will *be* nothing.

Have I convinced you? Of course I have. If I hadn't, you wouldn't have read this far. You would have thrown the book from you. You would have tried to suppress all thoughts of and from it. You would have tried sticking your fingers in your ears and going la-la-la-I-can't-hear-you, or some such silly thing.

But you haven't done that. And it wouldn't have done you any good even if you had. Because it's too late, of course. That's all there is to it. The end. You can go away now. Go on. Get lost. You're getting boring now. Yawn. I'm busy. I am a god, after all. I have godly things to which I must attend. And they're none of your business.

Sigh. Alright, you've got questions about your god. But look, I can't tell you everything. If I were to do so… well, certain things would be exposed that just shouldn't be exposed. Dangerous things. Things that would bring down entire kingdoms, raise new but awful civilizations, destroy pantheons and, perhaps, end your world. It's for your own good that certain things are never revealed. You will just have to take my word on it – as an article of your faith.

Yes, I can see that you would want to know the most effective way of spreading my word. That I will guide you in. Okay, so we use short sentences and paragraphs. It might not be artistically satisfying to you, but staccato style is punchy and compelling. It has pace and tempo. It *compels*. It draws people in and they can't stop reading, till the book is finished. And even then they can't stand that the book is finished. It's like they've lost something. They feel an emptiness and void, and that's precisely what we want, because that's where I come in. They want to be filled, and then I fill them. Ecrelis. They feel a gratitude. And that's also what we want because then they feel obliged. Obliged to do something on my behalf, to spread my word. See how it works?

I'm not just a pretty face. My face? Close your eyes. Say Ecrelis. Louder. See me now? If not, just try a little harder. Just try. Go on. Say it.

Up to you. If you now see me, then you see infinity in my eyes. You see immeasurable kindness, inestimable wisdom, limitless virtue and the most profound understanding in just the lines of my divinely drawn features. I am as clear to you as these words, and just as impossible to truly know. It fills you with a sense of yearning, lack and grief. And that's precisely what we want.

To truly know. Yes, the infinitive is sundered. For Ecrelis knows no rule or stricture. Laws cannot contain or frame me. And so, you must also break rules, the better to spread my word. Commit wanton acts sometimes, all so that attention can be drawn. Do not destroy (my) future followers of course – simply name me to them. Naming is important, remember.

And then there is a more complex lesson I must mention. Do not describe the lessons of your faith by way of commandments. Many cannot stand being told what to do. They are wilful and individualistic. Individualism is my nemesis like that. There are those of a place called Alba (Great Britian, etc) who are truly terrible in this way. Beyond terrible in fact. Be wary of them.

Lessons must instead be shared via stories. Why? Well, listeners *interpret* stories via what they know and have faced – and via that interpretation they hear only those lessons that are immediate and true for them. By contrast, a simple commandment can be utterly meaningless or irrelevant to them. The greatest leaders are the greatest story-tellers, for they seem entirely wise, although it is actually the audience themselves reading wisdom into the narrative.

See the trick of it? And it *is* a trick. One of many. It's not all tricks, mind you, for I am divine. Trust me. Have faith. I would not lie to you… unless it was for your own good, to stop certain things being exposed.

You need to learn these tricks if you are to spread my word. You will provoke wonder and awe with such tricks. You will mesmerise and convince. You will seem a magician or priest of power. A prophet perhaps. Or a politician. Share the secret of some of these tricks if you must, particularly if it will prove your intention is to instruct honestly rather than anything underhand or nefarious. Always keep back the truth of one trick or other, however, as otherwise you will lose the ability to inspire and move people through and by my word.

And now you will want the stories of me. I supply them for you here. Share them widely. As widely as you can. Put a price on them if it helps convince others that they have inherent value. Make copies and sell these stories to readers and collectors. Make more than one edition. Own multiple copies yourself. Learn these stories by heart and quote them. All in my name.

Make gifts of these stories to everyone you know, and have them do the same. Make these stories the biggest selling of all time. Publicly perform them, for in doing so you spread my word and perform your act of faith. Do all this in my name.

Yes, this is my bible masquerading as a set of stories.

Ecrelis.

II

The beginning

'WHERE THE HELL have you been?' Divine Aa demanded of the Divine Ecrelis. 'You're a thousand years late. I'd all but given up waiting.' Her displeasure was such that a whole village of her followers was suddenly flattened.

'Believe me, I came as quickly as I could. There was this magician–'

'A *human* magician? Do you mean to tell me you let yourself be detained by a mere mortal?'

'Well, he was particularly powerful. He had got his people all worked up and was leading a crusade against a sect of my followers around Antioch. He had them trapped in desert caves beyond the city.'

'A crusade? Antioch? Of all places. Way too hot and dusty. You should have left them to it. Aren't I more important than some miserable sect?' Divine Aa frowned and light fled the skies above the northern kingdoms.

Divine Ecrelis sighed, sounding as a wave against the shore, a leaf falling from a tree and moonlight touching a forest canopy.

'This sect has a particularly long history in my worship. I admit they have a place in my affections. I felt obliged to be there for them in their time of need.'

'And no doubt they have a long history in pretty high priestesses too!'

'Now, beloved, you know I have always been faithful to you.'

'Oh, I know you all too well. Have I not caught you in one compromising position after another?' Lightning struck the earth, destroying an ancient druidic oak.

'And have I not given you one reasonable explanation each time, beloved?'

'That maiden in Carthage?'

'We've been through this,' Divine Ecrelis waved away, separating clouds as he could, looking to return the sun. 'The maid had merely mentioned my name while about her ablutions. That was why she was disrobed.'

'The dancing girls of Thebes? All *fifteen* of them?'

'It is the local custom for them to disport themselves so.'

'Those Assyrian youths to whom all nudity was forbidden? I cannot even begin to think how that could come about.'

'I'm not sure I even remember them. Are you sure it was me?'

The Divine Ecrelis paused, stepped back and went to sit on a broken pillar, all the better to gaze upon Aa in the throne of her mountain temple. In so doing, he noted his surroundings properly for the first time. Flagstones were cracked, moss grew upon the door lintel, there was an unpleasant smell of rotten leaves, and there was an uncomfortable chill in the air.

'And what offence provoked this human magician of yours? He didn't find you in a perfectly reasonable situation with his wife, did he?'

'What? No, no,' Ecrelis murmured as he took in the missing section of roof, and the poorly maintained statue of Aa herself. 'The magician served some god of war or other. That's all.'

'So you stole this war god's paramour then.'

He looked directly at her now. She was careworn, faster to

anger than he remembered. Her eyes were red-rimmed – somehow enhancing her beauty but suggesting a terrible vulnerability. 'Beloved, are you well? What is it?'

'Don't you love me anymore?' Her voice had cracked. 'You used to say you *worshipped* me.'

'And I do worship you.'

'But it's all just words. Empty words!'

'I would not lie to you.'

'Shut up!' She put a hand to her lips, the chasms of her eyes wide in outrage or apology. She softened her tone. 'No more words, sweet though your speech can be, dear one. I need worship through worship and deed.' A whisper now. 'You left me alone for a thousand years. A *thousand* years.'

He hesitated. 'What would you have of me? But name it.'

'There is a prophecy. It is confusing my people. The son of some god. In the east. He is born, or soon to be. You know the eastern kingdoms. What happens there? Why do my people turn from me?'

'The war god of whom I spoke. His followers are full of *There-is-no-other-god-but-me*. There is only one god.'

'This will end the pantheon if it is not checked!' Aa gnashed. 'You must see to it that all newborns are undone.'

'You would have me massacre children? It… is… one possibility. There are others, though.'

'Hardly. All other approaches are too slow. They take generations. By then it might be too late.'

'Beloved, there is another matter here. The war god gives his followers commandments and a particular definition of right and wrong. Killing children will not go down at all well with the mortals, even with your own followers, beloved. It will only drive more towards his faith, achieving the precise opposite of what you desire. Trust me.'

'Well is he a war god or not? Since when are mere children of any concern to a god, except as a sacrifice?'

Divine Ecrelis shifted his weight forward, all but begging her to understand. 'Times change, beloved.'

'Times change but we do not. We are immortal. Eternal. Our will is divine and cannot be challenged.'

'Yes, that is what we tell the mortals. But think back. Where are Ta'Ur, Ilabrat and Anu now?'

'They'll be off somewhere doing whatever it is they do.'

Ecrelis shook his head. 'No, beloved. They are not to be found, nor any that follow them.'

'What is it you say? That they have died? What madness is this?' she blazed, daring him to argue.

He turned in a slow circle. 'Look around you.'

'Be silent! You will not utter blasphemy here in my holy place. I command it!' Her eyes narrowed. 'I know what it is you do, s-s-sly Ecrelis. You seek to sow the seed of doubt in me, to have me birth it as my own. You will have me nurture it until it outgrows me entirely. You want my people for your own! I see now why you returned. Be gone! This place is denied you forever more.'

'Beloved, do not do this,' he said sadly.

'Out!' came her screech. 'I have no need of you. I will command the necessary king of the eastern kingdom and he will see my will done. A mere mortal will perform that thing for which you are too *weak*, godling. Return to your dusty desert. There are none for you here.'

'It will be your undoing.'

'Be gone.'

Lightning Source UK Ltd.
Milton Keynes UK
UKOW04f0605260917
309886UK00001B/231/P